ENCHANTED
CLOCK

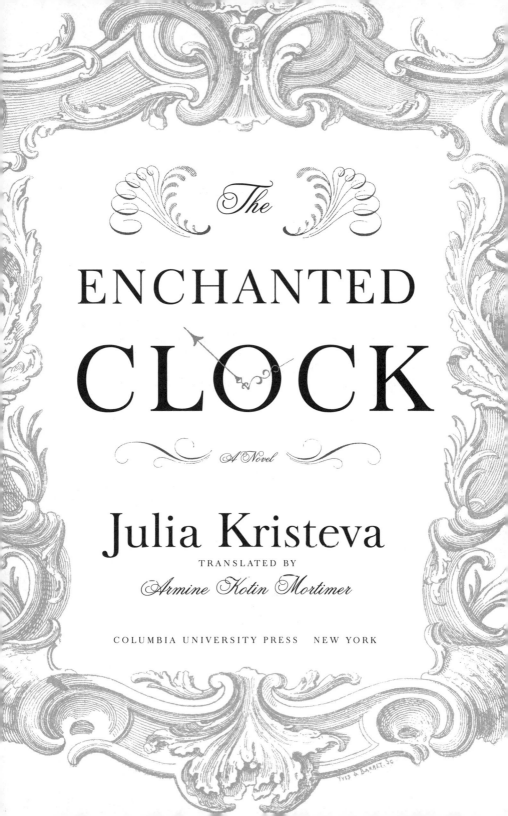

The
ENCHANTED
CLOCK

A Novel

Julia Kristeva

TRANSLATED BY

Armine Kotin Mortimer

COLUMBIA UNIVERSITY PRESS   NEW YORK

Columbia University Press wishes to express its appreciation for assistance given by the Pushkin Fund in the publication of this book.

Columbia University Press
Publishers Since 1893
New York   Chichester, West Sussex
cup.columbia.edu
Copyright © 2015 Librairie Arthème Fayard
English translation copyright © 2017 Armine Kotin Mortimer

Library of Congress Cataloging-in-Publication Data
Names: Kristeva, Julia, 1941– author. | Mortimer, Armine Kotin, 1943– translator.
Title: The enchanted clock: a novel / Julia Kristeva; translated by
Armine Kotin Mortimer.
Other titles: Horloge enchantée. English
Description: New York: Columbia University Press, 2017. | First published in
French as L'horloge enchantée.
Identifiers: LCCN 2017031553 | ISBN 9780231180467 (cloth: alk. paper) |
ISBN 9780231542739 (e-book)
Subjects: LCSH: Passemant, Claude Siméon, 1702–1769—Fiction. |
Astronomical clocks—France—Fiction. | Time—Fiction. |
GSAFD: Mystery fiction. | Historical fiction.
Classification: LCC PQ2671.R547 H6713 2017 | DDC 843/.914—dc23
LC record available at https://lccn.loc.gov/2017031553

Columbia University Press books are printed on permanent and
durable acid-free paper.
Printed in the United States of America

Cover design: Catherine Casalino

Before *and* after *are transitory conventions, but they can cause precious internal coups d'état. . . . As many thoughts as there are stars; the stars are there to remind us of it. . . . The word* mystique *should not be spoken here.*

—Philippe Sollers, *The Intermediary*, 1962

CONTENTS

ENCHANTED
CLOCK

I
VERSAILLES

1

WHEN?

Time stopped. When? I'm not familiar with this tight, round word. *The day passes, the hour strikes . . .* Time that flows for you is crushed for me, in an accumulation of presents. Vertical duration. I stand erect. Suspended, untouchable. Stylite in this overpopulated desert, in the midst of a cumbersome-encumbered throng: products, computers, e-mails, iPhones, trains, planes, videos, markets, supermarkets, hypermarkets, connections, depressions, corruptions, few conversations, miniscreens, giant screens, a few books, fast food, and more or less organic bars. Stingy nouveaux riches, insolvent-insoluble nouveaux poor. No men, but a mass of chargés d'affaires, entrepreneurs, bureaucrats, employees, artisans, artists, traders, bankers, philosophers, politicians, computer scientists, ecologists, extremists, wheeler-dealers, minimum-wage earners, temp workers in limbo, salaried show workers, monks (bearded or not), unemployed, homeless, and even poets. Women, a few—more and more—who hold, carry, and transmit. Words, silences, dreams, delirium. Everything. Nothing.

Petrified or enraptured, what's the difference. Taking refuge in the immaculate substance of time, I am outside time and outside the game in the great game. Play of skins, perfumes, syllables, accents, touches, breaths, waves, melodies, sparks, bursts of words, nausea, stench, suffering, migraine, palpitation, aggression, brutality, penetration, defecation, smothering, vomiting, bloodletting. Nothing.

In this everything, and next to it, I take a stand. I take a multitude of actions that explode time, pulverizing its flight. I swim in a whirlpool of endless challenges, failures, new starts, and new unfoldings. Indestructible founder, builder of what is required and urgent. I chase after the indispensable, the imperative, the vital, the whatever. I create, I believe in it, it exists, it has to exist, intoxication becomes reason, intoxication is reason, intoxication-reason: that's me.

Me? Nivi. "My language" in Hebrew. Spitting image of my grandmother Niva, only slimmer. Jeans and striking T-shirt, black skirt when needed, dark eyes, Chinese cheekbones, cherry lips, and well-rounded bosom. Not in the least androgynous. Ageless because time has stopped for me.

Have you ever observed the Luxembourg Gardens from the height of a bird? An intelligent foliage plants luxury in the heart of Paris. Florentine walls of linden trees, red beeches, chestnut trees, and skillfully pruned plane trees. Fir trees, fruit trees, *Ginkgo biloba*, and even a *Philodendron selloum* line rigorous lawns or are scattered across them. Flowerbeds in a moiré of iris, rose bushes, and tenderly disciplined pansies. Mirrors of water sleeping in patches, bursting in fountains. White sinuous or rectilinear paths, framing the first steps of babies and the rough-and-tumble of schoolboys. They offer chairs to expansive lovers and irreducible readers. This kingdom is because it thinks. A nacreous light bathes its logic, raises it from the ground. Bees, children, refugee and migrant fowl of all sorts. Marie de' Medici's pure caprice, the Carthusian nursery, the Haussmannian scissor-cut sacrificing the Philosophers' Valley and the Alley of Sighs. Tastes and actions follow one another and compose anew. The Luxembourg Gardens today are a sublime smile in the history of France, its imperturbable, serene resistance. When a bird soars and observes, it floats in the sky like the smile of the Cheshire cat: without a cat, without support, eternity goes with the sun and the mist.

I was that bird. It was by chance that I landed here upon my arrival in Paris, in a mansard room let for a song by a family related to mine. They lived comfortably above that time regained.

That was the age of the *Sputnik*. I dreamed of conquering the cosmos, astronomy, and nuclear physics, of joining the secret labs in Siberia. "It's out of the question, young lady, your parents aren't even members of the Party." The Red hierarchy had quickly put me in my place. In the East, I took refuge in the microcosm: language. French, English, Indo-European languages, and—why not—Chinese . . . Go with French! So much for interstellar spaces! I invent for myself an infatuation for France. It's still with me.

More in love with France than the French themselves? Possibly. Stan certainly has something to do with it. Infinite time will always have the form of the Luxembourg Gardens for me—the way migrating birds fly over it and such as I first saw it from the sixth floor of the home of my approximate cousins, the Vogels.

I frequently go by their building. I look at the lighted windows. Who could be living there now? Who sees what I used to see? I don't know. But I would be ready to kill the imprudent owners or renters of those premises so as to inhabit, if only for one moment more, the only place in the world where I could live with a smile until I die.

When the Six-Day War broke out, the Vogels left Paris for Jerusalem, and their apartment was bought by promoters who apparently ruled over the neighborhood. Luckily, the new owners, extremely rich, had underestimated—maybe even forgotten—my mansard studio, and for a long time I was able to enjoy it for a modest rent. Years of study, reading, music, mostly happy love with Ugo, until Stan was born. Then the departure of Ugo Delisle, who, having discovered that he was not made for fatherhood, went off to return to his native Italy, the country of his mother, the Red Brigades, and free love. I too left that bird's life at the Lux to devote myself to little Stan, who had decided not to grow up the way everyone else does. He sang better than he spoke and had only "orphan" diseases, which is to say, unidentifiable ones. Enough, though, to produce tons of worries and so-called atypical schooling. In short, life without respite.

My son X-rays me, entrails and bones. He knows what pain constricts my throat if someone happens to raise their voice. He holds my sweaty hands when words fail me. He perceives the tears in my dry eyes when I am struggling to remain standing. Stan is the only one who realizes *you* exist.

You are neither a passage nor a door. I have no need for light, no more than for night, oxygen, orgasm, even death. I have had it all; I still have it. With my ex-husband Ugo Delisle and with others. Times were like that, times are like that—that's life. Now you give me what was missing: the fullness of solitude, a solitude full of you.

Obviously I have always been alone, externally as well as on the inside. But that was an absent solitude lacking existence and flavor. Alone with myself. That solitude is not filled in by you now. You make it present, and I don't suffer from it. I've come to like it. Thanks to you. You alone with me, me alone with you—because you are almost never here—the two of us alone. Nothing obligates us. No need to speak to each other. No. You make me break with the untruths of solitude. You make it vibrant; I embody it. I don't think I'm trying to reassure myself by imagining that your solitude is an echo of mine—mute coincidence, silent fulfillment. Certainly not. In a more delicate way, your solitude diffracts mine. When you are here, we listen to each other, holding hands, but this handprint endures, and we also hear each other think, whether our bodies embrace or we remain far, far apart. I like this understanding, this taste for integrated absence, this pleasure in each other—"the pleasure in God," you'll say with your distant, almost funny seriousness.

Because you are alone, though less than I am, I don't come to you to rejoin you, the better to grasp my solitude and simply to feel myself truly alone. Not to expect anything from you. Other than that you exist and that you agree to think about me, with me. Two solitudes that are annulled only at infinity. You smile. "In Eternity." I don't know what that is. You say: "A world where time does not exist." A time-out-of-time, perhaps. "We have to forget time."

If you were religious or simply a believer, "eternity" would mean "the hereafter." But you live in the stars, "in perspective," Stan says. I think we're dreaming. I call this dream a fiction, a secret transport under the open sky. But you? I like to think that you carry me within you precisely when, to scrutinize the stars, you abandon us. For interminable days and nights. I persuade myself that I am the invisible depth of your giant telescopes, the very ones that confer visible surfaces upon celestial bodies. And that during your starry time, you think, you see, you live in a cosmic solitude. I am persuaded then that you are the most alone of us all. Or the exact opposite: at the limits of the All? My sole. What to call you?

Solus? The word seems too solar, exclusive and peremptory. It would be more correct to just call you You, without a name, a conjugate secret, me in you, you in me, my Asteroid, my Alone other, my A. I have no need to emphasize anxiety to discover that I'm missing you. I constantly tremble because of it; only at intervals do I lay myself open. For what purpose? For nothing. I have chosen gratuity; now I enjoy it a bit more. The furrow of your gaze in mine, osmosis of our hands that do not let go in the face of this film that the world has become, that we watch without seeing. Your breath, your odor, your voice from which I take food and drink outside time: when you are with me, while listening to your messages, when reading your texts and your e-mails. Dreaming about you, recalling you, reinventing you. Creating you.

"I am 300 million years after the Big Bang. With you and the red stars, those galaxies that I see now as they were 13.82 billion years ago. Because it takes time for light to reach us. These are very young galaxies, no comparison to the older spirals like the Milky Way or Andromeda. Witnessing this fascinating spectacle, I see time swallowed up. ILY."

You are convinced I understand what is happening out there, in the constellation Fornax, which you have just captured on your screen. Thanks to the Hubble space telescope, which was aimed at the desired target for at least 270 hours, you managed to obtain the most detailed image of the distant universe, an "ultra deep field" that puts you in contact with what took place 13.82 billion light years before.

"ILY" is our signature, as secret as Edgar Allan Poe's purloined letter, three compacted letters, to be written but not to be spoken:

"I Love You."

Magnetic field. Disk of accretion. Our star-baby. The first Earth-like extrasolar planet, habitable. Incredible but true: ILY.

More than 13 billion light years separate us, too. I, Nivi, am swept into the abysses of my patients, listening to their spiraling labyrinths. He, my Astro, not content to try out everything his state-of-the-art telescopes can offer, the most high-performing ones on earth—from Grenoble to New Mexico, from Toulouse to Seattle—persists in camping out day and night at some hundreds of millions of years after the Big Bang, a mere trifle compared to the origin of the universe. Obviously two realities that do not facilitate our nevertheless permanent meetings.

Since the day we met in the waters of the Atlantic off the coast of the Phare des Baleines, time has opened up, sweeping away limits and obstacles.[1] Whatever happens, whatever the weather report, genetics, or the Internet may say, ILY is felt and thought, ILY is translated into words, acts, patients, stars, lives, and deaths. ILY in everything, in nothing.

It was a violet morning, the garnet disk of the sun barely pierced the mist, the warm sand no longer caressed my feet, nothing at all kept me on the shore. Running toward the rolling surf of the rising tide. Embracing the nervous wave. It catches me, loaded with algae and iodine. I let it massage my face, my skull,

---

1. The Phare des Baleines is a lighthouse at the western limit of the Ile de Ré, the island where Kristeva and Sollers have a home. All notes are by the translator.

the back of my neck, my back. Force my arms, my thighs, my calves. Iridescent, warmed skin. I hear my heartbeat. I breathe in air between two waves. To be reborn has never been beyond my power. Why not? I burst out laughing, ô violet rays, I can no longer see the shore. Nothing but that circumflexed ô, no horizon. I go under, I am no longer cold, I am the iceberg that melts, the polar bear that drowns, I sink, I don't cry, ever, I will laugh to the end. What is there at the end of time? Lights still, sparks in my eyes, salt filling my throat. And my hand in his hand.

"Certain galaxies stopped making stars millions of years ago. Practically asleep. Drowned, if you prefer."

What is it? I hear an adolescent voice, its trumpeting, then velvety, timbre. I cling to the fear that's slipping away under this arrant audacity. I squeeze a hand, and always this voice; I don't give a damn what it's saying; it's as if it's trying to reach me, to grab me like a hand that does not want to let go of mine. A lifebuoy, sailor's hitch, caress.

"I think you're fine for the party . . . Oh yes. You know, there's always a handful of unrepentant revelers huddled together in the interior regions of the galaxy, celebrating new beginnings. They fuel the revelry while the galaxy takes a well-deserved rest. A new burst of stars is confirmed at 5,000 light years, and the celebration continues around the hub. Not in its core but at the margin. When the center collapses, the process begins again at the borders. Such is the life of stars. Ours too, perhaps."

The sun finishes drying my cheeks; it's burning my eyelids now, my lips. I open my eyes.

"Theo. Theo Passemant. You are on board my boat . . ."

"Passemant . . . I've heard that name before . . ."

"I fished you out near here. Very far from shore . . . You had to have guts. Or be unconscious . . . Do you remember?"

"Yes. Violet rays. I was dissolving from having laughed so much . . . Much too much, for no reason . . . Nivi Delisle."

He had wrapped me in a white peignoir and a plaid blanket. My bathing suit had come off.

"At first I thought that laughing seagulls were fluttering around a dolphin. Yes, there are dolphins that lose their way around here. Those mauve reflections . . . The tidal wind, the shadow that appeared and disappeared in the foam, struggling . . . But the cry was not that of a bird, that cry . . . could only have been the echo of a woman."

The wind had calmed, and the boat had stopped moving. I looked at his gray hair, his tanned complexion. How old might he be, this sidereal adolescent? Fifty? A little more? He shouldn't imagine, above all, that he has saved me from a melancholy suicide. That's all I need—that he should disembark like a hero at the Phare des Baleines!

"Very sorry to have scared you . . . I was having a wild time . . . I like to laugh in the water . . . Does that surprise you?"

He doesn't wait for silence to set in. Once again, Astro comes to my aid.

"Of course not. This encounter was inevitable."

"You don't know me."

"I waited for you to wake up . . . I heard you dreaming."

Am I supposed to say "sorry" or "thank you"? I am silent.

"I have read your books . . . certain ones. *Black Sun: Depression and Melancholia*."[2]

Am I supposed to say "thank you" or "sorry"? I am still silent.

"Don't worry. My job is to look at the sky. And to remain silent, me too . . . I don't talk a lot. Never about the essential

---

2. *Le soleil noir de la mélancolie* is a book by Kristeva.

things . . . I can chat, manage, communicate . . . Not a bit neurotic . . . I will not be your patient."

So much the better! I notice he has let go of my hand; I need him to keep it. His voice continues: "Besides, we both explore deep spaces, at the two edges of the universe . . . So distant one from the other that we have no chance of meeting each other . . . *Had* no chance . . . The probability was close to zero. But thanks to the violet ray, it was certain . . . You can keep my sweatsuit. You are here, madam."

He had dressed me.

I remember only vague sequences of the soundtrack of this film, and the beams of the lighthouse sweeping across the night in the Fier.[3] Theo must have quietly deposited me at my home. I found myself in an armchair on the veranda facing the ocean, dressed in his charcoal gray tracksuit and a plaid blanket. I didn't even have the strength to make myself some tea. I collapsed on the big bed and slept. Alone. Without Stan, without the telephone, without anyone.

---

3. Fier is the interior lagoon at Ars en Ré, on the island.

2

"THEO." WHAT A STORY!

I'm remembering: my linguistics professor is on the brink of death and asks me to visit him in the hospital. With a trembling index finger, he traces these letters on the mauve silk of my shirt. A cerebral attack. The old man I adore is aphasic. Three beds in a room at the Kremlin-Bicêtre hospital, rancid odor, noisy families. Does he hear them? His eyes tear, his white hair sticks to his prophet's forehead. No words. Only these letters imprinted on my chest, between my breasts: THEO. They are still there. At the time, I have trouble believing that this extremely well-known scholar, an Enlightenment enthusiast, has this word in mind. I hand him the notebook I keep at the bottom of my bag, with the red morocco cover, the one on which I have always sketched my constellations, the words and phrases that illuminate my days, my nights. And a black felt-tipped pen. Once more, with the same trembling gesture, the old linguist clearly traces "THEO." The prophet who explored Indo-European languages expired the next day.

I keep this precious notebook and my professor's last lesson with me. They accompanied me while I watched over Stan during his first illness, then during his coma, and even more at his awakening.

"Can we go see the clock, Mama, can we?"

Scarcely reanimated, was my son wondering what time it was? I must have looked flabbergasted.

"Don't worry, I feel fine. I'm okay now. How about you? Do you remember that clock and the pushing and shoving, at Versailles?"

At life's frontiers Stan is thinking about what time it is, what time it was, and what time it will be. He lives in time, Stan, and brings me back into it.

I have it.

Spring makes the sky iridescent. Versailles always dazzles me, that day more than any other. Nothing is annulled when we are transported into splendor and voluptuousness. On the contrary, the rest of the world, its challenges and sufferings, appear absolutely simple, elementary. Between Stan and me a new proximity is born, infantile and humble, the magic of this disorientation. My son blossoms in this magical world. Running in the alleys of Bacchus and Saturn, the groves and the Orangery; laughter in his eyes tickled by the waters of the Neptune basin and the Apollo baths; reveries along the Water alley, the North parterre . . .

Today we are not following the flood of Japanese tourists stifling in the Hall of Mirrors. Stan has always loved history and museums. Where other parents drag along their bored kids, he finds enchantment. Not really a gifted kid but an eternal child hovering in the body of an atypical preadolescent, who protects himself, gets around difficulties, avoids thinking about a father who no longer contacts him . . . He escapes from me too, so I follow him to protect him, share in the discoveries that absorb him. I love his face illuminated by astonishment. Stan has recently discovered a taste for science: Buffon, Jussieu,

Cassini, La Condamine. How much of that can one find in this king who they say loved celestial mechanics much more than he loved Madame de Pompadour? Stan wants to check it out, find out for himself.

The curator—head of an owl, peroxide chignon, eyes converging at the bridge of her nose—explains to our very private group (the extreme rarity of three or four enthusiasts on a guided tour of Louis XV's chambers) that a fabulous astronomical clock, the masterwork in this salon of magisterial *rocaille* décor, is programmed with the hours, minutes, seconds, and even sixtieths of seconds up to the year 9999. I'm barely listening to her . . . I'm thinking about Stan, who has lagged behind at a barometer made for Louis XV and who invents another world for himself: exceptional, solid, impregnable.

Outside the window a strange smoke rises. With my dog's sense of smell I've already noticed it, my eyes are getting irritated . . . The Owl is engrossed in her anecdotes about the Château. I don't have time to smile politely; the smoke is getting to my throat. Suddenly an alarm rips through the confined air: "Fire! Immediate evacuation!"

Where has Stan gone off to? I wasn't paying attention. The frightened Japanese invade the little apartments, mad scramble, I look to the right, then to the left. Where could my Stan be? No sign of him, unreachable on his smartphone. The human wave grows and carries me off. I catch hold of the Owl, her ear glued to her cell phone—"Have you seen my son by any chance?"—she doesn't understand, she's waiting for instructions from security, let's not panic, I am paralyzed, a guard has caught sight of someone, he grabs me, we attempt to push our way through the rush against the flow . . . At last we find him: in the famous Clock Cabinet, deserted now. Stan is in the middle of the room, in admiration of a Louis XV piece.

"Mama, look, look!"

"There's a fire alarm, my darling, let's hurry, we'll see it later!"

"Look at the time . . . 9,999 years closed up in a clock . . ."

"Really? . . . Hurry, it smells of smoke . . . We're leaving!"

There's an explosion, followed by shots. The guard rushes us toward the exit, we meet up with the Owl, she tries to take us down a little staircase, the Japanese, more and more numerous, converge on the same emergency exits, the Owl slips and falls, gets up without her glasses, her lip torn, blood all over her chic suit. "Run! Run! Don't stay in the Château. Quick!" She takes my hand, Stan clears a path for us. And we find ourselves outside, at the Café de la Place.

I hate these events that plunge you into a state of torpor. Only the media love them. Was the fire caused by a simple electrical short circuit? Or was it a terrorist act? The solitary wolves of al-Qaeda haunt the planet and threaten the Hexagon,[1] it's well known. Was the fire just a smoke screen? The gas explosion a homemade bomb that missed its target? What target? France, of course. Fortunately the police are on the lookout, and they are effective, sometimes. The proof: the damage was minimal, the inquiry takes its course, the smoke was just a provocation to distract attention, but from whom, from what?

The incident quickly forgotten, other news takes its place. No point in waiting for it to pass, it never passes, that's how it is.

Since then I've encountered the Owl several times, at the National Library, at the Café Marly, at the Carrousel du Louvre.

---

1. "The Hexagon" is a familiar name for France, in reference to its approximately hexagonal shape.

Didn't recognize me, in spite of her glasses. She didn't have any reason to, me neither.

Stan isn't giving up on his idea:

"Mama, I'm talking to you, can we go see the clock? Can we, mama? . . . Do you remember?"

"Vaguely. What clock?"

"You know, the Owl was leading us to a clock programmed to the year 9999 . . . Yes, that one, Passemant's clock, I've told you about it before."

My son's memory is as absolute as his ear. In my notebook covered in red morocco, I note: "An astronomical clock keeps Stan alive until he awakens after two weeks in a coma."

I don't tell Theo what happens to me when I think about him (I leave a few hints of it in my notebook). I just write to him: "Well before meeting you, Stan made me understand that an astronomical clock can restore life to someone."

The immediate answer: "Where you were, where Stan was, where you are, I am. An encounter of this intensity reprograms everything, from before as well as after. ILY."

Pure Astro. Understand it if you can.

As for me, I understand that at this very instant, billions of Internauts send one another words and energies. In the past, Theo claimed that these signals were lost in the atmosphere and loaded it dangerously with CO_2. Now he asserts these signals are not really lost. They accumulate and magnetize one another, encircle us in their networks, transport us outside ourselves, create zones of accretion where time and space are blended. As for lovers.

Often, ILY disappears from my screens for days, for entire weeks. Theo is working on a new ultrarapid camera capable of shooting 1,500 images per second in almost total darkness. He doesn't answer. In the end I get impatient, I send him a text: "How are you?" Finally he reacts: "They've just detected an exoplanet, baptized Kepler-186f, comparable in size to the Earth, turning in an orbit around a dwarf star redder, smaller, and less hot than the Sun, on which water can therefore exist in a liquid state. And now another team of researchers is on the verge of determining the speed of rotation of an exoplanet, Beta Pictoris b! Are you following me, Nivi?"

And how! I am following him . . .

A few days later (or maybe several weeks? When? I've lost my sense of time in these sequences that fix me in a single present), I write the following e-mail to Theo Passemant:

"The pleasure you have given me, our pleasure, comes to mind as soon as I think about you. In front of my computer, or swimming with the seagulls in the Atlantic, when I read your texts sent from I don't know what observatory in the Andes, whether we have a simple lunch at the Balzar or I imagine you in the sky, that pleasure returns. Ever since you entered my life, the pleasure that is called physical begins for me with a first name: yours. I see your face. Your hands slide along my skin, your voice pierces me, I feel it in my mouth, it opens my throat, warms my heart and my blood, makes my fibers tremble with the rhythm of your words. Belly, vagina, clitoris, uterus, anus: everything is inside and outside, fire and water, Nivi supple and on fire. You carry my entrails toward the heavens, as my Teresa of Avila would say. I take your penis in my mouth, it hardens, I caress it, it swells yet more, it penetrates me more and more until a single movement burns us to the same point, and our bodies dilute into one flesh, efflorescence and discharge. Animal embraces, baby embraces, embraces of chaste and monstrous angels, forever sated and always unsatisfied, endlessly to start over, all genders combined, all given names exhausted, your name, my name, no name, ILY."

I will not send you this e-mail. Our encounter, my rescue in the ocean, all those galaxies you inhabit, the universe I see in your eyes, your wanderings and your presence deep inside me and thousands of light years away; Stan's tenderness, who needs me and from now on you, because you love him through me, the way I love him, the way you love me: I write to tell you all this. I live again in our separation, which you confirm with a glance, a smile, or an exclamation point preceded by our cabalistic ILY. You feel the same pleasures at the same moments. The same ones as me, in your solitary male fashion, fazed by nothing, you say, converted to science so as to enter the order of the stars.

I will see you . . . *when?* In a few hours, two weeks, three months, Christmas Eve? That is not the time you are in, me neither. You are refractory to Time in your own way, which is not mine, yet it comes to the same thing. Could that be what makes us climax together, both here and there, in the Fier d'Ars and in the Astrophysics Lab, at Harvard or in New Mexico? I with Stan, who wants to return to Versailles to see the meridian in the King's Cabinets. You with your Advanced Camera Surveys, which reconstruct the history of the creation of the stars. ACS, which sounds like the abbreviation of an elite unit in a crime series.

"So where's the anxiety in this fine love story of yours?"

The metallic accents of my friend and colleague Marianne Baruch—still the same, I haven't changed since I left the Medical-Psychological Center (MPC for the initiates)—attempt to bring me back down to earth. Marianne lowers her gaze to Theo, passing through Paris on a flying visit. I swallow my saliva and don't answer . . .

My Astro's phlegmatic reflectiveness answers for me: "The Hubble observations are part of the Advanced Camera for Surveys Nearby Galaxy Survey Treasury program. Have you heard of it? We say ANGST, if you prefer."

Theo spins out this info without the shadow of a smile. And as for me I attempt to interest Marianne in the work of my A . . . I mention the ESA, NASA, the latest facts provided by the Planck satellite observing the diffuse cosmological background, also called fossil radiation: the first light emitted 380,000 years after the Big Bang! I also ask my friend to look up on the Internet what Theo pulls out of the active regions, those little blue spots that bear witness to the birth of stars. Or also the distorted images of ultradistant galaxies. The effect of shear that a universal gravitational field would produce allows us to distinguish the luminous mass of the amassed galaxies from mass that does not emit light. For Theo, this extremely weak twinkle, at the limits of current technology, serves to detect black matter and dark energy. Still mysterious, granted, but five times more abundant than the matter that constitutes us! These people are making maps of the invisible. When you think about it, Marianne my dear . . . Anxiety? What anxiety? *No feeling of angst, just ANGST* . . .

I sense that I'm making an impression on her. I too visit and inhabit secret regions, those of my psychoanalysis patients, regions active since the birth of I don't know what unknowns that torment them. I borrow Theo's vocabulary to give a name to this thought matter, where names, words, incredible stories light up, attract us, and escape from us. Little blue or yellow points, enigmatic, disconnected, and pulsating gravitational shears. I insert them into the words of those who take the risk of confiding them to me, until they catch up with me and become lives that encounter mine. Then I name them, I interpret; I share them, integrate them. Every day a new world. For me, for them. That is where I am focused with my A.

And with a few accomplices.

3

MY NAME IS CLAUDE-SIMÉON PASSEMANT

My name is Claude-Siméon Passemant, the king's engineer. Born in Paris in 1702, I died from a sudden so-called soporous illness at sixty-seven in 1769, twenty years before the French Revolution. I know this because time is my specialty. I calculate it, I live it, I can stop it down to the second, to the sixtieth of a second. I retain everything: numbers, words, colors, sounds, melodies, rhythms. My memory is infallible; my thoughts run at a gallop, like the horses of the king hunting at Choisy. Witticisms, vivacity, sparks, sparkling fires, my agitated soul nevertheless does not often get carried away. My thinking is quick and calm. Astronomy is my companion, my remedy, my religion. My relaxation, say my daughters, my sons-in-law, my wife, my *extollers*. What nonsense! I never seek relaxation. To flee sorrow by thinking about time is an infinite joy. I kill boredom by inventing machines that allow me to calculate the course of the stars, the rise of the tides, the strength of the winds. No rest, pure pleasure. In short, I speak less than I am moved to, and if my politeness seems too simple, it is never feigned.

I shun society; silence suits me. Bitterness or sorrow, perhaps. So they say, so they will say. *I'm indifferent* is more like it.

I find humanity's affairs tiresome. The court as well as the academy. What importance remains, after having calculated my clock with such precision that in ten thousand years people will see no deviation from the astronomical tables?

This is my refuge. The heavens can be calculated because time can be. I discovered this at the death of my father. This man, who had molded my heart more and better than he had ensured my subsistence, constantly encouraged what he called my "easy understanding." I have to admit that it brought me various prizes at the Collège Mazarin, where I did my secondary studies and initiated the calculations that would perfect that famous clock with the sphere that now resides at Versailles. But the heavens took my father before my education was finished.

At about age fourteen, I nearly succumbed to one of those so-called orphan maladies that take possession of your blood and your wits and imprison you in an irremediable silence. Nothing could appease me, then, other than a strange desire for the hereafter. My mother, who had promised me to a solar future at the Bar, wisely sought to distract me with books of history or amusement. Only Bion's work, *The Use of Celestial and Terrestrial Globes*, drew my interest. Ecstasy, beyond words. I abandoned my impotent body, tasted God's exterior, and embraced Him in the flights of my feverish mind. But since my only will was my mother's wish, my pleasure felt pain within itself, bitterness showed on my face, and people thought I was melancholic, whereas I was saved, I was elsewhere. I experienced the bliss of saints.

Let's not exaggerate. I willingly see myself in the celibacy of ecclesiastics, and I have read almost all the literature on the matter, the Latin as well as the French. Even yesterday I impressed Dr. Sue the younger, husband of my younger daughter.

I am more knowledgeable than he is in matters of celibacy. Doesn't spiritual passion equal the passion of the senses, isn't it even more ardent?

For a long time I thought I was alone in living like this, in this century enlightened by frenetic ideas and sensual audacity. Now I possess the assurance that our king the Beloved is himself not a stranger to these designs of Providence that grace has granted me the benefit of. How could I have such a pretention, as a simple commoner who is not even a member of the Royal Academy of Sciences? "Whereas in England, you would already have been in it," my son-in-law insists. "They have had their Revolution."

I won't tell him that human affairs leave me cold, whether they take place under my window or on the other side of the Channel. Although I am intrigued by the ideas of Voltaire, who launched the stellar word "revolution" into our world here below, for my part I am interested only in celestial revolutions. They surpass us infinitely more and better than our own, with all due respect to Monsieur Arouet, who has become the king's historiographer and whom I might have encountered on the stairs at the Château where he had his lodgings—it seems he found that His Majesty's current *favorite* possessed a philosophical turn of mind—if he had not left it to become chamberlain to the king of Prussia. I would not have told him—it goes without saying—that cosmic bodies obtain for me, humble engineer of Louis XV, a way to transcend myself. Besides, any other way scares me.

As for the good Dr. Sue the younger, who like so many people today has political ideas, he inevitably irritates me by wanting to converse, dragging speech out of me, seeking to make me agree to certain actions above my rank. In spite of my love of freedom and my indifference to wealth, I don't like to argue, and I say nothing to him, obviously. I just turn my back, when I'm not slamming the door in his face—because my moods are violent but short-lived, thank God. On the other hand, I am often seized by impatience, resistance, and the spirit of contradiction when I observe that the life of the mind, such as it is deployed by the sciences, scarcely moves the powerful of this world to passion. Except for our Beloved king, who has charitably manifested his interest in me, perhaps even an attachment. So my son-in-law believes, always overly keen on honors. He's wrong. God has simply given us a monarch with an affection for architecture, physics, astronomy, and mathematics. But those who know this fact number too few, and I fear it is not to the liking of his close relations.

"He lives and breathes for plots and drawings on his table," people murmur in Versailles. And Mme de Pompadour's friends are worried because they think she isn't able to keep this man of science as amused as he deserves to be. I *know* it. His Majesty prefers to reflect on his plots in the evening after dinner, and sometimes, before or instead of joining the marquise, he writes. On his campaign table, provided by Gaudreaux, I have actually seen a set square measuring six inches, with a plumb line; a large compass with six points, of which five are broken; a three-inch compass with a changeable point of pencil or ink; a small simple compass of four inches; a great six-inch proportional compass; a silver protractor and one made of horn; an ebony foot-measure decorated in silver; an ebony ruler; an ebony awl with a silver point; pencil holders; and paper clips. Are these not the tools of an architect? Drawings in his own hand covering the table, the annotations and modifications he has inscribed on the projects of his architects and engineers—I have seen these things. Also the mathematical instruments provided by Langlois. All the while Meissonnier, the Slodtz brothers, and then Challe compete and will compete in their zeal to design furniture, fireplaces, andirons, silver and gold vessels, festival decorations, and theater décor. His Majesty shows a great deal of kindness to his engineers, and the fact that he has deigned to manifest such beneficence on my behalf—for me, his modest clockmaker—is an immense privilege . . . Do I even deserve it?

I cannot imagine a greater happiness than the hours the king and the younger Gabriel spend together, sketching and discussing. His Majesty drafted continually with Jacques Gabriel, himself the scion of a long line of architects, and then with his son, Ange Jacques Gabriel, since this architect, endowed with exquisite sensitivity, possessed a dwelling near the king's. And when he doesn't go hunting, the sovereign is often found working in his private cabinet on projects for buildings and gardens.

Not exactly the kind of thing that interests Mme de Pompadour, and I choose my words carefully. I know the favor enjoyed by the marquise places her above events, sovereigns not being known for their continence. I also concede that the royally elect—whose beauty is *very* unique (for there are different kinds of unique) and whose intelligence is superior, for a woman— excels at running the household, at enlivening a supper or a soirée. As the queen's position is relegated to the official apartments and the grand royal homes, it is in fact la Pompadour who reigns over the little dwellings and the pleasure palaces. My work rarely takes me there, Providence having so decided, and that's a fabulous bit of good luck. The king's anxious character finds refuge there. But does the *favorite* truly love him? I ask myself because the duration of human affections is certainly not measurable like the time of celestial rotations, even if it is no less attractive to me, contrary to what my son-in-law imagines.

In this liaison I see a sincere attachment on the part of the marquise, but rather than a true love, I perceive a powerful appetite for domination. How could it be otherwise, since "la Poisson" (as she is called by her enemies, via a feminized allusion to her father François Poisson, though I never do so, except in this document in which I confide strictly personal thoughts that I wish to hold confidential throughout my lifetime and beyond) does not know that our well-educated sovereign can only truly take relaxation, other than in the hunt, through serious distractions. And I do mean scientific ones. Designing and discussing with architects, discoursing with scientists, performing mathematics, and even reflecting on the time of Apollo (the god he prefers as much, if not more, dare I say it, than our Lord) with a modest clockmaker like me. As for her, la Pompadour, she thinks only of stimulating him and enticing him to theatrical representations (which personally I avoid), in which, they say, the unfortunate woman excels. These frivolities bore His Majesty rather quickly, I presume. I sense it. And they are harmful in the end because they brand him with the bad reputation of a frivolous, spendthrift king. "He will end up angering his good subjects," asserts my dogmatic son-in-law. Yes, he again, always paying heed to rumors running around the city—and a great reader of lampoons.

Right away I understood that there is only one place where the king can be alone: his dressing room. Courtesans sneak in everywhere else. Connected to his bedchamber alcove, opening to it by a door hung with a tapestry and tiled with a colored marble mosaic, this place, which I have only glimpsed, marries the extreme elegance of tradition with the most intimate comfort. And His Majesty must feel this same harmony as he goes from his bedchamber into a vast room lit by three windows overlooking the marble courtyard. This room brings together the salon of his grandfather Louis XIV, by the little staircase, and a small room with niches designed by Louis XV himself, where there are astronomical dials built into a semicircular wall. Called the Oval Cabinet, with clocks set into the walls covered with magnificent white and gold woodwork sculpted by Verberckt, this room is pleasantly furnished with chairs and tables for quadrille, ombre, and piquet, prompting its designation as the Salon de Jeux. Oh, I have contemplated it, studied it, a great deal. I hold it in my memory, and you know why.

My clock, accepted by the Academy of Sciences in 1749, constructed by Dauthiau and presented to His Majesty, thanks to the intervention of the Marquise de Pompadour, on September 7, 1750, at Choisy, then at the court on October 10, 1753, was installed in this room at Versailles, but only in 1754. That's because the Caffieris took a long time to dress it in a case of cast and chiseled bronze from a design chosen by the king himself. But Louis XV is not one to stop at appearances, if I may be allowed an opinion, and it was for the pleasure of the mathematician king that I offered my automaton. I thought of his mathematics teacher, François Chevalier, an expert on fortifications from the school of Vauban, when I was working on it in my studio in the Louvre, generously provided by His Majesty, and then on the day when they did me the honor of exhibiting it officially. I have carefully preserved the draft I present here of the lines I wrote in support of my presentation to the Beloved king, explaining the clock clearly to the court and making myself understood up to the year 9999, a year toward which my thoughts never cease projecting themselves:

"The sphere daily represents the different movements of the planets around the Sun, their location in the Zodiac, their configurations, stations, and retrogradations. Each circle carries the orb of a planet and is inscribed with the time it takes for it to circle the Sun. During its annual revolution, the Earth sees the Sun traversing the signs of the Zodiac and their degrees.

"The clock beats the seconds. Marking true time and average time, it chimes the hour and the quarter hours of true time or Sun time, repeating, on its own, the hour and the quarter hour at each quarter hour. The movement of the chime works with spring, fusee, and chain, and the movement of the clock works with a double-weighted slotted pulley.

"At the front of the clock, above the dial, a planisphere indicates the Moon's age and phases. There one can see the day of the week, the date of the month, the name of the month, and the calendar year, in a singular new construction. The mechanism is made in such a way that it can continue to indicate the calendar year for ten thousand years, should the clock exist.

"The mechanism of the entire piece is designed so that each movement can be separated if needed, though they are all linked. The number of gear wheels that compose the mechanism of the sphere is so simple that there are only sixty, as many as there are pinions, few of which are on the inside. This makes it more open to view and at the same time more solid. The sphere is one foot in diameter and is enclosed in glass. The case of the clock is entirely of bronze, gilded with ormolu. It has four faces decorated with glass, of a very pleasant shape and fine finish, and with openings so one can easily see all the mechanisms of the workings. Its height, including the sphere at the top, is seven feet."

Here end the pages that Mlle Aubane Dechartre, assistant curator at Versailles, found in the archives of the Château—upon my request, to satisfy Stan's passion. No one had touched them since the clockmaker had written them. I was overwhelmed by this fragment of unfinished manuscript written with a lively pen, whose pages had yellowed. Of course, not as much as I was overwhelmed by Stan's reawakening after several days of being unconscious, but still. The guardians of the patrimony had no clue about its existence. A pretty coup d'état in museographic science, and perhaps beyond, in my humble opinion . . .

Way to go, Aubane!

4

NIVI CAN SEE HIM AS IF SHE WERE THERE . . .

So here he is. Claude-Siméon is presenting his astronomical clock at Versailles.

The man is vigorous, slim, rather tall. His face is diamond shaped, and his aquiline nose, long and hooked, betrays his obstinacy more than any nobility, to which he has no claim anyway. One also senses a certain penchant for pleasure. His sensitive mouth is drawn in the French manner but without the willful chin. His long fine hair, inherited from his German father, is the color of wheat. The look from his piercing Germanic eyes, of a beautiful steely blue, is furtive; his gaze fixes internally or on the stars. But if his eyes fall upon you, it's to make you cringe, as Saint-Simon would have said.

Because if the Duc de Saint-Simon had lived during Louis XV's reign, which is out of the question in a time where nothing stays in place, he would certainly have noticed this man of the most precise distinction.[1] No cruelty, quite a lot of rage, frequent bouts of anger revealing an inner-directed impatience,

---

1. The Duc de Saint-Simon was the author of famous memoirs about the court of Louis XIV.

a severe judgment of his results—mechanical results, on the whole, in a mechanical world. But no feeling, no inclination with regard to others. To the point that one wonders if Claude-Siméon Passemant even has any notion of what we know as "others." For him, only the stars count. But are the stars *other*? Or are they only his invisible secret, beyond his telescope or his own antennas?

At a time as despotic and directionless as this reign, where the whole court and through it the rest of the world regulates its actions by the movements of the king, prime mover among all things, Passemant is convinced that not only is the originating mover to be found in star time but that an artisan like him is perfectly capable of reproducing it in the form of an astronomical clock whose time is infinite. And that this fabulous clock, a product of his hands, *will be* the true sovereign body by which everyone must henceforth be regulated. Louis XV has no difficulty being convinced, the court follows suit, and soon so will the entire world. See for yourself, everyone, see how the automaton has the bearing of His Majesty, perfect Louis XV style, at once light, precise, erotic, and celestial. Therefore, *Mesdames et Messieurs*, who is the sovereign? The automaton or the monarch? That is the question! I'm the one asking it, I, Claude-Siméon Passemant, engineer of His Majesty the king of France!

You can find descriptions of the fabulous clock but no trace of the inventor himself. None whatsoever. Neither in the archives at Versailles nor in the National Archives, and not even waiting to be culled from some secret location by the continuing diligence (which I have solicited) of Mlle Aubane Dechartre, the Owl's colleague. Nothing other than the clockmaker's manuscript reproduced above, which I'm guarding like a treasure.

Rereading it, and lacking any other personal testimony from Passemant, I imagine him through Saint-Simon's eyes.

Why the duke? Because there is nothing more precise, slanderous, and correct than his implacable impudence in denouncing our society's ills, the cruelty of men, the devilry in the rituals of power. Well before the Red March of Parisians and the guillotine.[2] His music caresses appearances and skewers vices. The "Little Duke," as posthumous writer, would not have botched his portrait of my Claude-Siméon: a devil of a man, but of a discrete species, neither hellish nor romantic. Not even debauched—no wild license, no filthy dance of rumors, no scandals, and at the same time an understanding collaborator, a perfect witness, the duke would have said. Our astronomer clockmaker reinforces the scientific whims of His Majesty.

A stranger to the court, of which he is however the reflection, split off from the reflection within the reflection, Claude-Siméon takes part in the becoming-mechanical of the world—from afar, from above, from beyond, from time's astronomical infinity, which does not turn the king's engineer into a rebel, just a simple dissident, as prone to migraines as he is pitiless. Echoing Stan's passion and with Stan, I love him. I invent him as a distant double of my multiverse Astro. I combine them, I see two simultaneous faces of a reality that cannot be grasped entirely or in any other way. To achieve this, I have to avoid being an

---

2. In May 1750, rumor had it that children were being rounded up and kidnapped by disguised policemen and taken to the *hôpital*—not a hospital but an institution where undesirables were interned against their will. Parisians staged a revolt, the "Marche rouge" or Red March, and a repression followed.

obstacle myself; I have to yield up all mastery, seek a network of silences, of furtive signs, of logical crossings.

If Saint-Simon had not withdrawn from court in 1723 after the demise of the regent, the very year in which his memoirs stop, he would certainly have mentioned this new species of technicians, artisans, and great scholars, whether there would be an *Encyclopédie* or not. Hadn't he wanted to connect them to the power of the throne in the form of councils he called "polysynodia," which were intended to replace the ministers? With the vehemence of his arrow-sharp wit, in a defensive gesture like a cautious fencer, the excellent, terrifying memorialist would have understood this personage of the emergent "fourth" estate, a class not yet belonging to the "vile mushrooms controlling the highest places" whose "interest is in decomposing everything, destroying everything in the end." Not a poisonous mushroom, nor in the highest places, decomposing nothing but making himself a master in composition, Claude-Siméon the subtly uncouth, the celestially depressed, the sensitively robotic would not perhaps have served in the ranks of the polysynodia. But he might have been one of their experts, nervous, annoying, and innovating, and he might have made himself indispensable without self-praise or applause. A new personage endowed with the grace to live in this time outside time that unfolds, with his clock, between the Parc-aux-Cerfs and the guillotine.[3]

---

3. The Parc-aux-Cerfs was a dwelling in Versailles where Louis XV enjoyed gallant encounters.

5

EVEN THOUGH TIME
DISAPPEARS

In the world I inhabit with Theo, I remain informed about things going on at *PsychMag* thanks to my one friend and true, Marianne. The press is undergoing a crisis. I myself have stopped reading *Le Monde* and *Libération*. I find it sufficient to glance at the news headlines that come at set times, well before the newspapers are out, on the screens of my Blackberry or my latest-generation iPhone, a loving gift from Stan. The crisis, in the end, is doing quite well, in spite of what is being said by the hoodlums in the public sphere—chroniclers, journalists, and even me on occasion. Readers revel in it and ask for more: the disappearance of a female jogger in the country, suicides at France Télécom, drought in the Charentes, corruption in our ministries and even in the town halls, paparazzi disrobing politicos and their mistresses in their hotel rooms. For lack of growth the disenchantment expands, and pop-psych magazines like mine proliferate in numbers and press runs. The psychmags now have a decisive niche in globalization. "Better," Marianne amends, always more ambitious than I, "they have a prescriptive role." Not the most lucrative, but they're doing well, rivaling churches and all sorts of communities struggling to heal maladies of the soul. Multiplying approaches and currents, not counting charlatans and other crooked gurus, the psych press surfs on crisis and profits from debt.

"It was something to think about. The worldwide network of pop-psych magazines is our chance, I already told you." An easy victory for Marianne. "Okay, so it's about money, naturally. And so what . . . ? American capital or money from the Gulf. The Chinese are pitching in too . . . You have something against that? The pharmaceutical companies were already in the pot, that's to be expected, and there will be others . . . The troubles of the soul are not lacking for sponsors. The vast sector of leisure activities, vacations, cultural productions, shows, art galleries, showbiz . . . Obviously the Internet: Google, Apple, Orange, Bouygues, Free . . . You see?"

"Not really. How does this concern us?"

"Honey, come down to earth! Well I'm here, anyway . . . An international press conglomerate has just been created in London that includes the best publications in our area . . . With the City and the financial networks, their boldness, their freedom, and all the rest. It's win-win . . . The editorial boards will have complete latitude, and we will of course retain our independence."

Marianne is not really worried. She ought to be: let's be prudent, she knows we should, but since it's inevitable my friend launches into mechanisms of denial. She continues, goes with the flow, everything is for the best.

"Well, we are at the top of PsyNetOne, right? I tell you, the crème de la crème, darling! Within GlobalPsyNet, PsyNetOne covers France, Germany, Italy, and Spain . . . They acknowledge that we have an advance on the concept—in a word, the leadership. And the chief executive officer is a Swede, Ulf Larson, with an office in Paris."

"Ulf Larson? I don't know of any Swedish shrinks by that name."

"Wake up! I'm talking finance, sweetie. The sector has to prosper, secure and profitable. Shrinks don't have the vaguest idea about that."

With this I am in perfect agreement.

"Ulf Larson, who is only Swedish by birth, comes to us from the City, where he stood out in the Murdoch empire. He will be our president. He will relieve our dear Yves considerably, always overworked, as you know. Okay by you?"

The director of *PsychMag*, Yves Thiébault, is certainly not the brightest bulb, but, devoid of scruples and with a mischievous pen, he's so good at selling new mental illnesses without scaring mothers or business leaders that I cannot imagine a better publication director. Since my job as editorialist doesn't require me to follow any collective opinion, I am content to write my own papers; I rarely attend meetings of the editorial board. I agree to go only when Yves calls me in to keep himself up to date on research in psychoanalysis, "because I am convinced it exists thanks to you, my dear." Big smile—he doesn't believe a word of it.

"So, fine, our director will now have a boss above him, so it'll be Ulf. I guarantee this Scandinavian will know how to keep his distance and won't butt in where it's not his business." Marianne is fired up at having learned so much about our new structure.

"Are you interested in management? A new hobby . . . Better than contemporary art . . ." I try to rile her. She should stick to the point. "What's he like, this Ulf?"

"Nordic, handsome. They all are."

"Married?"

"And how! Three children, but he travels a lot. He has an apartment in Paris. His family is skiing."

"Are things moving, at Levallois-Perret?"

"How long has it been since you've set foot in here? Come back down to earth! At least quit this weightlessness, you're letting life pass you by! You know it, but I'm telling you anyway. Your affair with Theo is a kind of depression. You're obstinate, maintaining the impossible. You're going to tell me it's exhilarating, but it's a little limited, isn't it? The world is moving; you have to adapt to demand, that's all. Precede it, even. And for that, angel, you have to have antennas on this side of Earth, on current events, everywhere: in different milieus, the young, the old, women, sporty types, teens, mosques, churches, synagogues, sects, arts and crafts, artists, inevitably the media, politics . . ."

She's making me drunk. I can't see her eyes. Does she really believe what she's telling me? Maybe. For her it's a reason to adapt. I'm going to tell her I agree. I feel the vibration of my Blackberry. Marianne hears it too, raises an eyebrow. I'm not listening to her any more.

It's Theo. "*Kennst du?*" he writes while listening to Mahler in his ultradeep field. He's tracking some particle or other to prove the existence of the Higgs boson. Is it possible to be with Nivi, Mahler, and dark energies simultaneously? I will not reply to ILY. "Be silent and hope." That's not Mahler; it's Mozart.

6

I DREAM, THEREFORE I AM

Current literary events force *PsychMag* to cover the *n*th attempt to demolish father Freud. "Apparently the time has come to proclaim the twilight of this idol at last. What next! We ought to do an article about the murderer, don't you think? A philosopher who's making a splash on *France Culture*! That's for you, Nivi!"

Marianne knows I detest that sort of silliness—kill the father, save the father . . . Nothing doing, she's insisting, I'm resisting: "Thanks, sweetie, but you're not getting me. Now's the time for you to show your face. Nothing's better than a profile—it's your baby, okay?" Normally Marianne just writes little psychiatric chronicles: how not to abuse drugs while still supporting the pharmaceutical industry, etc. She's thrilled to get this more powerful role; as for me, I'm back with my Astro. Farewell, profile of Freud's latest assailant!

I duck into the Café Marly, order a tea. Which? Sweet Shanghai, do you have it? Certainly! I pick out the Owl in animated conversation at the other end of the terrace—in English, yet, with two fascinated young women. Art history students, I presume, foreigners, obviously, passionate about manuscripts and French civilization. The Owl, drunk on her knowledge, doesn't see me; she doesn't remember me. No spots of blood left on her blouse; today it's pearl gray, like the sunset behind Bernini's statue of Louis XIV. This devotee of art, deep into her seduction, keeps readjusting her glasses on her blushing nose. I leave her, walk toward the Opéra, the Galeries Lafayette, the Chaussée d'Antin, and a passage that leads to that strange church hidden in the heart of the commercial district, Saint-Louis d'Antin, I think. In another life, I had followed Marcel Proust here, who thought that this is where he had had his first communion. No proof, the priest had written me. Hell of a story!

"I dream, therefore I am." That's Stan's motto. He knows how to deactivate emotions. On this day I make his motto mine. Since Marianne wants to play her part in current affairs, I let the streets of Paris take over. The light is starting to fade, silhouettes of passersby grow long, but night is distant, and I roam in time regained.

An absurd time. Exploded, fragmented: each piece plays its part, communicating vases, the puzzle takes shape and is undone. My internal coups d'état tear me apart. I convoke love and phantoms—the king's engineer and my Astro. Who are they? The pains of these conjoined partners are contagious; as they are confused, so I'm confounded. Friend of junkies, if not of criminals? No, I am a chosen one, rather, visited by no ecstasy. I lean on my books, an astronomical clock accompanies me. My time regained does not elapse; it is erected within me, outside me. Rustling, exhausting, delirious, exciting, it metamorphoses me. I come back to life—a life of expansion, a stranger to myself.

This face emerging from the shadows, I have seen it somewhere before. This catlike air, the features of a man, or rather a phantom, with large, dilated eyes turning inward. Eyes that don't see me. They are fixed on the unknown. Like Astro. No resemblance, however. Astro has brown hair going salt-and-pepper, prematurely for his age. The phantom thinks it's normal; the worry shows through. The steely eyes scrutinizing the heavens are today like a cat's: green like water. Apart from the ironic gleam, they are not my Astro's. Scarcely perceptible, I perceive a vigilant detachment, almost amused. "What smile? I'm not smiling, I'm thinking about you." That's what Theo replies to reassure me he is thinking of something other than himself. That he's split in two.

Had the sea-green eyes already glided by the astronomical clock that Stan absolutely had to see after his attack? I must have carried them off with me while running in the alleys at Versailles during the bomb alert, toward the Bleu du Roi Café, rue Colbert, or the Café de la Place, I don't remember.

"Siméon," I say.

"You are mistaken," says the man with the cat's face coming out of Saint-Louis d'Antin. "My name is Claude-Siméon."

That is indeed the name I had heard before smelling the flames that threatened the King's Cabinet, targeted by al-Qaeda.

The king's engineer walks beside me. We leave Havre-Caumartin; I cut across via rue Gluck to escape the crowds. He's following me like a shadow. Or rather like a dress that sticks to my skin in the rain, diluting me, making me flow with it. I feel naked. I cross the boulevard des Italiens, my steps take me to the rue du 4 Septembre, I cross the rue de Richelieu. For reassurance, to recover, I think about my Astro and concentrate on his messages. My iPhone is showing nothing today. I never get lost in the streets of Paris, I expand in them, their timeless labyrinth is the organ by which I take pleasure in my exile. Have I at last rid myself of the obsessive Claude-Siméon?

Oh no, now he's in front of me. There he is turning around and heading toward me, at the place de la Bourse.

"You were eighteen when Law launched his system of bank credit," I say to him. "He ruined you, didn't he?" That man was the inventor of virtual money, the first trader in history, a sort of Goldman Sachs under Louis XV.

The Cat isn't troubled. He delves into his memories of the affair that determined his fate.

It's the month of May, 1716. John Law creates his bank. A madness, or an event that will change the state of the world. People fear a serious crisis, like the ones hitting Portugal and Greece today. France too, mutters the specter, but actually, I say, it will just be yet another crisis like many others. The Cat doesn't see it that way; Dr. Law is a redoubtable player. He says: "This banker had understood that gambling is a natural necessity like drinking, eating, and making love."

I answer that it's common to think so—since when, now? The Cat thinks that Law goes much further, that he shakes up the system, the state of the state, everything that exists in and of itself: the solid, the absolute, power, order, the kingdom, cold hard cash.

"His bank is both a bank and a business, a trust and a public service, a commercial bank and a lending bank. Abandoning precious metals, he launches paper money. What's the difference? *Circulation*, of course. Circulation is easier and quicker when the material isn't weighty. Folding money announces the era of cash."

"Soon to be followed by the virtual era and along with it the digital, the hyperconnected . . ." I'm finishing his reasoning. He's thinking for me.

"You can say that again. And money goes worldwide. In 1718, his bank becomes the Royal Bank, while his Company of the West, now called the West Indies Company, absorbs the East India Company, the China Company, and the Africa Company. 'Money is for the state what blood is for the human body. Circulation is necessary for the one and the other,' proclaims this Scotsman soon turned Doctor of Good Offices of an ultraspendthrift Regency."

With a feline flair, Claude-Siméon senses that everything under the sun ends in crisis. The crisis alone is eternal. Terrestrial time plays out in the stock market with virtual money. Shares at a total loss and colossal gains. The roulette stirs up coups d'état and puts the state in a fragile state. Boring, isn't it, when you've grasped its logic? That's what he thinks. What remains is to track the only unknown worth thinking about: time in another world. Star time.

"You know it yourself, Nivi. The public, quickly accustomed to this paper money, prefers not to know that the circulation of banknotes is infinitely preferable to cash reserves. It's easy, billions in paper nourish a torrent of transactions! Right here in Paris, rue Quincampoix, between Saint-Denis and Saint-Martin, the stock market has been set up in the open. People buy and sell on the pavement, in the boutiques, in the cellars, in the attics. From seven in the morning to nine at night, the area teems with crowds that sometimes get rich, sometimes lose their shirts."

The cat-faced clockmaker is proving to me that you can't save the system, that it's been sick from birth.

"You knew that already," I say to Claude-Siméon.

"God does not pull men from the abyss any faster," he observes. "The nouveaux riches marry daughters of the nobility, and everyone disappears the next day. The duchesses attack Law the magician: 'Come now, hurry, we want money, paper money. Where are you off to? To do your business? What rot! What business do you have doing your business elsewhere? Take your piss right here and listen to us!' Nobility lets itself go; it no longer exists, under pressure to have the money that no longer insures the state, you see . . . Then everything collapses, confidence is destroyed. Speculators want to exchange their banknotes for cash, and they discover the fault in the system— so quickly! The insufficiency of metal reserves. The teeming crowd that fought to buy now fights to sell."

I must have displayed a questioning look.

No, says the steely-eyed specter, he is not a prophet. He's just spooling the film of the crisis as his father, Theo Passemant, my Astro's homonym, told it to him. Lackeys-turned-millionaires strut about in the carriages of their former masters: abbots here, waiters there, beggars, chimney sweeps, haberdashers. They gain or they lose—10, 30, 40, 70, 100 million. Plebes on top, plebes on the bottom, all greedy, all the players in a heap and all swindled.

"When the bank was transferred to the rue de Richelieu, my father was nearly crushed to death in the garden by a stampede to the teller windows, barely contained by soldiers."

Claude-Siméon emerges from his memories, somewhat surprised to have shared them with a passerby, and his gaze is now direct, as if he is finally seeing me there in front of him. Light skin, a blond quality, high cheekbones, an Eastern air. "German?"

The cat-man doesn't answer. He is thinking about his father, the mercer, master tailor at Clèves. *Klive* in German.

"He was called Theodore, known as 'Lallemand,' the German. I'm not making this up; that was his real name. Mistrust of the Germans only came later. In Law's time, they were considered nothing much. So Theodore was naturalized as French in 1704."

He changes his name to Passemant, as in *passementerie*, embroidery. He is a mercer and a tailor. Claude-Siméon's father transmits to him the insecurity of the immigrant. The son will be afraid. Afraid of society, of those who live near the Saint-Michel bridge at the corner of the Marché Neuf, and of the other students at the Collège Mazarin. Afraid with his father's fear, who fears he will be unable to leave anything solvent and durable to his only child.

So Theodore Lallemand-Passemant, to obtain as much money as possible and bequeath it to Claude-Siméon, nearly suffocates in the crowd assailing the banks on the rue de Richelieu. How much money? He would have liked at least ten million. After Law's bankruptcy, all he has left is ten thousand. Virtual capital is born. But the son of that Theodore, Claude-Siméon, already has his head elsewhere: in the clouds. He speculates on the heavens—always higher, always farther, always more alone.

I ask him if Theodore Lallemand-Passemant really was called Theo. The Cat stares at me with fixed eyeballs. What a question—since he has already said and repeated everything.

Suffocating and depressed after the stampede, Theo the tailor doesn't ever really catch his breath. The disastrous spring of 1723 begins. The ruined speculators in Paris envy the fate of the plague victims in Marseille.

"They thought you were dying too. At your father's death, after the Law affair, you were like twins, father and son."

The revenant's smile relaxes in contempt. Because the son of the master embroiderer had decided to have a look elsewhere, well before that sinister Law bankruptcy. Descartes, Newton, and the revolution of the planets. So much for Voltaire, who dreams of the revolution of the kingdom. Claude-Siméon will go seek his treasure elsewhere. In something the naked eye can't see. Something invisible, that treasury of Love with a capital *L*, which can be measured in stellar time. Much more reliable than the excessive distension of fiduciary circulation. The astronomical clockmaker is going to try. To make people's dreams last longer, go further than the desires of men and the will of God. But what blasphemy such a pretention is! An apocalypse! Shh! Do not pronounce that word! Instead, keep in mind the figure 9999.

We arrive at the rue Quincampoix, a mere tunnel of a street, narrower and certainly more nauseating than at the time of Law.

"Do you work in the stock market?"

Claude-Siméon pretends to take an interest in me. I say, "In a sense." In the stock market of souls and proper names. He says again that one should not play at that game, even less *with* that game. Too dangerous. Worse: insane.

I don't have the time to make it clear that I basically agree. The king's engineer disappears in the flood of employees emerging from nearby offices. It's five o'clock; the downpour catches everyone by surprise, and I take shelter in a doorway to answer Stan's call on my cell phone.

7

AT THE COLLÈGE MAZARIN, DURING THE REGENCY

I rarely leave my neighborhood: Saint-Jacques, Port-Royal, the Observatory, the Luxembourg, the rue des Écoles, Jussieu on occasion. Since Astro entered my life, Stan says I've broken off with the human race. I've lost my way. I scarcely stop by the office; I delegate. I browse the scientific journals, I walk, I cross the Seine, the Tuileries, Café Marly, the Louvre, the Palais Royal, the former National Library, the Bourse . . . I don't know much about the engineer Passemant; no one seems to know of him, but the man intrigues me. And it seems to me that my Theo is even more mysterious to me than that somber subject of the king to whom he is apparently related.

No one would think to be called Passemant these days. I'm sure of it. I checked on the Internet. No one. This family name no longer exists. Theo doesn't want to know whom he is descended from. "That question is without interest," he proclaims. Denial, defense for some childhood trauma or other (speaking like a shrink). That's his business: I'm not getting involved in everything. Of course he has encountered the name of the enlightened inventor and his famous clock; of course helpful people didn't hesitate to tell him what they were able to gather here

and there about the character, which is not much. So how important is it? "Madam, it's of no importance whatever!" my Astro
repeats with a Spanish accent, like Picasso replying to the lady
who claims to be an art specialist and states nevertheless that she
doesn't understand a thing about his work. "Besides, did your
Claude-Siméon, who seems very astute and clever, really invent
something, or did he simply copy the English and the Dutch?
That's what I was told, we'd have to check, history of science is
not my thing, I don't know the first thing about it, since I am
light years ahead—or behind, depending. You know that," he
concludes, with a paternalistic smile at the corner of his lips.

Oh yes, I know it!

My rambles take me to the Tuileries today. Regency teens
would not have failed to take in this stylish corner of Paris,
which has always attracted youth. There the serious and the
surly exchange smiles and kisses, rumors and vices. It's summer, it's hot, people huddle in the shade of the nearby cafés, and
I can imagine that the king's clockmaker could have met my
Theo there on a day like today . . .

"Every evening, the regent hosts a supper at the Palais Royal."
Jacques Germain seems to know all about it: one of his cousins,
like him lacking in renown but reputed for his wit and his
debauchery, claims to belong to the close circle of the regent.
Jacques Germain believes it. Claude-Siméon would like to
believe it, but really . . .

"They talk, they laugh, they drink. They shout obscenities.
They're as blasphemous as possible." Alexis d'Hermand acts
like he's one of them.

"And the regent's favorite daughter, the Duchesse de Berry,
who they said was 'as wild as the rabble,' was she there?" Charles

Joachim wants the details; the two others don't know much. "Yes, really, they say she drank like a stable boy, to the point of falling down, and would throw up on the table, splashing the diners. She's had scores of lovers. The latest, Rion, takes his pleasure in debasing and humiliating her, but he is so ugly, covered in yellow and green pustules and abscesses." He blushes with shame.

The Cat listens but adds nothing, just a nervous laugh that momentarily bursts from his larynx, his lungs, his belly. He laughs with all his neurons, a staccato hilarity, glottal expulsions of a convulsive breath, asthma sublimated in reclusive pleasures. Is it the Cat's laugh or my Astro's? A torrent of little bells, Papageno ripping off the padlock stuck on his lips, a numberless outpouring in a cascade of puerile joy, child or teen half goth, half crazy, Milos Forman's Amadeus. Sometimes he tells me about his "Berkeley period," his crazy years as a student who "learned everything and did everything" on the campuses of the East Coast: science, drugs, and the rest. Few words, always this unbridled baby laugh. Masturbation in hilarity, furtive testament to a body that "did everything" when it could, when it wanted, when it was needed. A body buoyed by a wave of candid laughter to recount it all.

If he had been here in the Tuileries with these boys from the Collège Mazarin during the Regency, Theo would have been as dumbfounded as Claude-Siméon by the debauchery at the Palais Royal. The future clockmaker must have been of the Astro type. I can see him as a fan of Watteau, another face of the Regency: pleasures that are graceful, reserved, innocent. His favorite painter dies two years before the regent, and the *Embarkation for Cythera* has nothing to do with the roundup of loose girls for

Mississippi.[1] All the same, the entire band from Mazarin is dumbstruck by the drinking sprees and other misbehaviors that the great men of the Regency loved, beginning with the regent himself, so intelligent, so progressive . . . And depraved, surrounded by the Dubois, the Broglies, the Effiats, et cetera, a lot more war-hardened and desensitized than the supper guests who excite the boys . . . Frenetic, feverish, sick with pleasure, some of them soberly so as not to harm their health—the height of vice . . . Others, spendthrifts or misers, greedy, jealous, persecutors, persecuted, always keen to blaspheme . . . Their disgrace takes the appearance of grievance, remonstrance, revenge, insurrection . . . A sort of infrapolitics? Or a comical settling of accounts, as meticulous as it is absurd? Claude-Siméon rebels in vain; the world is moving against false rights and for true rights, the unique right to progress, the right of nations that should win out, that will win out . . . No one's listening to him.

"The priests are horrified, the police had to intervene. You know what it was: a profanation, for God's sake!" Jacques Germain quivers with envy. "It's true! The body of the lawyer Nigon, in its casket at the cloister of Saint-Germain-l'Auxerrois, was desecrated by the Duc d'Arenberg, who was staying not far from there. He comes in with his friends and his lackeys, carrying bottles and glasses. They jump up on the casket, straddling it, tip up the font and spill holy water on the head of the cadaver. 'Here, have a drink, my good Nigon, since you died of thirst!' Death itself is no longer respected . . . What do you think about that? The example comes from high up . . . That's how boars and sows behave . . ." He hasn't stopped quivering.

---

1. To populate the Mississippi region, girls and women without status or means were rounded up and shipped to America.

"And the regent's minions, you know? Alexis, do you know them?"

Alexis mimes the antics of the minions with a smirk. The Cat doesn't intervene: he's ashamed, he's thinking about his father. "Stories are told, let's wait and see . . . Let's wait for the memorialists . . ."

Claude-Siméon isn't laughing anymore. The other three don't know that their dirty stories excite him so much that it disgusts him. Enough to vomit—the minions, the sows, Alexis, Jacques Germain, Charles Joachim, himself. Disgusted enough to flee, to drop them, to throw himself into the gray mirror of the Seine, the Seine that also wallows lasciviously—would it be possible to discipline it, to tame it one day? Something to look into later. Today, the Cat wants to fade into those tense reflections, drown the rise of blood beating in his temples, his lips, his penis. But no, he will control himself, govern himself. He composes his face with an air of superiority, above himself, older than his age. Astro would have done the same, he always does. Claude-Siméon floats above it, no longer laughs.

Never mind, he continues: "What's important is to govern the state, that's what my father's friends say. Instead of that, each faction has its libelers who drag the opposing faction through the mud. The regent Philippe d'Orléans, the cardinal Dubois, the royal princes, the dukes, the bastards . . . And Parliament is chafing: cessation of activity, the height of disorder, a strike, you know! People are getting irritated, my father can't take it anymore: he paces about saying 'Order, France, order is going out the window!'"

Papa Theo, new French subject and proud of it, likes to throw out political predictions, but people can't really tell if he thinks they are optimistic or catastrophist. Claude-Siméon thinks about those English and Dutch visitors, artisans and merchants eager to share the secrets of their trades and of the philosopher's stone while speculating on the fate of the world. Although Mme du Barry has not yet arrived to taunt the monarch with her *bons mots*, Papa Passemant isn't far from coming up with them himself. The revolution might be under way already, he mutters to the future astronomer-clockmaker, upon leaving discussions with his colleagues in the Harmonie Divine. And Claude-Siméon begins to sense its arrival. This event would not burden itself with government by monarchy—that's what the most audacious members of his father's lodge predict, as if they were imagining ten thousand years of universal fraternity to come.

"The regent has brought in financiers of the old school, the Pâris brothers," says Jacques Germain, clearly better informed about the reality of affairs. The three others envy him.

"And that's not all. The regent Philippe d'Orléans preferred the Jansenists because Louis XIV had persecuted them. Now Dubois has brought him back to the Jesuits. They're negotiating a settlement." Alexis d'Hermand contributes the latest news of significance, and that's logical; his family is involved.

The future engineer is overcome. He thinks his father is a dreamer—a German. The infinite is not dreamed; it is calculated. Newton and Leibniz, they're what's serious, some are even talking about them at the Collège Mazarin . . . On the other hand, his mother tells him over and over, every evening, that he has to get ready for his future—in the judiciary, for example. Not go out with those rather undesirable boys, even if they are students at Mazarin. But these days no one respects anyone: money itself has lost its meaning; anybody can attend that school if they have relations. Such is not the case with her own son, the son that Marie-Madeleine Canaple, wife of Passemant, raised like a real treasure: knowing how to economize, respecting order as concerns things and people.

Meanwhile, the German tailor labors to support the modest household while frequently escaping for occult discussions with friends whose visionary aspirations are a mystery to no one. But the young man is not really bored. He breathes in his mother's fresh-smelling skin. He imagines a world above the world. "My son has an organized intelligence," Marie-Madeleine exults in front of the entire Canaple family, reunited on Easter Sunday. "His fingers are so obedient that there is nothing their skill and their suppleness cannot accomplish." Unconsoled about never seeing him become a magistrate, she recites her son's praises the better to persuade herself of them. While the family stands in awe of the sphere Claude-Siméon has constructed. All alone, but not without having read a great many scientific books. It's a fact: he reads too much, that boy . . .

Claude-Siméon, imperturbable, lets them argue, just as he listens to the boasts of his schoolmates with a detached air. Naturally, he takes them into account, but he in turn takes leave, farther and higher than his German father did. Marie-Madeleine's mouth seeks his cool cheeks, disdains the forehead of her aging husband. The regent's misbehaviors as detailed by Jacques Germain and Alexis d'Hermand blend with his mom's perfume, with her breasts that she doesn't cover, with her thighs that innocently brush against the adolescent's skin. This woman deserves much better than the status her Theo provides. Her large nut-brown eyes avidly beg the son to make her shine in high society. Marie-Madeleine believes the future is for the Nobles of the Robe; that's what she wants for Claude-Siméon. Does she sense that a government of judges will one day take root against the authority of the king?

The young man says nothing. He doesn't succumb to passion. Neither to the passion of his mother nor that of his wife, when he has one, nor to his male friends, administrators, or ministers. He barricades himself against human passion, and this withdrawal splits his head in two. Painful border, indispensable purity. A sort of celibacy? Not really. But something approaching it, and he is going to study the question. The vices that fascinate Jacques Germain and Alexis he sees today as in a dream, beside the rosy body of Marie-Madeleine.

He will hide them one day in his automatons. Music boxes like the ones Papa Theo had brought from Clèves, which he will perfect for his daughters (he will have two). He is going to program the automatons with the popular melodies the old tailor used to hum. But to get rid of his migraine, he will need more than music boxes. No remedy beats the supreme effort of calculating the stars, the hours, the seconds, and the sixtieths of seconds.

8

NOW

Marianne is not wrong: I'm refusing to get involved. Not at *PsychMag* or anywhere else. Nowhere. I avoid going to Levallois-Perret. Those offices in glass cubes, carpeting, movable partitions, and the staff glued to their computer screens give me the chills. Ever since the editorial offices left avenue Bosquet in Paris to settle in the Hauts-de-Seine department, I have been boycotting it. Of course I know that rents are skyrocketing in Paris, that print is hardly selling anymore, but *PsychMag* in a building for the *hedge funds* of the digitized globalization causes me more anguish than the empty towers in Shanghai or the freeway-boulevards in Beijing. Machines and smartphones thrown into the void, and *what else?*

"You're exaggerating. In our location it's cuter. Beauty salons and bakeries *à la française*," Marianne corrects. She has adapted perfectly. Not me. Everywhere a calculated transparency is rushing headlong toward some point of PR. But without the childlike naivety, the charm of colors, this unmistakable re-minder of carnival that brightens the concrete mastodons of the Chinese metropoles. I don't have a feel for it, this new *Psych-Mag*; I'm obstinately absent. Yet an inexhaustible sense of efficacy inhabits me and leads me to the editorial office in spite of my-self. I close my eyes on Levallois and back into it. I sacrifice myself.

It all began with Stan. I've caught fire and I'm holding on. I had to. And it continues even more with my patients, it's only logical.

"How do you manage to keep all those balls in the air, from one thing to another, from one second to the next, moving heaven and earth?" When she forgets to be jealous of Theo, Marianne evinces empathy, she tries to encourage me. "You're living in the present, is that it?"

Weird present. With my Astro at 300 million years from the Big Bang, with Passemant soaring above Versailles at ten thousand years minus one. Theo, more knowledgeable than Marianne, tells me that my strange *present* is called *now*.

"Yes, *now*. There is nothing more specifically human, but no one realizes it, nobody gives a shit. You didn't know it either? Okay, but you're in it. Science, on the other hand, has no grasp of the *now*, it's a shame but it's inevitable, Einstein said. Is it really? Saint Augustine, who was not a physicist, saw only the present, naturally. That saintly man was concerned about souls; a present relative to the past: memory; a present relative to the present: perception; a present relative to the future: expectation. Can you guess why? Well it's obvious, since the talking animal knows that he is talking and thinking, or at least can have this consciousness that makes him present to himself and to the world, agreed? I'm not saying there don't exist patients who, because of physical or even psychic lesions, possess neither this unconscious knowledge nor even the consciousness of themselves. It's clinical, all that,

pathological. That's another story. I'm talking about the presence to oneself and to the world, *before* which lies what we call
memory of the past and *after* which we envision the future.
It's understandable why Einstein was disappointed, because
scientific reason has nothing to do with that properly human
presence."

I don't see what he's getting at.

"Well, today, in astrophysics, instead of commenting on past-
present-future, researchers are content just to calculate. They
measure before-during-after and put time in parentheses. Not
only the *now* but *time* itself does not seem fundamental; instead,
it's a human, all-too-human artifice."

I'm thinking good riddance—but what's it good for?

"You, Nivi, are never in one place for long. Neither in your
present, nor in the past, nor in the future. Why? Well, it's because
you're living on love and fresh water. I'm exaggerating—you're
not averse to champagne. You're in love but not stationary, you
'travel yourself,' as you yourself put it. You espouse the presents
of those whom you desire, of those whom you love; you are
invested in them; you inhabit them. You are living *hic et nunc*.
All in all, I'm not sure your *now* is the one I've mentioned, that
Saint Augustine and Einstein talk about. Your now is not a
consciousness, it comes from your love, it is imperious, tyrannical. Porous, definitely. That's it: you are unique in floating and
holding on like that. This is why ILY."

Theo always starts out instructing me: "Why? Well, because," then he flatters me and ends up making fun of me. This
is what he wrote me from an observatory someplace in Chile
where he is detained by a "fascinating program"—yet another—
that prevents him from attending another colloquium, just as
fascinating, in Hawaii. So he analyzes me by e-mail, it's his way

of paying attention to me. I read it, I laugh too, and it makes my day.

This specifically human "thing" speaks to me. Yes, the instant dilates now, and I coincide with what I feel, think, do, and say. The before and the after surge up, seized and incorporated into this *flash*, written as they are in amorous interlace. Though absorbed, resorbed, the course of time does not become a point on a horizontal line running toward a goal. *Now* has neither duration nor end. My dilated present is also not the vertical straight line that carried off my roommate of ten years, Teresa of Avila, toward the Infinite Love of her Beloved Spouse, all in capital letters.

Now: the expanding instant gathers together distinct universes from scattered times. It holds them together. Neither flees nor passes, neither captures nor effaces. Immobile, fleeting, singular, permeable, changing, persistent. All these traits from the explosion of time interest me. I desire them or detest them. Momentarily, locally, they constitute the spaces I inhabit (Levallois, Versailles, Fier d'Ars, the Lux, Shanghai) or the stories that attract me (Louis XV, Claude-Siméon Passemant, Theo's labs). Appearing suddenly and recomposing, these versions of time bind together in my *now*. Thanks to them, I settle down and travel myself; I lighten and re-create myself, disappear. I am their vibration, their copresence.

Is it a fiction, this *now?* Certainly, since in it I am telling of my Astro, Claude-Siméon, la Pompadour, Stan, and Marianne with her new Swedish CEO. Time is not eclipsed; it is accumulated and maintained. *Now* is not that *time-out-of-time* of the unconscious according to Freud, in which series of events, as in a dream, do not relive the past or predict the future but reveal vigilant desire. Nor is it the time of depression, which *fails to pass* because desire is frozen and in which speaking withers into silence, the body drowns in tears, life is annulled in suicide.

Neither dream nor depression, yet I know all about it. Emerging times cohabit and are distinguished in my *now*, spacetimes that encounter one another without being abolished. In the encounter between Theo, Nivi, and the king's clockmaker, we are in tune body to body, heart to heart, autonomous and correlated. Through the narrative I'm making of them, I do not take on values as my own: I adjust drives that escape me, and I escape the present. Thanks to traveling desires, *now* is not outside time, does not flee like an arrow, is not absent; it spins tendrils. From its plural atemporality there emerges an extreme time: the now of fiction. Madness at a breakneck pace but under strict surveillance. Everything is possible, and everything eclipses. Fullness of the self outside the self.

9

WHERE ARE YOU,
ASTRO OF MINE?

Y ou haven't written me for a week, but that doesn't mean I've left you, since I am with your ancestor Passemant at the time when Mme du Deffand was writing to Voltaire: "If you don't write me, I shall say you are dead and have all the Jesuits say Mass." These days we don't joke about death, and neither the Mass nor the Jesuits have any authority. We love each other in a density made of silence, of unbreakable complicities, of sensations enflamed to billions of billions of billions of degrees Kelvin. I'm trying out metaphors, appropriating your vocabulary to translate our way of being together: invisible to others, inconceivable for our friends, insane for ourselves. When you last came down to Earth in Paris, you said we approach the infinite condensation of the initial singularity that astronomers daydream about when they become philosophical. A sort of faith, in the end, this singularity. When I recover my wits and return to this side of the Big Bang—okay, it's done, I'm here—I know that you are not as far as all that. You are in the depth of the sky.

The "sky," at 13.82 billion light years, where you are looking for the seeds of galaxies and that dark energy that constitutes the greater part of the universe. You are so far away from me, in

Kourou in French Guiana or somewhere in Mexico, that I neither receive nor send you e-mails or texts. You'll get in touch
when you want to.

Apparently you and your team are now 300–400 million
years from the Big Bang? I'm only 500—poor me! At this rate,
my A, how far are we going to get? You were saying exploration
is not difficult; it's the philosophical quest accompanying it that
poses a problem.

I was expecting that. What happened before this boundary
of light? That is the mystery. The Nothingness that preceded
the All, couldn't it have already been a latent Being? All right,
but how to go from one to the other? By hierarchical growth or
by dissipating collapse? The one or the other, unless it's both at
the same time? Do you desire me, or is it that you are interested
in my philosophical extravagances? I would like to believe you
will say *both*, is that it?

At the degree of intensity where I am with you, we draw our
reflections from intimate darkness, and I am not surprised that
being apart brings me so little suffering. Living at a distance in
space and in time spares us the anguish of separation. This is
well known (speaking as a shrink). Before us, someone had already asserted that an intimate knowledge of interstellar space
dissipates the unhappiness of departure. Was it Pascal? Or
Rimbaud? In any case, that's where we're at.

Each in our orbit, travelers always under way. We don't have
to uproot ourselves like plants, and no need for animal warmth
like mammals. Our "us" is not really terrestrial, in short; it is
interstellar, you think. Cold? On the contrary: incandescent.
That is the paradoxical advantage of our presence in spite of being apart: nothing can separate us.

At the very instant when I think I miss you, remembering
you brings me joy. After a few minutes, without my having said

or even written the slightest word, you reach me with a vibration of the background radiation. Then I know your penis comes to me. And somewhere in the vicinity of the Cosmic Microwave Background where you state you are living right now, the pulsations of your neurons carry off both your tongue and mine, your skin, my skin, our blended blood. Your neurons arrive here in the waves of the Atlantic and the sands of the Conche des Baleines, where I'm constantly making love with you. Neither real nor virtual, we are *attuned*.

Right after meeting you, I thought I would be able to suspend the copulation that transports us as soon as we think about each other. As of now, this is beyond my strength. I don't want to, I am not able to. You have no need to tell me it's the same for you. I know it. IT IS. It is like that. The pleasure of desire at will, without conditions. The inner experience plays out for two, whatever the supposedly real exterior may be. Finding you in Seattle, Grenoble, Paris, Mexico, Chile, anywhere, anytime, nowhere or never, neither presence nor absence counts. Only the explosion takes place, and the place continues its expansion into innumerable human and inhuman variants. We live its magic permanence, 13.82 billion years extending to you and me, as you say, in the 4 percent emerged matter, 74 percent dark energy, and the rest, 22 percent, which is just dark matter. I am replying that that's called love. ILY.

10

KING, GOD, AND COMPLEX TIME

There's nothing scientific about it, is there, A of mine?"

"In astrophysics, we have equations to describe this outpouring of multiple universes. Elementary particles permit their emergence. But the reasoning that imagines these unthinkable limits seems too abstract for those who have not known an amorous alchemy like ours. It is foreign to our senses as soon as we leave our labs. To such an extent that none of my colleagues wonders if there is a human experience that would be in unison with this ultratime that conjugates time that passes and time that passes by the wayside."

I like it that Theo gives his lecture course for me, but really he asks himself questions, seeks to justify himself, has doubts, and doubts his doubts. As is often the case, his teachings end with a question.

"Besides, is it possible *to personally experience* all those times of the complex universe as revealed to us by current cosmology? Do we really need those intimate coups d'états to thaw disappearing time, to instill its absence in the provisional time that emerges? Can these times resonate in the heart of hearts of a man or a woman? And if that can happen, where is the cause, where is the effect? Do scientific discoveries modify our way of thinking and feeling? Or, on the contrary, is it the inner experience or our wandering fictions that leave their imprint on fundamental research?"

As for me, I know what to call this human experience of the *now*. Quite simply, it signs ILY. No need for words—too romantic, pathetic, ridiculous. ILY is enough. I'm not going to tell Theo; I'll write it to him one day, perhaps. To love, like to believe, *credo*: I give myself, you give yourself. To love from afar, at a distance, close by also, thoroughly, from the depth of the bowels, from everywhere, without security, with complete security.

"There is time: That much is clear for everyone, isn't it? Newton himself was of that opinion: he thought the universe was equipped with a master clock, as it were. My homonymous ancestor, your Passemant, read Newton, and not content to adopt his science, it seems he was its everyday artisan in that Society of the Spectacle that was Versailles. You know that aging, elegant society better than I do. In any case, Newton and Passemant listened to the tick-tock of that cosmic time clock, which for them replaced God but which they continued to call God. Newton and Passemant believed in it, projected themselves into it, into time; they were persuaded that this tick-tock proposed a more certain future than the revolution. Their vision lasted how long? Two centuries, a little more? Order, continuity, duration, simultaneity, absence, crises, perhaps, and new departures, necessarily. Catastrophic or fluid, it flows, it outflows and rebounds, always moving forward, obligatory. Everyone was educated like that, everyone believes in Time!"

The twentieth century dismantled such self-evidence, but people don't want to hear about it, and my Astro is amazed! Have they not demonstrated the asymmetry of matter in the universe, confounded absolute simultaneity, revealed that the observer determines the observed? All these discoveries should have knocked us sideways, but no, people prefer to recycle the deceptive evidence of the everyday, the old thinking. Why?

"Quite simply because the binomial space/time seems incontrovertible. But gravitation deforms time. So long to a single temporal parameter! Newton's time decomposes in general relativity. With that, how can you expect king and God to endure!"

"That's not the point we're at now. Didn't the Republic replace them?"

"In appearance. But they did not really disappear under democracy's laws. Kings and gods are still here to manage time. Not just through tyranny, dictatorship, Holocaust, or extraordinary endemic crises. But because spectators and Internauts believe the universe is stable, that it has to be, with time that progresses in a straight line toward capital-*M* Meaning. They lack security, illusions, traditions. They need time to reestablish the order of things, the social model, security, life! They need things to *last* according to their way . . . So they ask for time; they will keep asking for it again and again!"

While Theo is philosophizing, Nivi thinks that Internauts are children, that we are all children. That Oedipus wants to settle a score with a father before seating himself on his right or taking his place.

Astro continues: "So that's what your patients tell you? The anxieties of the couch perpetuate monotheisms, I suppose . . . But you've noticed it yourself: the Oedipus crisis is just one of the possible psychic spaces. Humans invent others, unless I'm mistaken. They say shrinks notice it themselves, that other spaces, other times, are heard from the couch . . ."

No point in intervening. Although Theo's monologues are teeming with questions, I sense that the moment is coming when he is expecting no echo. Here it is. I am silent. I will write to him later that ILY is our quantum state. Yes, ILY evolves in time, so Nivi and Theo cannot know at any moment—none can know—what resolution, what choice or event to expect. Except by a calculation of probabilities, and even then. Nevertheless Theo feels and knows what I feel and know. If ILY is an infinite power, my duo with Theo reacts like a pair of quantum particles. What affects me affects him, wherever he is. ILY is our "spooky action at a distance," an instantaneous correlation. Is time abolished, then? On the contrary, ILY provides another master clock to the universe.

"There is no *now* in physics. Duly noted! But when the black body of the thermal equilibrium is linked to evolution, the quantic system enters a transitory state (the KMS state, according to the initials of its inventors: Kubo, Martin, and Schwinger). Its inherent time ceases to exist and is transformed into a complex, hypothetical time in two dimensions: real time and imagined time. A minute can last an hour, or jump from noon to 9 p.m. . . . ."

"This complex time has no chance of existing in our reality." I think I've understood, and I want to reassure him. But he outstrips me, more subtle than I.

"Other than for Nivi, the tightrope walker! You incorporated it into your very own *now*. A *now* not like the others, the Nivi *now*. Nothing like that astrophysical time that emerges from atemporality when we attempt to unify general relativity with quantum mechanics. My colleagues are convinced of it, I know their reasoning: I practice it; it goes without saying! And yet . . . I don't let them in on what I tell you, what we experience, you and me. Don't worry! Maybe some people will understand me. That's not the problem. Nivi, I like your way of living in this *now* that belongs to you. My mind is at home in your complex time, my senses too."

I take his hand. His hand in mine. And our bodies, free of each other, in each other, limitlessly. And Astro would not be my Astro if he did not try to initiate me into his science so I can follow him to where he has got to with time. Not without maintaining my fiction, while smiling at the white hieroglyphic swan that watches us make love from the other side of the veranda. And thinking about his labs, Versailles, Claude-Siméon, 9999. That's his way of being in love. In cosmological terms most of the time but giving of himself with his entire body now.

11

LOUIS THE BELOVED

Today, Claude-Siméon Passemant, the son of the German embroiderer, is not afraid. Usually crowds make him sick to his stomach. But during this dry August night, with lighted windows, tables set up along the streets, fires and dances, he feels safe and warm. The moon is full. The Big Dipper shines in the heart of a celestial ceremony. With Charles Joachim, Jacques Germain, and Alexis d'Hermand, his day-student pals at the Collège Mazarin, he threads his way through the mob as far as the Conciergerie. Claude-Siméon, mixed in with the people of Paris—who, having apparently forgotten the bankrupt bank and the bottleneck of taxes, are shouting at the top of their lungs, "Long live the king!"—finds himself shouting it as well.

Jacques Germain, the most assiduous of the three in their philosophy course (which is what they call theology at Mazarin), wants to go to Mass at Notre Dame the next day, but Claude-Siméon protests: "Forget it, it's for the regent, the court, the red robes!"

At the festival of Saint-Germain-l'Auxerrois, the king, who is only ten, felt sick during the service. He developed a strong fever during the night, and twice they had to resort to bleeding him. Everyone in the city feared it was smallpox. Now that his recovery is certain, joy is overflowing.

Charles Joachim's cousin, a woman from Les Halles, is among the deputation to the Louvre. She takes an eight-foot sturgeon there, and butchers offer beef and mutton; there are also the coalmen with their cockades and their drums. Accompanied by his favorite in the group, Alexis, who is keen on geographical maps and strong in mathematics like himself, Claude-Siméon decides to attend the free performances at the Opéra and the Comédie-Française. They will have their opera glasses, will try not to miss anything happening on stage—whirlwinds, masquerades, fireworks, words falling like rain and pulverized into farce.

Louis is only eight years younger than Claude-Siméon. That's a lot; that's nothing. But he is the sovereign, and all the adolescents at Mazarin celebrate the royal recovery the way they venerate a god—that god they will not become, even if they secretly wanted to, but who knows, things shift, times change.

"Never has a people loved their king so," says his father with a learned swagger, playing the part of the respectful nobleman.

Papa Lallemand (speaking of him) is taking his time to die. He remains cloistered at home, though not without following events, above all the coronation. He pushes his son to seek a position higher than their modest condition, as do his lodge brothers, who come from Austria, Aberdeen, or Exeter, who speak of a certain James Anderson and are fired up by the idea of translating his Constitution.[1] Claude-Siméon barely understands

---

1. James Anderson was the author of *The Constitutions of the Free-Masons*, written in 1723 and published in America in 1734 with Benjamin Franklin's name on it. This was the first Masonic book published in America.

what they are saying—the same thing and its contrary, it seems to him, a world before or beyond the visible world. Moreover, Papa Theodore is so careful with his words that scarcely has he pronounced one than he reverses it, enough to give you the headache that will become chronic for his son.

"Never has one seen such love, nor heard such a fuss," says he about the crowning of the young king. Mysterious, Papa Theo? As always a sidestep: Theodore Passemant is not really comfortable with the terrestrial order of things. Nothing can be done, that's destiny. Passemant the son, Claude-Siméon himself, is certainly taken with the young sovereign. When Louis is twelve, he will be fully king, crowned at Rheims in 1722. Good riddance to the Regency!

A tumult of love: three thousand tables, eighty thousand bottles of champagne, a gigantic buffet where everyone helps themselves and their hunger. Today, we admire the child-adolescent, bursting with youth, grace, beauty, among the diamonds, the flowers, the cries, the incense . . . High Mass at Sainte-Geneviève . . . Competition for the Saint Louis prize at the Tuileries . . . Too bad for Theodore, who grumbles in his corner: "Never has one's health been celebrated to this extent. And far too costly . . ."

Claude-Siméon will always remember the portrait of this Louis XV as he imagines him then—already sovereign, though a child. Obviously he didn't see him; he's in the parade of celebrators with Jacques Germain, Charles Joachim, and Alexis d'Hermand. But he's able to imagine him all the better. And he will respect him, since Theodore wants him to. He sees Louis in his mind as the young monarch of not quite twenty that Jean-Baptiste Van Loo will later glorify: with boots and a breast plate, his left hand on the hilt of his sword, the right resting on his command staff. Louis poses, his body stiffens in the attitude of majesty. His high forehead and the acute line of his nose are marks of nobility. But the pink cheeks betray the incurable spleen of the orphan and a furtive feminine gentleness. Under his elongated almond-shaped eyelids, large dark eyes languish, already blasé or turned inward. Inaccessible zenith. Depression mixed with the empire of the senses seems posed upon the head of a body raised for dancing minuets, hunting stags and women, being saluted by the troops.

In this mirage of the young Louis that Claude-Siméon imagines while celebrating his recovery among the crowd, he cannot help painting his own wishes. Under the sovereign highness that transcends them, in the fog of the mournful gaze, the long eyelashes like a young girl's, the flaccid flesh of the jowls, the feverish adolescent from Mazarin caresses unavowed temptations. Too passive, ready for somber cruelties, bloody angers to suppress unavowable abandon. Who guesses so? His ambitious mother, who bears her name Marie-Madeleine to perfection? No chance. Alexis d'Hermand certainly, the close friend and more than that who scarcely hides his attraction to the male dancers at the Opera. "Are you coming?" he cries, aping the minions of the Tuileries. Claude-Siméon thinks Alexis is overdoing it, it's not funny anymore. "His society is not ours," the mercer and his spouse have always warned him. Passemant the son is going to cut into the flesh of his daydreams, of his weakness for Alexis, for Marie-Madeleine. What remains is royal seduction, bolstered by readings, halted by evasions into the stratosphere. Interminable fumbles, adjustments, finesses, and feints worthy of a royal clockmaker-jeweler. One could hardly put it better, since he will become one.

As for the fragile Louis, destined from birth to a shorter life than even that of his parents, he cultivates muscles and passions, suffers no fatigue, kills beasts and humans in his hunts with hounds, thinks only about the next day's conquest. Between the head of the melancholy androgyne and the haughty body of the commander-in-chief, he shelters a secret garden, to which the somber memory his gaze reveals bears witness. Invisible to all, courtesans and even mistresses. But not to Claude-Siméon. The future astronomer will see intercontinental and interstellar spaces traverse the suave and painful unspoken royal thoughts, the promised land of geographic and astronomical maps, numbers, calculations, altitudes, scales, stars, plants, zoology, all sorts of science. No art. The king refrains: art dispenses pleasures to the senses, and His Majesty's are as volcanic as they are fragile. There are places for that, discreet if possible—the Parc-aux-Cerfs, for example, which will be notorious.

Claude-Siméon, too, has a single passion: light. That is what saves him from his own "black holes," migraines, and untold rages. The gentlest of men, the most docile of spouses, the most tender of fathers with his two daughters (after a son who died at an early age) and with his sons-in-law, to whom he will transmit his science, his daydreams, his enterprise, light. The light that Louis shelters in the velvet of his eyes, that he explores in his private cabinets. That he shares only with the great scholars of his kingdom. And also, sometimes, rarely, with the unranked chosen, those outside the game, outside the times, like this Passemant who brings him his fabulous clock, the one he had presented as a project to the Academy of Sciences on August 23, 1749.

On October 10, 1753, Louis is waiting for him at Choisy. The clock conceived by Passemant was constructed by the clock-maker Louis Dauthiau in a new case of gilded bronze, which the king ordered from the famous bronze smelters Jacques and Philippe Caffieri. The Duc de Chaulnes is charged with presenting the wonderful object as well as its inventor. A great honor. An event. But what's this? The inventor is late. An offense. Calamity! Catastrophe! The courtesans panic, scandal threatens. His Majesty doesn't wait. Will not wait for long. What time is it? This is too much for a king, even one who protects the sciences. Finally the man arrives!

12

THE FAMOUS CLOCK

C laude-Siméon has a horrible headache that day. Is it the rain battering the Château de Choisy? Is it the grandeur of the royal person? The engineer can't move, hasn't a single word to say. Prostrate.

Many of those who helped him complete his various works, crowned by the already famous astronomical clock, have been gathered before His Majesty for some time already, struggling to distract him as best they can. The Comte de Maurepas should have been the work's sponsor. Was it not he, the state secretary in charge of administering the Royal Academy of Sciences, who granted to the hardworking technician a privilege from the king for the construction of his reflecting telescope? But Maurepas, in disgrace for several years now, is no longer among the scientific counselors nor in the circle of invited personalities. He is the declared enemy of the king's mistresses, noted for his witty sayings, suspected of being the author of an epigram directed against la Pompadour in person. It's the Marquis Charles François Paul Le Normant de Tournehem, director general of buildings and close relative of the *favorite*, who, seeking to associate himself with the prodigious jewel, advances toward the

king as a connoisseur to remind him that solid walls are indispensable for this kind of work.

"To be able to attach his instrument for observing the stars on the walls, in line with the Meridian," he concludes in learned tones, thus letting people believe he has been involved in the entire project at the desire of the king and thanks to his protection.

Louis XV is not an expert in communication. Most of the time words refuse to come out of his mouth, other than banal canned phrases relayed by a distressing mutism, an absent air. His mechanical questions call for no answers. At times one senses that he would like to speak more, but without taking the risk of granting or soliciting affection.

A few succeed in drawing him out of his reticence: scholars, his children—and his angora cat. And then, surprise, while waiting for the clock and its inventor, the king recovers his presence of mind along with the pleasure his scientific knowledge brings him, a presence well served by his grand style and all the colors of his expression. His Majesty approaches the object.

"What exactly is it? A clock? A mockup of the universe? An androautomaton? A priapic sculpture?"

"The clock made into a man, Your Majesty!" says Chaulnes.

Indeed. An enormous head and not just one sphere but two—the solar globe with all its planets atop the ball of its clock face. But the silhouette of this automaton lacks arms. All its cleverness is elegantly constricted in its waist, svelte like the dancer of a minuet. Male strength is planted in the legs, sporty thighs and calves, spread wide the better to encircle the treasure of this personage: its gigantic pendulum consisting of a heavy mass of gilded copper suspended from its stem, able to oscillate around an axis of rotation and thus regulate the movements of the clock.

Their eyes riveted to the crotch of this astronomical android—on the pendulum of the clock, to be exact—the (male) guests are also swinging back and forth, not at all sure if they are supposed to admire the exploits of science, rhapsodize about the beauties of the art, or envy the virile powers of this being as rigorous as it is eternal. Had one wished to give His Majesty a mirror of his own gifts, one could not have done better!

"An astronomical male, Majesty!" says Tournehem.

Obscenity is hardly in style, but everyone still has in mind the *Ode to Priapus*, which resulted in its author, Alexis Piron, not being elected to the Académie. La Pompadour offset this failure with an equivalent pension, but still.

"Perhaps not Priapus, but it's really *Metromania!*" Luynes takes it upon himself to whisper the title of the play by the same Piron that caused a scandal at the Comédie-Française.

"It's fortunate Maurepas is missing. He would have recited Piron's poem:

Priapus, give me breath,
And for a brief moment into my veins
Bear your fire . . ."

Tournehem is definitely not planning on being bored.

"Enough, gentlemen! Maurepas is a *witty* man, but for the moment astronomy is where we are, and before you is a masterpiece conceived by M. Passemant." As Chaulnes never fails in his role, the ceremony becomes serious again.

Overwhelmed with pain, embarrassed by his lateness, Passemant comes forward, more haggard than ever. Only his two eyes, used to staring at the stars, express the curiosity of a fascinated, inaudible intelligence. His Majesty, so close by today, seems nothing like the imagined adolescent whose coronation he had followed as a schoolboy. No connection either with the whimsical sovereign whom rumors charged with burlesque exploits—walking on rooftops at twenty-one, accumulating acrobatic feats along the gutters, shouting like a savage to scare guests in the Château. No more of that mischievousness, that great cordial pummeling. To the sudden inconsistencies and the legendary mutism of the young monarch have succeeded an apparent reserve and insatiable, less and less secret rituals of pleasure. The voluptuous hunter has been refined into an enthusiast of science, skilled with his hands, master of his memory. And that is the man, King Louis XV, whom the engineer of time contemplates by an unheard-of chance right here, in this very instant, before the best of the court gathered here for the occasion.

Today, Louis XV looks more like the portrait by La Tour than the one by Van Loo. Piercing gaze, trembling masculine beauty, sensual lips and nostrils, the desire for and the practice of carnal domination. Precisely what Claude-Siméon fears and flees, he the ascetic who reads and rereads everything he can find as testimony about the life of monks, saints, and hermits. As if to justify his disgust or dismiss his vices.

When he sees his automaton dressed like Louis XV, in the case fabricated by Caffieri, Passemant thinks he's having a nightmare. The infinity of time contained in a human carcass, even a royal one—that is surely a scientific absurdity, he thinks. It's a monstrous stupidity! What demon, what infernal alchemist can have fomented such an offense? Unless it's a farce, a joke—but by whom, on what?

Before this unbearable vision, the engineer wants to cover his face; shame is drilling into his brain. But he is struck by one detail: this homunculus has no arms. Did that idea come from him, from Claude-Siméon? It doesn't seem familiar. No, had it escaped him, he would have disavowed it at once; he will never assume its paternity. Perhaps Caffieri made 9999 armless precisely to remove from it the mad pretention to seize hold of the passing years and, why not, of the expanding cosmos? Or did the furniture builder want to draw attention to the sovereign crotch? Or was it just a fantasy?

In any case, in taking note of the automaton's handicap, the inventor immediately feels his anguish diminish. He brushes a light kiss on his own hands, as if he is discovering them for the first time. These hands that will never hold anything but the pen, the compass, the square, the plumb line, books, and metals, screws, and nuts. He looks at this work of his that does not capture passing time but tries to adjust its inner being to the cosmic race that transcends it. And a certain pride touches his heart, which doesn't even last a second—perhaps a sixtieth of a second.

Chaulnes tries to excuse the unfortunate inventor's tardiness: "Majesty, M. Passemant suffered a headache so painful that it prevented him from presenting himself before Your Honor at the given hour."

Tournehem tries in vain to obtain a few words from the engineer about his prodigious clock programmed to the year 9999. Aaaah! sighs the audience. With the position of the planets, the hours, the minutes, the seconds, the sixtieths of the second. Aaaah!

But it's the sovereign who comes up with the right words to put an end to the malaise of his talented servant. Who was it who said His Majesty had complexes? His very straight stature, his head held high, and his robustness, sculpted by the outdoor exercise that Louis enjoys and recommends, grace him with a masculine manner and a noble grandeur. But it is "the expression of his magnificent head" that Giacomo Casanova himself, a keen connoisseur in matters of seduction, finds overwhelming, "when the monarch turns it to look at someone with benevolence," writes the Venetian. At this moment the someone is none other than Claude-Siméon Passemant.

"He mustn't worry. Like him, I have been subject to headaches that have not had any consequences."

The ice is broken. Who was it who said His Majesty was not an expert at communicating? Passemant feels the blood flowing in his veins once more; his voice resonates in his throat. His gaze encounters the eyeballs of the king.

"Sire . . ."

The inventor has forgotten his notes. Fixed in his diamond-shaped face, which betrays obstinacy more than scientific nobility, his piercing eyes scan the draft consigned to his memory. Clearly this technician is in breakdown mode. After tardiness, forgetfulness. Will the chain of accidents never stop, then? Luynes, like a canny psychologist, comes to the rescue and fills the silence with a sententious tact: "Our scientist pronounces more sentiment than words. His politeness is simple, but never false. We are listening."

The description will be brief and precise. The two men—the king facing his engineer—and their two worlds are suddenly joined in this instant of *becoming*, named 9999 that day. One of those majestic spectacles, like the ones the Duc de Saint-Simon immortalized in the past, "where nobody thought to budge, and deep silence reigned."

A brouhaha and a little applause follow. Passemant looks out for the grudges, the jeers of the ignorant, the bigoted, the jealous, and such. He glimpses only delighted faces. His Majesty is pale with concentration. He walks around the clock several times, remarks on the position of the planets in the solar system, with the eclipses. And notes the time—"a lot of time"—that will elapse until the year 9999, its hours, minutes, seconds, and sixtieths of seconds.

"You are hunting the sixtieths of the seconds all the way up to 9999, Passemant, congratulations!" he says with the smile of an experienced reveler.

"This clock is the most beautiful in the world!" Luynes exclaims. "I believe it's a miracle of science."

"One that gives us a headache!" says the marquise, the only woman in the audience. His Majesty's face darkens.

General stupefaction. Suddenly the assembly hears the clear, resonant voice of the king, who carefully avoids looking at Mme de Pompadour: "This masterpiece would more likely make mine go away, as far as I'm concerned."

"May I be permitted to agree with His Majesty?" Passemant hears himself pronounce these words, at once realizing their temerity.

"You may, my good man. Nothing brings people closer than the body's pains. And the light of Apollo, right?"

The king's supper punctuates the presentation of 9999. Passemant is present, against all etiquette. Louis XV's hungry curiosity is beginning to shock even the most devoted of his followers; the traditionalists of the court seize upon the slightest reason to plot. Never mind, Louis bombards his engineer with questions.

"Luynes, you will have this astronomical clock installed in the grand apartment in Versailles, next to the bedchamber."

"Yes, Majesty . . . Well, the changes to the interior apartment of the king have occasioned some contestation. I have requested that M. de Gesvres be so kind as to inform me of the details . . ."

Luynes makes certain that entries to the king's dwellings are strictly regulated. When the sovereign goes to morning Mass, for example, only the grand chamberlain, the first gentleman of the chamber, and the captain of the guards have the honor of following him, as well as any princes of the blood who are there. All who wish it are presented in the throne room, but none are presented in the bedchamber . . .

His Majesty is not listening.

"Did you hear me, Passemant? You will be well lodged, my good man. I speak of your clock, naturally. As for your person, you will have a pension of one thousand *livres* and an apartment at your disposition in the Louvre, in the galleries. Be assured of my benevolence and of all my protection."

"Those persons who have the honor of following the king cross the interior corridor only after him; the door is always double-locked when the king passes there . . ." Luynes continues to murmur.

"Go now, you may leave, Passemant."

The inventor bows but doesn't lower his head in front of the sovereign.

"Don't look at me like that. It's surprising, I know, but that's how it is. I can be gentle, polite, amiable, speaking a lot, even speaking with exactness. That does happen, with wit and charm, contrary to what they say. Oh yes, oh yes! Cheerful and affable, talking and talking well, it will be said; you will see, or your descendants will see." The monarch is more and more at ease with his engineer. "We have time, don't we, you and I? At least ten thousand years; that is what you calculated, isn't it? Afterward, we'll see. Luynes, rest assured, this astronomical clock will be installed under Apollo's rays. Where exactly? Its place is in the Petits Cabinets. Where the Meridian will pass, one day, later, obviously. You will do it, won't you?"

Whereupon His Majesty veils the homosexual languor of his eyes, shuts up his orphan timidity within his royal pause, and leaves the clockmaker, who has had the privilege of counting among his intimates for the space of only a few moments.

You who doubt this encounter, read Louis XV's letters to his grandson, the *infante* Ferdinand de Parme. They bear witness to the realism of the scene and the comments of the sovereign, which would galvanize the body and mind of the inventor until his death.

It is certain that His Majesty is quite seduced by the masculine beauty of the clock. It is true also that his trauma as an orphan found in the sciences a refuge to heal wounds. One also knows that with time heaven transcends the risky charms of the *favorites*. The astronomers' heaven as well. But it is the sensitivity of an *old child* that advances, in Choisy on this autumn evening, toward the visionary servant who prowls around his clock and talks to it. A Louis who knows how to flow with the weather, who cares daily for his "generative parts" like a baby, in the anguish of his death and much taken with survival, riding beasts and mistresses, mixing women with auroras. Who deprives himself of nothing, seeking the "most desirable," which is found only in "peace" and "the state of nature," though his people do not really see it. And which only the good work of men of science brings him with certainty.

Father and son, sometimes the one, sometimes the other, both at the same time, neither the one nor the other, difference of age and social rank fused in a primary humanity. At such a game the loser wins, but before losing the affection of the nation,

His Majesty writes sentences like these to the son of his daughter Elisabeth de France and Philip II:

> "The cold has returned almost as bad as before, and everything is white as if dusted with sugar."

> "Did your surgeon, who they say is good, see the problem with your organ, which could only have come from your prepuce being too long and difficult to pull back?"

> "My arm is still very far from its natural state, but since it deprives me of little, I pay it little attention. Nevertheless I have taken a bath and a shower, and I think I will continue to do so for a few days."

> "I am very glad that your generative parts are better, and that you are enjoying yourself as much as you can."

> "What is this disease in your wife's breast? Does she have much of a bosom, because she is thin, they say, and do you find her pretty; it seems to me this little illness should not prevent the rest."

> "I am delighted that your wife is better. We have also had several auroras [that is what the king calls rainbows], but as they are rather frequent, people no longer pay much attention."

> "Hot weather has arrived here, and it is excessive, which could bring us storms. They are cutting the wheat as fast as they can."

> "I am not pleased that Antoinette is too fat at her age."

> "My indigestion is gone, but in the last few days I had a bit of a stomachache from having drunk, or rather tasted, a cup of white chocolate with cream and ice."

"You mustn't despair of anything, my dear little one."

"On Wednesday we had a phenomenon at ten thirty [the comet of 1771], which frightened everyone."

"I don't remember having heard of the rumor [of war] you are talking about. Peace is what is always the most desirable."

Louis is afraid of death. His parents poisoned—no proof, of course. By the Duc d'Orléans himself? No indication of that either. All he can do now is live life to the fullest: in herbs, passions, rainbows, sex, breasts, births, rebirths, peace, war (to be avoided). To protect himself from attacks! Was Damiens a sign of the Last Judgment? To live on hygiene and pleasure. To live: ten children with the queen, Marie Leszczynska (almost a child a year), of which three dead at an early age, and thirteen adulterous children with his mistresses. We don't count the others.

Was Louis XV a sensual bioautomaton, a tireless rower in the Tao of procreation? Shattered at the death of his son Louis-Ferdinand, upset when his daughter Louise, called Madame Seventh, enters the Carmelites, he "cries in private and affects tranquility in public." It's been attested to. At that time, depression is not French.

After the loss of the dauphin, courageously putting on a good face, Louis lies in his armchair for eight days in a row, heartbroken. The only thing he can bear is the presence of the famous Cassini, much to the displeasure of the courtesans who smother in ridicule the astronomical distractions of their sovereign.

And at this tearful father's side, the fabulous astronomical clock 9999 and the specter Passemant, his elder by eight years, his good fellow and his double, his son, his brother. This protégé of the same Cassini has surpassed himself; he has surpassed them all, both the court and his king. His only purpose in life was to capture the time of survival, that time of the stars, in a body of bronze and wood in the purest Louis XV style, his own body. A royal engineer whose headache His Majesty humors at hearthside on this day in January 1754.

The lover of la Pompadour, a sinner and hence all the more a man of the faith, finds peace only with men like this one, men of talent and perseverance, whatever their birth. Those qualities he lacks, but he doesn't complain; he leaves it to them. Such is his religion, his revolution. "If I have committed errors, it is not for lack of volition but for lack of talent and for not having supported as I would have liked, especially in matters of religion," he insists in his private testament.

His heart saturated with anguish and none the less admiring.

13

AMONG THE CONVULSIONARIES

The spring daylight floods the courtyard on the rue aux Fers, where Claude-Siméon has set up his workshop as a mercer. He's a mercer only in name. A dreamer, rather, besotted with astronomy and clockmaking, stranded among honest artisans. Surrounded by the richest silk merchants of Paris, this son of the venerable German spends the bulk of his time immersed in scientific books, calculating the paths of the stars, and constructing telescopes, sundials, barometers, and thermometers. Then, seeking reflection, he goes to Saint-Eustache, his parish church, which saw the baptisms of the Beloved king, Richelieu, and Molière. Claude-Siméon is thinking only of filling his soul with the polyphony of Rameau, transcribed for the precious sixteenth-century organ. The stained-glass window of the south transept is a circus of sonorous colors, a divine jewel that diffracts universal clarity to infinity. There is only one retreat—the chapel of the Virgin— that pacifies this solar madness, brings order to the bedazzlement and transmutes it into time for oneself: into quietude.

The faithful clients of the respectable *passementier* are starting to distrust this heir who scarcely listens and frequently sends them to his father's colleague Louis-Onophre Ollivier on the rue Mazarine, a member of the famous Ollivier clan, all suit tailors acquainted with high society. Publications of the Academy of Sciences are piling up on top of the astrological treatises Passemant junior prizes. Like his father, he is very skillful with his hands; his work is more than adequate, but everyone can see that his mind is elsewhere. If he's become a cabbalist—no big deal! It's what people are talking about a lot these days. Instead of working at cutting cloth with his scissors, he polishes glass, cuts steel and copper, inserts screws and nuts, spheres and dials, goes from one book to the next, and would rather cover his notebooks with microscopic writing, numbers, and sketches than calmly take his clients' measurements while conversing with them, as he should.

Especially since as night falls—does he take himself for a magus?—this individual trains spyglasses on the moon. He's visited by secret societies, it's a fact—the neighbors have seen them. This coterie exchanges writings and calculations and goes about melting metals. They build machines; they aim for the sky.

A great friend and protector of Passemant the father, Niels van Klim, or rather one of his relatives, a clockmaker and co-worker of the famous Julien Le Roy, who works for His Majesty at Versailles, crisscrosses Europe and brings him, at the rue aux Fers, the latest inventions of the English, the Dutch, and the Italians. It's not surprising that the fingers of young Passemant see, that his eyes feel, that his mind knows how to calculate to the millimeter the magnifying glasses, the number of wheels and pinions, the turns of the crank, the teeth of the gears necessary to make the sphere of each planet turn. Earth, Jupiter, Mars: no detail escapes him. This Niels van Klim knows the calculations of Huygens and Newton inside out. "It's indispensable," he convinces the already quite knowledgeable young man. "Learn them and apply them, and you will have all Versailles in your corner," he promises. "You will have God in person, since He is the Great Clockmaker." Their god is not our god, people whisper. What can you know? They worship Time, or rather the Great Constructor of Times.

Claude-Siméon doesn't listen to the gossip. He is inspired by the Dutchman's mechanics, the Englishman's optics. As if he had written them himself. He re-creates them truly and better, always more precise. Nearer to the time of the stars, which he has spent the entire night doing nothing but recalculating. More and more exact in each millimeter of steel, of copper, of silver, of gold. His lenses are peerless for enlarging celestial bodies, which they capture and lodge in music boxes. Baroque ballets and cosmic precisions, what difference is there? It is possible—better: it is urgent—to reproduce the exactness of the Divine Clockmaker in a childlike, fair-inspired, human merry-go-round. To tame the order of the world.

No one stops time, it's obvious; so one has to marry it. Claude-Siméon is persuaded that attraction is beautiful, that's what he feels. Gravitation is not only grave, it is also desirable, gracious. And the effort to think becomes a felicity. The man is happy only at that hour of the afternoon when he has refined the night's calculations into a finely worked object and the frowns of the forehead yield to the joys of the eyes, the fingers, the entire body.

The son of Ollivier, Pierre-Antoine, who has left the paternal shop to become a lawyer in Parliament and referendum reporter in the Chancellery in the Palais de la Cité, understands that Claude-Siméon also takes his distance from the quotidian. A little fanciful, all the same, at some distance from ordinary matters, and absorbed as if at the will of a vocation in all his bizarre innovations as astronomical clockmaker. Pierre-Antoine becomes impatient, the dear man; he doesn't seem to grasp that this new science that engulfs Passemant demands patience, also distraction, a sort of absence, it goes without saying. But the two of them have an understanding: Claude-Siméon will marry the older sister of Pierre-Antoine, Louise, and take the younger brother, aged sixteen, as an apprentice to help him with everything.

A true gift from God, this Louise. She has the skin of Marie-Madeleine, the same large brown eyes, and a flair for business. Better than Mme Passemant, the mother, who is always only aspiring for more. No, Louise is content to be the perfect wife of the mercer, of the master draper, of the *passementier*. That's all, that's good, that's a sure thing. She will handle the affairs of the two united families, just as they are, no need for stars, what more do you want? It's exactly what's required to leave Claude-Siméon free rein with his sky and his automatons.

Today, Pierre-Antoine Ollivier is into the fad that has all Paris in its grip. He lands at the workshop with his two sisters, Louise and Aubine, and absolutely demands that Claude-Siméon go with them. "Everyone in Paris is going to Saint-Médard to see the miracle. Are you coming?"

Not interested, but he complies. Claude-Siméon is only thinking about the quarrel of the Cartesians and the Newtonians and about inserting the mathematical principles of natural philosophy into a music box. He's not planning to transport the Olliviers into that territory, of course, but he also doesn't want to disappoint Pierre-Antoine, Louise, and Aubine. The time seeker already senses that he is going to have a very bad headache. Never mind, he'll go. He won't stay very long; he has an appointment at the Observatory with his teacher from the Collège Mazarin—you know, Louise, that great man I've already told you about, Jacques Cassini. He has been admitted into the Royal Society and the Akademie in Berlin; he's a friend of Newton and Halley.

Louise raises her eyebrows. She doesn't understand a single thing about the astral calculations of her fiancé and future husband. What on earth is the meaning of those peculiar prayers that plunge him so far, so deep inside himself, that he is truly lost for her? A sort of witchcraft, for sure. But he returns and is saved again; that's how it is. Her Claude-Siméon is a genius; Louise will do everything necessary so he can live with and for his stars. It's perfect. Claude-Siméon will be a great clockmaker, and we will all go see the *convulsionnaires*!

They cross the Seine, take the Pont Royal, walk along the quai des Grands-Augustins; farther on they will take the rue Saint-Jacques toward the Latin Quarter as far as Saint-Médard. The previous night, his eyes had not left his telescope, and now, with this walk, the incessant chatting of the three Olliviers, Claude-Siméon again feels that bar cutting into his skull. But he continues on.

"You never talk about God. It's as if you can do without Him." Pierre-Antoine Ollivier has no intention of provoking him; he just wants to mention what the people and the three Olliviers are excited about these days.

Claude-Siméon takes no notice. How can he make them understand that you can't talk about it; you think about it, write it, compose it. The Olliviers are used to his silences; besides, Pierre-Antoine is not expecting an answer.

He carries on: "You know, the Jansenists are forbidden. By a declaration of the king. Maneuvered by the implacable Fleury, Monsieur le Cardinal, who was directing His Majesty's spiritual life. But Parliament is having none of it, nor is our parish. And you, at Saint-Eustache, are you with us? You know about it or not? The police aren't able to prevent the *Ecclesiastical News* . . . Never heard of it? Too bad. The gazette of the clandestine Jansenists, that's what it is!"[1] Breathless with pleasure, Pierre-Antoine knows lots of things, clients are talking, for or against; they pity the king, who is weakening as a result of being contested by Parliament. "It's over, the Jesuits are back. Don't you know about it? At Saint-Médard it's something else again: those people are opposing the anti-Jansenist papal bull, but they also hate the Jesuits, for whom Jansenism is just boiled-over Calvinism."

These imbroglios seem so absurd that Pierre-Antoine is not sure he understands it all. The clientele are also lost, to tell the truth. The budding lawyer strives to ferret things out; he has a talent for complicating everything.

"My dear brother, what are you talking about!" exclaims Aubine. "There are extraordinary healings at Saint-Médard, after . . . I actually know of a deacon named Pâris, a man of great piety, who sleeps without sheets, eats only vegetables, and distributes his wealth to the poor. At his death, a woman paralyzed for twenty-five years throws herself upon his coffin and suddenly is able to move again." Aubine is on cloud nine.

"And a fruit seller who had an ulcer on his leg was healed by applying a piece of the wood of that same deacon's cot on the wounds." Louise is awestruck, her voice sweeter than ever.

"Now people visit his grave like a saint's grave. The sick lie down on the stone, and they're seized by convulsions. They froth, they drool. Sometimes a hundred people convulse together.

---

1. In 1713, the papal bull *Unigenitus* by Clement XI proclaimed the interdiction of the Jansenists at the request of Louis XIV. The *Ecclesiastical News* was the weekly Jansenist publication.

Others are into self-flagellation, like at Saint-Benoît." Ollivier warms to his subject, gourmand, intrigued now.

"And then, secret organizations of *convulsionnaires*, more than five thousand people, meet to pray, sing, make sacrifices, have orgies . . ." Aubine's cheeks are aflame.

"Can you imagine, darling? They slit the throats of animals, and with the blood they mark the houses of those whom the Exterminating Angel should spare, even in Versailles." Louise is in love and docile, but transported.

"And there's a visionary who draws straws to decide who among them will be sacrificed to expiate the crimes of the others." Ollivier, slightly disapproving, after all: too much is too much.

"Look! Look! A *convulsionnaire*." The crowds make it hard to see, but there must be more than one. "She's drawn a design on her skin; it looks like a chalice. And she is speaking in tongues!" Aubine is enthralled.

Claude-Siméon's head hurts more and more. He has read practically all the books from Port-Royal, beginning with those by Nicole. So the Jansenism at Saint-Médard is not the Jansenism he was taught at Mazarin? This affair is madness. The clockmaker is decidedly not of this world.

"Okay, friends, it's time for me to leave you. Don't wait for me for dinner; I'm not sure I'll be on time. I will do my best, but there's a chance I'll be late . . . You can tell me what conclusions you draw from this visit to the good Lord . . . or to the devil! I'm kidding . . . A bit . . . I'm leaving your company . . . Adieu, dear Louise! Ollivier, look after her for me."

14

SOMEONE HAS WHISPERED
A SENTENCE IN MY SLEEP

Y ou have to let the poor folks sleep, I've prevented them from sleeping too often."

I frequently wake up at night. I read or listen to the radio, news and music; I wait for sleep or for the idea of a new sentence for a book in progress. I know that certain dreamed words are forever lost, inaccessible upon awakening, so I get up and consign them to my red notebook with the graph paper. I dreamed about Passemant—but which one? My Astro or the clockmaker?

I was reading a book: I heard words; they rose before my eyes, unfolded into spaces, tortuous labyrinths at first, then more and more distinct.

Two or three stories of low-ceilinged rooms, staircases, corridors, delightful nooks, libraries, and map storage. Coffee kept warm over embers. A studio with a tower, a distillery, high bay windows with little panes. I am in the private apartments. Pearly light, chandelier pendants, reflections to infinity in facing mirrors. The large *Holy Family* by Raphael, Holbein's *Erasmus*, some Poussins, a Veronese. Bouquets of sculpted flowers and fruits between the gilded foliage on the white woodwork. Trophies of war, hunting, and love.

After the cabinet attached to the bedchamber, where Passemant's astronomical clock reigns, I go through the hunting
cabinet. Only the nobles and the king's wardrobe keepers are
allowed to enter here. Courtesans remain in the staircase or the
marble courtyard. The King's Chamber becomes the Council
Chamber. The sovereign uses a little interior corridor where I
see there's a door opening into the Throne Room.

During my night's sleep, these labyrinthine spaces fashion
the brain of a man in 3-D. The king of France, said to be hypo-
critical, is an office man here. Notes, documents, files. He takes
Passemant by the shoulder, leads him to a separate cabinet. "I
like papers, study, reading. And even writing, a lot—at Coigny,
Noailles, Toulouse . . . I write as I will, but I warn them all:
there will be no rattling on about my letters!"

His papers are arranged in order on shelves, labeled in his
handwriting: descriptions of products, scales, expedients, means,
plans. Inventories and catalogues of all states, grades, and
charges.

"An impenetrable secret nook," says the king.

"A clockmaker's work, Sire."

"As it were." Louis does not seem to disapprove of his subject's audacity. "You understand, my friend, this comes to me
from my ancestor: 'Have neither favorites nor Prime Minister,
ever. Listen, consult your council, but decide.'"

How can this be possible? My dream is wondering . . .

"Chauvelon's taste inspires me in spite of his disgrace, what
can I say. 'Everything too well known is scorned, thus it is a
rule for royal authority not to let it be seen what the king can
do; soon one would know what he cannot do.'"

They join a little group of intimates, before whom Passemant
will describe the clock conceived for the king of Golconda,
which was ordered by Dupleix, the governor of Pondicherry.

Ordinarily taciturn and frivolous, the undecipherable Louis XV speaks freely. His Majesty looks to his astronomical engineer for confirmation: "You have an idea, Passemant? Tell me. Yes, yes, I'm interested! I listen and I decide. What else would I do? A great and noble monarchy like ours, which holds the attention of all Europe, should be governed by orders with full and ideal knowledge of the laws that constitute it. Such laws are just only on the condition of being in harmony with the laws of the universe. A good king, in short, would be ill-advised to ignore those laws. And if Apollo is his patron, the sovereign owes it to himself to regulate the time of his subjects with his eyes fixed on the time of Apollo . . . The time you call cosmic, is that the scientific word?"

Louis recites as if he is reading a book . . . The one I may have read the day before, found among Stan's documents or those of the little Albane Dechartre . . . ?

Whereupon my dream branches off into flames, a brazier, the smell of burnt wood (memory of the stampede Stan and I lived through at Versailles?). His Majesty kneels down as if nothing were more natural, among his royal functions, than to maintain the fireplace. He relights the fire for his stupefied guests. Claude-Siméon tries to take hold of the poker, but, brushing his shoulder, the king stops him and stirs the embers himself. "It's my pleasure, Passemant. I prefer to listen to you describe your new clock than to see you lend a hand for the fire. *And we have to let the poor folks sleep, too often I prevent them from sleeping.* Come, tell me everything, I want you to."

Intimidated, dumbfounded, finally emboldened, Passemant stands before the fireplace as if transported and describes in a loud voice his project for a new clock, "The Creation of the World": "Since such is your desire, Your Majesty, it will be a singular clock. Approximately five feet tall, encased in gilded bronze, it represents the different moments of Creation brought together and seen from a single point of view. The Earth is a bronze globe of fourteen inches in diameter on which all the countries are engraved, with the principal cities. This globe is situated among rocks and waterfalls that serve as a universal horizon. Behind it rise clouds that end in a gilded bronze sun of three feet in diameter. In the middle we place the clock; its communications give the terrestrial globe its various movements. Its first movement is turning on its axis; and as the sun, which seems to light it, can light only the top part, the bottom part is plunged into darkness. Thus all the cities that begin to appear at the edge of this universal horizon made of water and rocks enter daylight. Those that pass under the solar rays are at noon, and those that reach the other edge of the horizon enter night, and the sun sets for them. Days lengthen and shorten during the year. The seasons follow each other, and one sees the countries that have six months of day and six months of night and the time at every instant for all the peoples of the world. A moon placed among the clouds waxes and wanes regularly. So that this machine, whose revolutions are of the greatest exactness, unites the useful with the magnificent."

I thought my dream ended there, but now the Owl appears. "The scene is taking place at the Trianon Palace," she says, feeling it is her duty to instruct Stan. I awaken.

"It's well known, Mama, the *Gazette de France* recounts this event on March 2, 1754: 'His Majesty was so pleased that he expressed his desire to see this mechanical construction again.'"

Of course. I did not know. Who would know that today?

15

"YOU ARE MY DEPTH"

There you are."

My Astro doesn't open his arms; he takes my hands, squeezes them as hard as he can. His eyes converse with mine. Wordlessly. There remains the imprint of our blended skins. And soon that of our genitals. "Your depth." That's all he'll say. Digging, fathoming, turning, licking, sucking, palpating, palpitating, kissing, spurting, sparkling, enveloping. Tasty, toxic, exorbitant. Outside of me, in me, indefatigable, timid, resolved, incisive, decisive, concentrated, impulsive, explosive.

Now, holding his hand, I smile at the only adventure that seems possible today: solitude with him, the leisure to let myself go to the point of craziness, to explore madness. A sort of prayer. Stendhal thought of the novel as the comedy of the nineteenth century. I consider it the prayer of the twenty-first. Is it still possible to speak of the novel? Concepts one thought of as solid take bodily form, become apprehensible. And among them is Time. Let's go with prayer.

My A is a tormented soul. He is mistrustful about everything, everyone, Passemant in particular.

"Your ancestor? A relative? A homonym?"

No answer, never any answer. Vague smile. "You're interested in that? What's its importance?" says Theo, icily.

He thinks it's meaningless to connect oneself to a family name—it's just a pastime at best.

"Not for me!" Now the cold is turning to anger.

Could my A be one of those new soulless terrestrials who manipulate cognitive strategies to adapt to digital language elements? No. Not he. Had he been, he would of course have saved me from drowning, but without taking the trouble to cover me with a blanket and hold my hand.

This tormented one is a fugitive uncoupled from his roots who has chosen the sky as his refuge. His great dark eyes leave you at the very moment when you hope to gaze into them; they flee toward the light that bathes the façade of the Palais Royal.

"Do you see that illumination giving depth to the décor?" He's changing focus, changing theme.

Never speak of yourself—it's too vulgar—at the risk of losing your privacy. Or very rarely, by allusion. And especially do not burden yourself, the better to burn body and soul between the infinitely great and the infinitely little.

All that's left is for me to gather up the precious pebbles my Astro scatters inadvertently or on purpose and follow him in this adventure, which is less extraterrestrial than he imagines, since it is ours, here and now. I, Nivi, need it to compose the puzzle that takes the place of my interior being, my survival equipment.

For Theo, the exodus probably began at the death of his father, the jeweler and clockmaker Jean Passemant. You know of Passemant & Nicolet, master clockmakers for ten generations, rue Vieille-du-Temple. Ruptured aneurism at thirty-eight. My Theo is only five then, an orphan clinging to his mother, Irene, who sheds no tears and says nothing. Too much pain. No fuss, no fuss at all, nothing. Only that mortal dilation of an artery making holes in the past, annihilating it. And indifference for a bandage: coldness made woman. Tied to her little Theo, single child encapsulated in the maternal embrace, as in the arms of a Virgin confusing Nativity with Dormition.

My Astro's mother, whose maiden name was Irene Rilsky, is none other than the older sister of Police Chief Northrop Rilsky. Yes, the same Rilsky I met during my investigation of the decapitation of my friend Gloria Harrison, the incorrigible translator of this planetary village where no one reads, even though each year, for example in France, eight hundred novels are published, of which four hundred are translations from English.

Rilsky, the dear man, later investigated a murder in Byzantium that occurred in the cathedral at Puy-en-Velay and was intended to lead to an explosion at the Louvre pyramid. Several times I went to be with him in New York, his Interpol functions having led to his living for many years on the other side of the Atlantic. A very close friend, a provisional lover.

At the death of Theo's father, Uncle Rilsky couldn't let Irene wall herself up in her frigid mourning. He had read Freud a bit and knew what melancholy implies, also thanks to me. Irene's brother—there was only a difference of five years—took it upon himself to take little Theo under his wing. This odd recomposed family formed a trio that was not really incestuous but was clearly incestual, as it is said among shrinks. Irene, Nor, and Theo. Nor never talked to me about it, and I had decided to put this story aside as insignificant. The hinterland of Nor: how did that concern me? Until Theo fell from the sky with his savior's voice, in the waters of the Ile de Ré, his eyes fixed on the microwaves from the cosmic background, which penetrate me and save me.

Theo disengaged from the instant glue of Irene and abandoned the tortuous investigations of the police chief. Obstinately turning his back on the darkness—enough with the lamentations! Farewell, "night where no conceiving is done" and "horrible unfeasible love"! Not to ask too many questions, to observe the world and oneself at a great, great distance, to keep to the right, to keep to the left, protect the right, protect the left, remain vigilant, impermeable. "Theo? In search of his dead father, needless to say, pressurized and airtight in his space suit," the uncle diagnoses, having become an apprentice therapist.

An invisible target, this loss of the paternal history, imaginary Planck Wall and Big Bang. It makes your heart ache, dilates your pupils. Nothing terrestrial is viable with such a heritage. "He doesn't have a girlfriend?" The Passemant-Nicolet family doesn't mince words. Irene blushes, still glacial in her incandescent black body. "You're gay, my man!" Nor prods his nephew, trying to provoke him from time to time. But the guilty party doesn't hear. He's content to get up from the table without a noise, his mind on other matters. "Maybe a monk?" Irene hopes. In vain. And a joyless laughter cascades from her, the matrix of Theo's laugh.

I don't like this vibrating laugh of Irene's. Her triumphant depression, the protestant denial of deep-seated feelings, the compressed anguish of the American-style feminist she claims to be: I hate them all when they pierce through Theo the birdcatcher's little bells. He cohabited with this spasmodic hilarity of the mourning female, then shredded it into a thousand stars and refashioned it into nonsense, a child's game. Into a pure delirium that relegates you to the margins of humanity or just before the birth of visible matter. Yes, Theo chose this last flight, the most absolute possible at the present time. It is not enough to explore time, which amounts to suffering from it;

time machines are machines for suffering, it's well known since Proust or even H. G. Wells, and women know it better than anyone; no, it's out of the question to start over. Theo prefers to decompose time; he claims it can be forgotten, he frees himself of it. His laughter is the radiance of this absence, the wave of a sigh.

I think I loved my Astro definitively from the moment I understood that his laughter was his second birth, wresting his Papageno score from the swells of maternal dissatisfaction, from the poison of his feminine lining.

As nothing human is truly desirable for him, young Theo drops everything. Goes and surfs the waters of La Rochelle, wins the MIT competition, gets married to the *zero-point* where energy no longer exists and the *Instanton* contains all the information of the Great Universe. I dwell in a time that is not real, he thinks.

Without telling me, as usual, my A is transfused into this time-without-time, trapped in immense gravitation, a terrifying density that contains nothing solid. Since he thinks about them and calculates them, he lives them, he is *of* them, and I participate too. As best I can, in my own way. For all that, Theo does not succumb, and he pursues his investigation. What lies beyond? A preuniverse? Not really. And before? He envisions an eternal existence, "origin" of origins, with plural potentialities, well before the Beginning that will lead to particles, to bodies, and to our Word. Ending with it in a new initial Singularity that will dilate in turn, engendering bubbles of white universes sustained by multiple existences—billions of further universes. A hypothesis, as required in the sciences. Theo made it his thesis, his doctorate, his profession, his cosmology, his theology. To be discussed. To be innovated. To be abandoned, perhaps.

At this point in the adventure where physical energy links to sensorial and mental information, Theo wants us to think that he himself behaves like a *Big Bounce*. Then Rilsky attempts to bring his nephew back down to earth. He has no notion of the singular equilibrium that ties me to Astro. Unless he has detected it? He only tells me I am far away—me, Nivi, far from him, the police chief of my metaphysical detective novels. Without flinching, no reproach whatsoever, nothing but a nostalgic and resigned smile. I smile also, without comment.

As for Theo, he is categorical: "You and I are at the first nanosecond of the Big Bang. So far there is nothing but light, but it is invisible."

In times past, that was called a *coup de foudre*, love at first sight. I squeeze his right hand, which keeps hold of my left. I know my Astro ignores nothing of the politico-police matters that the police chief is passionate about, nor of the anger of his uncle-father toward him, the extraterrestrial acrobat. He has judged them with his Astro's anger, savage and cold, fed by that black energy that causes or accelerates the expansion of the world. Of all the worlds, and ours.

"You are my depth," he says—from time to time my Astro becomes human. He touches me, he embraces me, our bodies come together, the collision pulverizes our singularities, they simply don't take place.

Only afterward will we go discuss the news of the day with Rilsky.

Have you noticed the absolute silence that resonates on earth just before nightfall? Only an ear attuned to the deep radiance of beings captures it, escaping parasite noises. What one calls a "couple," in the inaccessible meaning of this term, is formed when two people hear this radiance in each of themselves, reciprocally, and in the world around them. No one else can mix in. We have indeed become a sort of couple, my A and I.

16

MAMA, ARE YOU FRENCH?

France lost eighty-eight soldiers in Afghanistan, six in Mali. Should our armies continue to parade on the day of the storming of the Bastille, or is it sufficient to have the people sing, women and children included? Such is the question raised by a representative of the Green Party while the funeral service at the Invalides is being prepared. The national banks appear to have withstood the stress tests for the time being, but both the voters in the upcoming presidential election and the abstentionists know that no man or woman invested with universal suffrage will keep us from the fate of the Greeks, the Portuguese, the Spanish, the Italians, and others. None of our current leaders, here and across the Atlantic, will receive my Astro or one of his colleagues the way Passemant was received at Versailles. Customs change . . . Unless there's an awards ceremony, and even then . . . Overbooked, wrung out by the media. Science goes overboard; the banking system turns out to be untouchable; Taliban, jihadists, and company are out of our grasp. World summits are overloaded, and they don't even have the time to put space shuttles and stem cells on the agenda, while those at the levers of globalized power like to relax by collecting Rolexes and listening to evangelical preachers—except when they prefer to amuse themselves with call girls, all instead of sharpening their minds with cosmological research.

I am aware that Louis XV ended up provoking the people's indignation. That while dreaming of inscribing the longevity of his country into universal time, and in spite of his military successes in Europe, he was satisfied with little: the Hexagon. So much so that his "home turf," his *pré-carré*, as they said and still say—namely, France—shrank rapidly, already degraded. The misery of the poor and the cacophony of power. The Treaty of Aix-la-Chapelle brought harm, and the magnanimous pacifier of Europe that this hunter wished to be lost a large part of the French empire—New France and much of India—to the profit of the British.[1]

His principal glory remains the conquest of the weaker sex. After the queen, Marie Leszczynska, it is public knowledge that His Majesty honors *favorites* and obscure mistresses, among whom the four daughters of the Marquis de Nesle et de Mailly: Julia, Pauline, Adelaide, and Hortense; the Marquise de Pompadour, his preferred mistress for twenty years; Marie-Louise O'Murphy, followed by nine "little mistresses" whose names are forgotten; and finally Mme du Barry. Those times know nothing of feminists or of violence perpetrated on women. At Versailles, the legend glorifies sex as a ballet of pure pleasure, the Parc-aux-Cerfs has not yet been replaced by some Sofitel, and no plaintiff has been found who would dare to testify. Our royal Apollo, a fan of astrophysics, finishes his reign among general discontent. Death and poison are spoken of,

---

1. By the treaty of Aix-La-Chapelle (1748), France lost "La nouvelle France"—French holdings in North America—as well as a preponderance of its land in India.

and toward the end broadsides threatening the monarch appear even in the Hall of Mirrors.

For Nivi to exhume him along with 9999 and Passemant, this monarch, premature orphan under a regent and eternal libidinal young man, had to discover in himself and cultivate a taste for numbers, for celestial fires, and for mathematics. Within the folds of those comical rituals and his sensual extravagances, the man manages to shelter an ardent desire for knowledge that sometimes pushes him to ignore the rigid constraints of the absolute monarchy. He opens his court and his heart (secretly, in passing) to a few of his subjects from the new class of renowned scientists and sometimes even to modest technicians. For the pleasure of being informed and taking enjoyment by thinking with them. For the pleasure of knowing. A pleasure as voluptuous, as intimate, as his lovemaking with his *favorites* and other mistresses. More, indeed. Precious to hold forth with at the fireside, under the stuffed heads of stags and boars, not far from famous astronomical clocks. Memorable trophies to abstract speculation and sensual hunting.

Am I exaggerating in showing Claude-Siméon conversing with this king? A French exception? Premonition of 1789? Go look at his bathroom, his bathtub, his dressing tables, among other accessories. All duly immortalized in paintings on the walls, in case these furnishings happened to disappear. Which did happen, as you know. As a height of refinement, this culture of the body is ornamented with signs and coats of arms from all the artisans and trades that contributed to the beauty of the royal person. Why?

Visitors coming from the world over had to leave Versailles without having seen the nudity of the Beloved, but certainly, necessarily, they could only be thunderstruck, as they left, by the minute technical details involved in the maintenance of his body. There too resided his glory and the glory of the crown of France. This feudal logic was not just an accommodating paternalism. By the same token, it exhibited a curious maturity, which intimated that he should affiliate the excellence of his servants with himself. Technicians who know, who know how, and who proffer their science to the service of magnificence. Exactly what I dream of!

Fabulous *equilibrium*, fragile *moment*, to which *Passemant* bears witness. All three will be swept away by two enemies: automatons and the Terror.

Already in the time of Mozart, excessive virtuosity and artisanship in the service of the technical illusion promise to replace the anxieties of men of taste with the omnipotence of the machine. Robotics is under way, for better or for worse.

Too costly at that time—and it always will be—to construct astronomical clocks for *all* the schools, destined to become lay, compulsory, and republican. Along with the tyrannical and arrogant royalty, democracy was to guillotine that moment of grace where calculating thought (let's call it "technical prowess," Faust not yet having signed his pact with the devil) was still able to join together the beautiful, the powerful, and the magical.

"The Passemants of today are doing much better. Wake up!" My friend and colleague Marianne Baruch is always breaking my toys. I'm used to it.

True. Astrophysicists build spaceships not only going to the Moon and Mars but ones already leaving the solar system. How far will they go? The Americans are tired of it; they've just stopped! Not so interesting as all that, space conquest? Yes it is, because we are developing telecommunications and other military and technological successes thanks to it. For the rest, let the Russians and the Chinese make do! But Europe is keeping an eye open, and her cosmologists are making an impression on the world. We are also interested in the infinitely small, in labs and in the living. Our biologists, descendants of Buffon (another of Passemant's acquaintances), are making test-tube babies, surrogate motherhood, artificial uteruses, soon human clones. You can't stop progress. And that changes life, that's for sure. In what sense?

"Mama, what is the subject of History?" Stan has a paper to write. I'm supposed to know how to answer, since I write in *PsychMag*.

I hesitate. It's no longer the working class, because of digitization and unemployment. Stem cells, that's debatable. Religion? Allah? That would be more like the end of History. The Chinese? Remains to be seen.

My dream of Passemant drawing the king to his timepieces prompts me to hazard a reply. Couldn't the subject of History be the desire to know, when it makes the sky descend and punctuates time with magnificent usefulness? Not bad, but when History reaches this layer, it risks repeating itself in robotic techniques and exploding in terror. Perhaps we have not reached that point. We hope automatons, the automatization of the human species, "spin," and virtual money will spare us the apocalypse. The end of dominations, of the exploitation of men by men, of fundamentalism? Certain people return to the need to believe. Is that all?

Passemant and Louis met among beauty: infinite promise. Having opened French time, did they not go farther than us?

"Mama, are you French?"

Stan surfaces from a reflection that he summarizes with this question. Is it even a question?

French like whom? Certainly not like the native-born French. Stan's question bothers me. Am I French? Do I want to be?

Like everyone else, the French can be stupid and lazy. And devout, for fear of being nothing. Like you and me, and even more than that. Devout about sex, the nation, the kingdom, republican values, security, acquired advantages, their income, their retirement.

Passemant perfected the hinges of his time. Émilie du Châtelet, his contemporary, who did not know the clockmaker but who the Cassini brothers and Nivi and Theo will not fail to remind her of, detected the illusion and took pleasure in the black fire beyond the fantastic nights.

"French, French . . . Like whom?"

"You have so many facets . . . Like a Picasso portrait."

I thought so: only Stan knows me.

II
BLACK MATTER

17

INSIDE-OUTSIDE

Outside, the sweltering sun slams the polluted air of Paris down onto the crowds. Phantom drivers slumber at their steering wheels. Others pretend to keep moving, disabused, tired of this rigor they keep harping on. Nothing moves forward, and no one notices that I've left this world. Where I am there are two translucent membranes with veins of mauve silk threads that separate me from life. I feel them shiver, inside. I try to cross the border. My bodyless body rejoins an opaque flesh and infuses it. Pierces the darkness. It resists. I'm smothering, I push. I let myself go, I come back up, breathe, dive in again. I return from an artificial coma.

I'm not dreaming, I know I'm keeping vigil by Stan. He is the one who comes back to me. I tell him I'm looking at his trembling eyelids—pale indigo petals, you remember, the color of the citronella geraniums that perfume the rockery of our garden by the Atlantic Ocean. His swollen lips attempt a smile; I hear him and volley back: "My little bird, where are you hurt, where did you, while flying about . . ." His eyelashes come unglued, tears or sparks, fireworks, garlands of light, words, images, memories. At the Phare des Baleines, we were buying pink panthers, inflatable or stuffed. The torchlight parade, the

Fourteenth of July, the village square, the bouquet of rockets setting the steeple ablaze. My voice oxygenizes his oxygen, my film distills sensations of happiness into the glucose IV, life is a cascade of birthings and rebirths, to be and not to be—who notices that?

Doctors and caregivers today are astrophysicists. They claim they are trying to "externalize" our brains into the dematerialized IT cloud. Professor de Latour, eminent specialist at my son's bedside, explains that to do this they have to manage the thousands of billions of biological facts that science now has available for each of us. Especially when things get rough, he adds with a lovely smile. As we wait for the experts to appropriate the hundred thousand genetic mutations they discover daily, what are we doing here in the coma limbo, behind or in front of Stan's eyelids?

The smile becomes sympathetic.

I attempt a hook, a "reliance"—my own way of externalizing myself in the digital (or not) storm of these internal coups d'état that come upon us, that we fabricate, that make us live or die. My cloud computing operates by poetic language. I make myself into mother and baby, take your pick and all at once, never one without the other. Stan understands me as much as or more than I understand him.

Once awake, he will have had enough of my citronella geraniums and their little discreet flowerheads.

It's done. He forgets me in a burst of laughter. Later. Forever. Outside time. Without time.

I will find him again. You will find me again. You can count on me. You too.

Until the next internal coup d'état. There are so many, there will always be some, we won't need to wait long: that's life.

18

WHAT IS AN INTERNAL
COUP D'ÉTAT?

Whether the violence of the shock is internal or external, illness or aggression, your intimate state explodes; you are dispossessed of it. Neither being nor nonbeing: annihilation. If you do not succumb to this attack, as a furtive escapee from the succession of intimate coups d'état, and if you succeed in reinventing yourself through these cumulated trials, you acquire a flexible constitution. Because even though you are powerless, deprived of all mastery, you nonetheless possess the science of rhythm, the conviction that you are nothing but an apparition in the thread of time. Thus all the coups d'état themselves, wherever they may be in the world and in History, join with yours. United around your debacles, which become *coups de théâtre*, new beginnings, however scandalous they may be. Impromptu flashes of inspiration and survival.

You think of a coup d'état as an illegal and brutal seizure of the central offices of power. But such situations do not occur in politics alone. They can happen during any time of one's life, and their goal is to expropriate or at least deviate a life to the point of destroying it. They can also become a paradoxical motivation of this life, here and now, if one traverses such situations by means of rebounds, exiles from oneself, transubstantiations.

Marianne thinks I'm dreaming. She hopes I'm not boring the professor stiff with my fantasies; she warns me Stan might suffer.

No danger. Once I've tamed the coups d'état, my reality becomes something else. I am a neorealist.

Nothing will keep my friend from diagnosing me: Nivi has been traumatized. By exile, love, maternity, everything. The tiniest pinprick pierces right through, ravages her like a solar explosion. Isn't that right, Nivi? It's not wrong. Things take hold of me and reduce me to an unnamable state over which I have no power, and that makes me get involved in other people's traumas. I accompany them; from time to time they accompany me, in spurts, in waves, in as many rebirths.

"Resuscitation, so that's it! Pardon me, I was forgetting that you believe only in the revolution." Marianne is humoring me to spare me her psychiatric verdict.

Not at all, a coup d'état has nothing to do with a revolution. While revolutions are often punctuated by coups d'état, they cannot be reduced to coups d'état. The storming of the Bastille, for example, is a true revolution: brutal damage to the prior state of institutions, inevitably to bodies and souls. Heads are cut off, though in the name of History—a wildly enthusiastic fight between faiths. But the coup d'état is more underhanded, it decontaminates and decapitates rather than shouting from the rooftops; it is possessed with the desire to possess, provisional occupant of the vacancy. For example— and the memory of them is sinister, grandiose—the coups d'état of the 18th of Fructidor year V, the 22nd of Floréal year VI, and the most famous, the 18th Brumaire of Napoleon Bonaparte. Many others exist: Catherine II against Peter III,

Lenin against Kerensky, Hitler against Weimar, Castro against Batista, Neguib against Farouk, then Nasser against Neguib, Boumedienne against Ben Bella, Oufkir against Hassan II, a failed one . . . The blow, usually military, is brutal, no point in arguing, on your way, nothing to see, nothing to say. The hour has struck, that's all.

Often a bloodbath is enough. It disrupts the political clock, and then another tick-tock restarts the gearwork of the routine, the turnover of the states. It strikes, it cuts. How long will this succession of scansions, blows, and Big Bangs last?

Coups d'état do not restart time; they don't modify the calendar. In contrast, changing the calendar is revolutionary. Revolutions without coups d'état exist: the Gregorian calendar proves it. Pope Gregory XIII, who was to increase the power of the Inquisition, made his mark on History primarily by replacing the Julian calendar. A revolution made to last: the Gregorian calendar is still ours.

Let's not let these classic coups d'état make us forget those that, though hidden, are no less harmful, shaking up internal regimes without overthrowing them. A cunning coterie, a rebellious undercurrent, an ambitious clan, even a single magnetic, spellbinding, glamorous personality suffice to eat away at the status quo more or less surreptitiously. They end up seizing a ministry, imposing a change of course, undermining a program, shaking up a cabinet, sacking a dignitary, if they don't succeed in replacing the sovereign rulers themselves. They are chastely called "palace revolutions," so as not to be confused with the routine succession of governmental teams (the first, the second, and so on), who care only about remodeling the façade. These coups d'état ruin a state, disfigure it, discredit it, decimate it till all it can do is float with the current like a headless duck, lacking any efficacy.

Nivi is thinking not about such intestinal evils, as she considers her possible escapes, but about the corroding catastrophes, the fatal aggressions that affect the condition of life and its intermittent intimacy, lacking which nothing exists.

Internal coups d'état seed your death. They leave you no other choice but to walk in death's footsteps while trying to disperse it in shooting photons, sunny spells, and encounters. Nivi emerges from her internal coups d'état like Stan from his comas, finding them again in the dilation of cosmic time— temporary victory over mortality, which takes shelter in a jewel of French history. Oh yes, Nivi and Stan recognize its pulsation in the astronomical clock, whose obscure inventor becomes their hero. Naturally!

While Versailles seeks pleasures and Aix-la-Chapelle celebrates the dream of peace in Europe, Passemant foresees the blows to come: Red March, decomposition of the state, massacres, spears, and guillotines. New regime—which one? Apocalypse? Unknowable, unnamable; philosophers call it *revolution*; the enlightened clockmaker prefers to say 9999, an alchemical figure. Blow for blow, blow after blow, obscurely but surely, Passemant sees them arrive; he senses their rhythm with the same intuitive precision that tightens screws and bolts on his parallactic telescopes. He's not terrified, not amused either. He feels he is *part of* them, of these blows of time that carry, that carry off; he assumes them—better, he reproduces them, engenders them, gives birth. But to what, exactly?

Certainly not the *Encyclopedia* of all knowledge, song-filled tomorrows and the rights of man, terror, democracy, clash of religions, globalization, hyperconnections. These are inevitable. They will happen with or without him, it doesn't matter. Passemant is elsewhere, on the Moon, Venus, Saturn. Laborious, living among courtesans, having survived the pleasures of the enchanted isles, eclipsed by brilliant scholars and philosophers? No doubt, but not entirely. He replays the scene.

His secret love—less secret than it appears, when one observes the clock carefully—plunges him into such distraction that he no longer knows where he is. So Passemant *composes himself*, as they say at court. He seems penetrated with respect and embarrassment. He prostrates himself and pays his respects, thinks of his social position, to be sure, but speaks of his birth in carefully chosen terms the better to emphasize the goodness, the kindheartedness, and the power of the king. Without in the least praising or applauding himself, the engineer knows how to express himself without stopping, without stuttering, without looking for his words, just getting tangled up in the musicality of his sentences. Attentive, with the countenance of an embarrassed person, then turning inward. A man who suffers from strange moments of violence, which he also forces upon himself the better to feel them. This finely nuanced mechanism is in fashion; the little duke portrayed many other examples. And the regent, who sensed the coming of the "whirlpooling abyss," was the absolute master of such subtle disturbances. Today, His Majesty observes his clockmaker's organization with indulgence and answers that there are things that time erases, others that time imprints. The engineer bows. Yet another internal attack. Exquisite.

No one notices that this visionary in love with his prince is prey to a condition of timelessness. He accompanies all the times that preceded him and all those that will follow. Outside passing time, Passemant hears cosmic time beat for the benefit of those humans who know how to listen.

Passemant seeks no escape from his internal coups d'état, which split his skull and unsettle his stomach. Neither psychological, nor political, nor social, nor juridical, nor moral. Either he will have them or he will not. It is absurd to ignore them and criminal to be disinterested in them; they are as indispensable as they are ineffective. The engineer merely tries to make people hear the pulsation of supernovas, of neutrinos, of dark energies, to be identified after him. This subtle rhythm does not relativize explosions. Passemant puts them in perspective so as to make people feel their cosmic breadth, to externalize them and make them visible and audible to the present, to those present—to the court, to everyone.

From there on, with those 9,999 apocalyptic years held in the clockmaker's hand, encased in the male body of the Beloved king, his astronomer's step becomes lighter. Nivi's too. Walking itself becomes almost dancing, and nothing seems to her more desirable than to "travel herself."

19

I HAVE AGAIN DREAMED OF
YOUR ANCESTOR

No, Astro, not Theo the German whose first and last name you bear though you won't admit it. There is only one Theo for me, and that's you. This time I only dreamed of Claude-Siméon, the one Stan is always telling me about, since he's so keen on clocks, telescopes, and whatever. I was somewhere between the Louvre and Saint-Germain-l'Auxerrois—we were there recently, do you remember? The last time you were in Paris we had a drink on the terrace of the Café Marly, we made love, then we strolled around the neighborhood. Claude-Siméon was coming out of the National Library, I think.

I see him heading down the rue des Petits-Champs, then the rue du Louvre; I follow him, as one does in a dream, as if I were he, as if I were you. His staring eyes are translucent, testimony to entire days spent in the greenish aquarium light of the lamps in the former library. I didn't know you at that time. I was looking for constellations of ideas in the pages of "continental philosophy." Your black curls fell to your shoulders; it was the month of May. Not the May of the "events," but the month of linden trees and promises of honey.

Now I see him on the rue des Prêtres-Saint-Germain-l'Auxerrois. He is coming toward me, holding against his hip a packet of books and notebooks tied together in a beige strap decorated with red and green threads. I notice the main title of the book visible on top of the pile: *Poissonnades* (1749). Did the strap loosen, or did Claude-Siméon make a false movement while embracing me? *Poissonnades* escapes from the package, and the title of another book appears: *Réveillez-vous, mânes de Ravaillac!*

Passemant looks at me with an anxious air like yours, about which I don't know if it's contemplating the end of the world or acting a part. A glance to the left, a glance to the right. In a hoarse voice, he unloads his anxieties onto me: "Look out for the cops, special agents are on the lookout everywhere, the police are omnipresent."

"I know it."

"No, you don't know it."

Fear brings people together. I see us: Claude-Siméon Passemant pulls me into the corridors at Versailles; now he's using the familiar *tu*.

"Argenson and Conti's men, the devout party, are railing about la Pompadour. And the people are imitating them. Explosions everywhere! Do you know the pamphlet, *Melotta Ossoupi, histoire africaine*? An anagram of La Motte Poisson . . ."

Does he imagine himself—a misogynist, moreover, like everyone else—a rival of la Pompadour? His Majesty's technician, more and more agitated, knows of every slanderous attack launched against the *favorite*.

"It seems the marquise has the most haggard, unhealthy look in the world, they say she has leucorrhea! Madame had a miscarriage, she spits blood, gets a cold whenever a door is opened, always has a sore throat, nothing helps relieve her fevers. And that's not all! The marquise keeps the war going out of self-interest, sells regiments and passports to move the kingdom's wheat abroad. She buys up all the diamonds she can get her hands on, distributes at the price of gold appointments as underfinanciers and supercouncilors. The courtesans take her for a pretty prime minister (so they say in the gazettes, it seems). She is afraid of being poisoned, it's understandable. An obscure working girl, a *petite bourgeoise*!"

"Is it possible duchesses agree with the people? Look out, revolts are expensive!" I manage to get a word in, seeking to share my experience. But he continues his wild harangue against la Pompadour.

"She never goes anywhere without antidotes to poison, she has her kitchen under surveillance, drinks lemonade only when served by her people, and has her doctor sleep in her antechamber. Can you imagine!"

"Mr. King's Clockmaker, the ends justify the means, and power is never where one thinks it is."

"We risk the Bastille and Vincennes prison!" He's not listening to me, wrapped up in his terror as a persecuted man. "The Château d'If, Maastricht, the Mont Saint Michel, Charlemont. Watch out!" I follow him as he takes refuge in the church.

A priest passes, discreetly. He looks at us, seems embarrassed. I have a feeling of weightlessness and seek a sort of moral support, but which? The organ remains mute. I had found myself in this same place one Sunday afternoon after Astro's departure for Lima. Wandering in Paris on a Mother's Day. Chance had brought me here; when I went in I had heard the singing of the *Dialogue of the Carmelites* by Bernanos and Poulenc. The words were unfamiliar to me, a little out of date, but I understood them. (Like now, in my dream, where I bathe in the flood of words from another time.) Vague memories of some readings came back to me. Voltaire's Pompadour, yes, a bit. But Passemant's? What connection with time, the clock, the heavens? And with this Claude-Siméon panicked with jealousy, with plebian hatred, with unrequited love for his sovereign?

I ask him again: "You have no settled place in life."

"Everything is politics, believe me." He's still using the familiar *tu*. "Look. Maurepas, the minister of the king's house, had granted me a privilege for the construction of the eight-foot reflecting telescope, the latest. Because to be completed, this work requires suitable lodging. But Maurepas has been dismissed; it seems la Pompadour does not find him efficient enough . . ."

"Yet Voltaire said she liked to be of service. That she 'thought philosophically.'"

"She couldn't do anything for Diderot. Neither get him out of Vincennes nor get him into the Academy. But as for philosophizing, oh yes indeed, Jeanne-Antoinette does philosophize! Buffon will testify to it."

Claude-Siméon murmurs that he also has privately sought Buffon's support in his need for money. I say I understand.

No need to worry, says the suddenly smug phantom of my dream, a relative of la Pompadour is getting him lodging in the Louvre. This Tournehem, moreover, knew la Pompadour's father and also her mother. The illustrious financier general knew her so well that he could even be Jeanne-Antoinette's father. Oh yes, so the rumor has it! Besides, the official father of the king's mistress, François Poisson himself, was nearly hanged . . . You can see what a fine family that was! But the poor fellow's cunning, he agreed to be the scapegoat in a murky financial affair implicating the Pâris brothers. He took exile in Germany, and from there he has continued to provide important services to the royalty while also attending to the education of the person who passes for his daughter. He placed her in an Ursuline convent in Passy with a sister of his wife. His wife, the mother of the marquise and mistress of Tournehem! Can you imagine?

The man of the automatons is indignant. Is he pretending, or is he naïve? That's the Regency for you, Mr. Engineer! Intrigues and French follies found everywhere, from the lowliest of cottages to the summits of the state.

He senses that things are falling apart everywhere. The only stability lies in the sciences: that's what he thinks, this phantom, and perhaps he is right. Otherwise there's a risk of migraine, madness, maybe Hell.

"Madness or Hell. Me, I prefer science."

We hug the walls of the church. It is deserted, like today. I sense you are reassured. This Passemant, in the end, is you; I'm merging you two. I'm scrutinizing the woodwork; it's the same as Saint-Eustache, where we went recently. In the end you put down your packet of books, you forget it. Color has returned to your face, your voice has become silken.

"In forty years we will be in 1789."

Are you speaking, or is he?

I ask you to repeat the number. Passemant calmly spells out the fateful date.

"That will be the French Revolution, Monsieur."

He looks at me without flinching. "What is your name?"

Suddenly he's using the polite *vous* form, as if to extract us from the dream . . .

"Nivi. Nivi Delisle."

He asks me to spell my first and last names. Places his hand flat on the lectern. Frowns. Looks away. Visibly, my name means nothing to him. No more than the date does.

"Have we already met? The French Revolution? Why not . . . Louis XV is afraid. 'I can see I am going to die like Henri IV,' that's what he said to me.[1] The eclipse will take place, it's programmed, and others will follow. Not right away . . . My clock will not be in danger in 1789, it will function until 9999, no problem . . . After that, they'll need five digits."

A group of Chinese tourists rushes in under the arches of Saint-Germain-l'Auxerrois. Passemant doesn't like crowds. We hurry out to the sunshine, breathe the humid air.

"Were you born on an isle, Delisle?"

"Not really, but I like islands."

"Chinese?"

"I would have liked it. Who knows? Do I look it?"

"I don't know . . . That first name . . ."

"It means 'My language.'"

"Aha . . . French of French origin?"

"Sort of, yes . . . Now, yes."

"You understand . . ." He stares at the air above our heads, asks himself . . . "A revolution . . . A revolution, you can't stop it . . . Whether it's French, English, German, Russian, or Chinese."

He speaks to me with compassion. Is concerned to solicit my curiosity, careful to avoid upsetting me. Nations are so susceptible. I hasten to help him. Like with you, my A, when you leave your interstellar speculations and try to find the words to name our "affection," as you say. That expression seems more

---

1. Henri IV was assassinated in 1610 by Ravaillac, whose latter-day emulators are alluded to in the title of one of the books Passemant is holding.

neutral to you, more scientific than the usual words. When you become terrestrial again, you hesitate, awkward. I move closer to the clockmaker.

"There is time, and there is time. You are from another time."

He would like me to give him the details, but I am silent.

In a sudden burst, he turns toward me and cries: "But I don't yet know how to measure the diffuse cosmological background!"

Whereupon I burst out laughing. Claude-Siméon hesitates a second, then abandons his seriousness and starts laughing with me. Gone is his long hair; he is you, completely you, the way you are today.

That's it. We wake up. Where are you? ILY.

20

PASSEMANT WITH THE CASSINIS

The Cassinis are a veritable dynasty of astronomers in the service of science and the monarchy. How often has Claude-Siméon been in their apartment? This location, attributed to them by rights, is situated on the second floor of the Observatory. The day student from the Collège Mazarin is fascinated by the great Jacques Cassini, who, not content merely to transmit the fire of the stars to this mercer's son, becomes his *extoller*, does his best to support him. This Passemant may not be a scientific genius, but he's certainly a Cartesian who knows how to combine his mathematical talents with his skill at diffusing Newton's God into Versailles's amusements. This boy's instruments are worthy of the best astronomical tables, and one day they will be capable of diverting intelligent people who abhor boredom. As Claude-Siméon is the friend of a cousin of Mme Cassini, anyway, it is not surprising he is welcome. In England, people are far less fussy about birth. They know how to appreciate individual gifts and merit, whatever their provenance. All the better for young Passemant.

Not so young as that anymore: he must be well into his forties; he's the father of a Louise-Françoise and a Marie-Aubine. The astronomer Cassini leaves it to his spouse to take care of the courtesies: Suzanne-Françoise de Charmois does not fail to ask about her little cousin Charles Joachim and about the visitor's family.

The engineer wishes to speak of the divisions of a quadrant, a project he is getting ready to present to the Royal Academy of Sciences. Cassini has not been involved in scientific activity for four years, leaving astronomy to his son César-François. The elder Cassini is snowed under by his numerous administrative duties: Chamber of Accounts, Chamber of Justice, Council of State. But still a scientist at heart, he makes sure to keep people like this young Passemant under his wing. From the start Cassini recommended him to Julien Le Roy, the esteemed clockmaker of the king, who has become accustomed to the technical talents of this fine lad.

Jacques Cassini is not one to waste time chatting. This somber dark-skinned Italian, in the elegant beauty of his sixty-seven years, absently studies the postulant from bottom to top, without animosity. Claude-Siméon hands him his calculations, numb with admiration and humility. Is this host who has welcomed him really the great Cassini, the one who drew a perpendicular to the meridian of France? He, the author of the fabulous work on the inclined orbits of satellites and the rings of Saturn?

Suzanne-Françoise has a square jaw, rarely smiles. Her transparent blue eyes, like those of Charles Joachim, the classmate from the Collège Mazarin, have nothing to say. Stiffly, she asks about Marie-Aubine, Louise, his comrades from school, then turns on her heel and leaves. The other members of the family, equally stiff-lipped, barely pronounce a few words. They are deep into their occupations: the first doing accounts, the second focused on a military tract, the third on a score for voice, the last on a novel. Each ignores the presence of the others, shut up in their own worlds. With the exception of the second son, César-François, who, aware of paternal attentions, asks to read the pages of Passemant's thesis.

Silence.

"Excellent!" Jacques Cassini looks up from the manuscript.

"Excellent!" So does his son César-François.

Claude-Siméon feels himself come back to life—in another world than his, it goes without saying, but a world far beyond this living room. By any chance will he be admitted to the Observatory for good?

"You are one of us, Passemant. Every day, with your techniques, you are accomplishing for Newtonians what Voltaire achieves in the world of ideas. No need to tell me you are a diffuser of knowledge, I know it. A Hermes. That's not nothing, believe me. You bring the god of Reason into everyone's time."

Jacques Cassini is alluding to Voltaire's book, *Elements of the Philosophy of Newton*, which is intriguing scholars and scientists. Everyone here knows it. A work reprinted several times and still at the heart of debates after more than ten years. Claude-Siméon lets it pass, looks down. Lowers his head.

"Oh no, I'm not overvaluing you . . . What has Voltaire done, actually? He goes to England, where he becomes a deist after meeting Clarke, Newton's disciple. From the natural order—or more precisely, from Newton's gravitation—he infers a principle of transcendent order, namely, God. Which our M. Arouet encapsulates in an expression that has become famous: 'I cannot imagine how the clockwork of the universe can exist without a clockmaker.' Voltaire, as he likes to call himself, then settles at Cirey with Émilie du Châtelet. He invites my compatriot Algarotti, who has adapted Newton for the ladies. It's important—oh yes, oh yes, you can be sure! Voltaire steals his idea but adapts it for everyone, including women, and with a genius far superior to his guest's. I have to admit that France today is much better than Italy . . . This philosophical debate frightens the church, as you know . . . *Ergo*, we celebrate—you celebrate—the natural theology of Newton. Or of Voltaire. Such is the meaning of your calculations on the divisions of the quadrant, my good friend, and of your telescopes and clocks in the works. But then, does Descartes lead to . . . impiety?"

"Sir, certain people accuse Newtonian physics of lending strength to materialism." Claude-Siméon hesitates, attempts to stammer as if to prevent emotions from taking over, then lets himself go. "We know that the gravitational force is not only mathematical in nature. It is a quality of matter. And I can reproduce it in an astronomical clock. Up to 9999, for now, indeed more, if . . ."

The visitor is ashamed at boldly launching into abstract arguments. Yet he does feel at home, as if no longer in the company of the illustrious Cassinis. Almost as comfortable as he is at La Pomme d'Or, the little observatory he has built for himself on the rue de la Monnaie, having left the rue aux Fers the better to observe the moon and the stars. Almost. He can't manage to think about Newton and Voltaire, or even to think at all . . . As the Cassinis do . . . As he should . . . Shame makes him sweat. At La Pomme d'Or, Louise has placed an enamel plaque representing the baptism of Christ. And Claude-Siméon himself has hung two paintings on wood, *The Flight from Egypt* and a *Descent from the Cross* . . . Things should be clear: Passemant is a man of precision. The only thing that interests him at this time is to be better lodged so his equations will be fair and true, appreciated just like those of the great scientists here in their Observatory.

Cassini continues; he takes a stance, rewrites history as an astronomer and politician. "That's it, that's it. The debate is just starting. Look, even if everything were just information, how would this Everything be any less real, or less material? Starting from when, and where? Call 'that' God, up to you! As for me, I'm just a scientist. I believe only in experiments. You engineers are the ones who make science available for everyone's use. Let's do a bit of daydreaming and start with the greats of this world. With the king's graces. You know His Majesty spends long hours with science. In the vicissitudes of life—because God does not spare monarchs—science is the unique distraction of a fine soul, that is, one as fragile and sensitive as his, understood . . . The frivolous courtesans don't give a damn; they see only ridiculous manias. No surprise for you, these things are becoming known . . . I myself have witnessed them. His Majesty is capable of the most difficult observations, measurements, and calculations . . . There's more than one step from there to saying that the Newtonian party is going to win the metaphysical and political battle, no doubt about it. Let's take that step, and one more, come now, with a bit of hope!" A faint smile. "In contrast, His Majesty has a devil of a distrust of the literati . . ."

Claude-Siméon doesn't have a word to say. Clearly the world is not precise enough for him. From Port-Royal to Furetière and Voltaire, God is present everywhere. Without really being present. He's slipping through his fingers. Is it God, or is it Nature yielding and withdrawing? An engineer should not ask himself such questions; an engineer owes it to himself to stay in his place. Humans are artisans, clockmakers, it can be said. Passemant grasps this. Then are clockmakers gods without a capital letter? It would be dangerously pretentious to think so, certainly a sin. Or are they the outcome of the Incarnation, its definitive reality . . . for the moment? The despair of solitude. Unless one has faith in the Great Clockmaker. Or performs like an automaton . . . The visitor isn't quite sure.

The Cassinis, father and son, continue the debate while the other members of the family progressively disappear in the light of the afternoon.

"Descartes is far from building a physics independent of metaphysics," says the son, César-François.

"Perhaps, but Newton deduces God from his physics. He puts forth the perfection of the world. A single law, immaterial and not mechanical, suffices to explain all terrestrial movements: gravitation!" Jacques Cassini is more deist than a moment ago.

"Of course, father, but you must admit that gravitation reinforces materialist thought. Monsieur Passemant seems to be saying that man is capable of being the perfect clockmaker, infinitely, with time. On the condition of having enough time! And he does have it, infinitely, since he thinks it infinitely . . . Man can construct the infinity clock up to the year 10,000, and why not beyond?" César-François, the future cartographer of France, the author of the beautiful map of the kingdom, becomes the accomplice of the engineer, who wasn't asking as much.

"That's serious, what you're saying, my son. Serious because without issue. We need an external principle, without which man is crushed by responsibilities. Or condemned to nothingness. I remain a creationist, what can I say! And Voltairean. Although I do not deserve to be thrown into the Bastille! 'The universe confounds me, and I cannot imagine how the clockwork of the universe can exist without a clockmaker.' That's by Voltaire? If it isn't yet, it will be!"

Here Cassini the son is bolder. "I follow you, father. But with your permission I'd like to point out that a woman, the Marquise du Châtelet, predicts a counterweight to gravitation."

"The one they call 'Pompon Newton,' son? You mean it's genuine?"

"Only the future will tell. Science, your science of the stars in particular, is advancing by leaps and bounds. This woman pictures things before calculating and proving them. She has just deposited a thesis about fire at the Royal Academy of Sciences. Not really scientific, in my opinion, but such beautiful logic! Anthropological, and I would say also theological. Who knows, won't this fire she talks about provide a new energy, a different kind, one day; maybe a name will be found for it, a color, I don't know. For the time being, the Marquise du Châtelet's thesis calls it 'fire': without matter, without weight, this fire will supposedly give the world lightness and movement. Do you see? A very special force without mass or weight."

Jacques Cassini is not sure he follows. Could the Royal Academy of Sciences be into literature now?

"A momentum of sorts, I daresay. The soul of the world? Sublimation? Levitation? I agree, father, science has not yet found the exact substance that would correspond to this hypothesis, but it won't be long. I can sense it, if you will. No need to wait till 9999; probably we will know it before then. For now, I wonder: is this woman proposing a dream? A passion inherent in matter? Or in God? It's happiness, she says. Fine, she speaks from intuition. But in cosmic terms, what is this expansion that englobes and surpasses attraction-gravitation? Another God? The same God, but with two faces? Will its mathematical formula be found? Its precise measurement? The map . . . The clock . . ." César-François, half serious, half ironic, definitively impassioned, he too. Uninterruptible.

"Unless this fire lies outside time?" Passemant interrupts him, as if in a dream.

Claude-Siméon is not sure what he is saying or why. Could this technician who works to calculate time let himself be shaken, in front of these people more learned and more competent than he, by the hypothesis that there could be a "nontime"? A "fire" that consumes time? Something like a lining doubling the universe, on which the clock would have no hold? Aberrant! How can one be sure of it without an instrument capable of taking the measurements of this "time-out-of-time"? Given that humans speak and think only within time, would it be possible to think and speak outside of it? How can one even imagine it? Unthinkable—but is it so absurd, since they are thinking about it at this precise moment at the Observatory in Paris?

Curiously, while taking such a risk, the engineer no longer has a headache. In fact, Claude-Siméon has never felt as serene. Calmly but with complete humility he'll gather up the pages of his thesis, which the Academy is going to accept without a problem. Will he really read the *Dissertation on the Nature and the Propagation of Fire* by this Mme du Châtelet, who is not of his world either? In the city, people talk a lot about this author, much less about her fire. As for the happiness on which the lady in question is said to be a specialist as well . . . Could it be some sort of frivolity? A discretion, certainly, a concentration, impenetrable secret . . . Passemant is going to think about this along the route that takes him back to the other side of the Seine to his studio, La Pomme d'Or.

21

HERE I AM AT THE PLACE
DE L'ÉTOILE

I take the avenue de la Grande Armée, cross the periph-
eral highway, and escape past the parade of signs: l'Oréal,
Hachette, Filipacchi, Alstom, Altran, Carrefour, Butagaz,
Disney, Hachette Press, Epson, Guerlain, Plastic Omnium,
Mineral Design Strategy, it's endless . . . I turn right, then
left, turn again, and I arrive at the rue de Lesseps. The old town
of Levallois, or almost—what remains of that little provincial
burg of the nineteenth century. Away from the big Paris publishers
but right near that golden crescent of liberalism, the Défense and
its nouveaux riches.

"GlobalPsyNet will be able to give us more. The Chinese are
getting themselves psychoanalyzed via Skype by our British
colleagues, and we will soon do the same . . . It looks promis-
ing!" Marianne doesn't lose sight of her objectives!

Our new colleague, Loïc Sean Garret, is in charge of a
brand-new concept: "The Show Business Correspondent—we
say SBC, which the president Ulf Larson brings with his position, among other innovations. Loïc Sean is perfectly bilingual,
and we credit him with estimable reliability and an admirable
reputation. In exchange, this man is going to align us with the
large-circulation presses."

"Do you understand the plan?"

LSG (that's his moniker) worked for *Sunday People*, for the *Sun*, for *NoW*. "He's reached a stage in his career where he needs to go deeper, you understand, to find himself, in a sense, by meeting others . . ." Marianne, heavily maternal.

The Franco-British LSG has the melancholy eyes of a guru from India under the light chestnut hair covering his forehead and the back of his neck.

"Tea? Coffee?"

"Mineral water."

He sketches his self-portrait: gay, approaching forty. Breton mother, English father—"but with mixed blood," he wants to insist. The paternal grandmother of Loïc Sean was a beautiful Indian woman from Bombay. Our new colleague's parents, both in business, died in an attack by Muslim fundamentalists, the mujahedeen in India and the Lashkar-e-Taiba based in Pakistan. It was in Pune, in the west. The explosion struck a packed restaurant, causing nine deaths. LSG cried for three days; he's still crying—"Can't you see?" He is controlling himself, but his heart is no longer in it; life has disappeared. Since then it has been a torture for him to speak English and even more to write it. He doesn't understand: "Okay, the paternal tongue, but why?"

"It's true I love French, not Breton, no. 'French is a royal language, all else is bloody gobbledygook.' Someone said that before me . . . French is my maternal tongue, can't you hear it? English came much later—the language of school, university, bank, but not of milk, you understand?"

Mr. Garret is jubilant: he thinks he's speaking our psych jargon; he's making himself at home.

"I'm normal, don't you think?" He clowns; so lovely. "And I'm going to tell you: I don't understand people not liking France!

How can we be reproached with being *too French*? That's what they say among Anglo-Saxons, as you call them, right? Ridiculous! Well then, I'm *too French*, I would like to be. Ok, it's a pretention, and it will not be my last, that's a warning."

He wants us to like him; he's laying it on a bit thick.

"France is royal like its language, of course, and even better! How cold England is in comparison! Sober, dignified, grandiose—but dry. Taste lies on this side of the Channel, it's well known . . . Your cathedrals, your castles, your cuisine are on display at the head of the aisle. Even your Republic is royal. So it cut off the heads of a monarch and some aristocrats! Pardon me! At Brussels and at the UN, France takes itself for a great power."

He stops abruptly, swallows his cappuccino, cools it down with a Perrier, then all in one go: "With the Élysée Palace at the summit of a pyramid of rebellious parties—blatant feudalism, isn't it? I'm not making this up. It was *le grand Charles* who said it, and he made it. Brilliant! Ungovernable! As if the Sun King, or what's left of him, could take control of our digital and laboriously narcissistic spider webs that now strangle all the so-called democratic—or undemocratic—regimes." A little pause for breath. "Oh, but the French model is better than the others, it's exceptional! Frankly outstanding, no? At this point it's unique, sympathetic! Didn't I tell you? I'm a realist, I adore the impossible. Oh yes, it's absurd, it's beautiful . . . France . . . I adore it."

LSG's voice, in the upper registers, sparkles; his face remains like marble. Not displeased with his number.

So when Larson, the president, offered him this job in Paris, he accepted right away. "A way of coming back to mother, don't you think?" He's teasing us. A psychoanalysis is out of the question—

LSG doesn't think he's intelligent enough for that. Not as if he were fishing for compliments, he's simply very sensitive—too sensitive, no doubt. This job at *PsychMag* will give him the chance to take an interest in others, a new thing for him, and bandage his wounds . . . "That's what you say, isn't it, you shrinks?" President Larson had moreover given him a push in that direction. "A true father, what are you suspecting . . ."

He doesn't believe a single word of what he's telling us. One is not born a man; one becomes one, and masculine homosexuality is not a homogeneous category. I observe Loïc Sean, I decipher him. Little Loïc is always two years old, clutching his Breton mother. Lost in India, she cradles him in her native language and devours him with kisses. He escapes her arms only for those of his sari-clad grandmother, whose gaze implores the vacuum, just like his, inherited from her, the Indian woman. Loïc Sean was, still *is*, these two women who cohabit within him, love each other and hate each other. He is so dependent on them that no third person is admitted into the fold, especially not a man. Poor Papa Garret wedded to his business, white shirt and black tie, neither Indian nor British but both at the same time. Darker than Loïc Sean, naturally, and not proud of it.

Make room for the man? That would be the height of pain and the height of pleasure. On the condition of swallowing him up in ecstasy, LSD, ephedrine.

"You catch on quick. Of course he's a druggie! The King (for the initiates) is addicted to designer drugs, the ones they call Meow-Meow, M-CAT, drone, bubbles, or White Magic. He intends to get clean by taking this job in Paris, from what he says . . . We'll see." Marianne is hopeful.

"Is Ulf Larson his lover?"

"On that you're mistaken! Mr. Ulf is a predator, my dear. He likes the little women of Paris, including our young and beautiful interns, haven't you noticed? No comparison with seduction *à la française*, none at all. A real wolf, this Ulf, a savage, I'm telling you. Brutality and rape."

"S/M?"

"My information remains incomplete, but it seems our director doesn't go that far. He just likes to screw the chicks, if you will." Marianne the connoisseur.

If I were our CEO's shrink, I would be looking at the maternal side. Really, the Western male is so into revenge! But that's none of my business, and the wolf has only just arrived in the sheep's pen. As of now, LSG is working on a portrait of the new techno star, the irresistible Zina Z., Russian-born, the body of a goddess and the voice of Amy Winehouse. Zina is packing them in at the nightclubs, and her album sales are through the roof.

"LSG uses his own methods, it's logical, he's not a therapist. He's a close friend of Zina's and shares her whims, goes out with her, powders his nose with her band, unearths some scoops about her private life . . . He even went to see her shrink."

"Zina has a shrink?"

"You know, she was in detox at Sainte-Anne Hospital, she escaped from there and took refuge in Saint-Sulpice . . . The press had traced her route back to the psychology clinic after the rehab . . . Now the ball is in the King's court; he'll do anything."

"He looks fragile."

Marianne is hardly listening. Ulf is calling on her cell.

"We're as *speedy* now as a daily. You can see I have to go. Ciao, sweetie, love you."

While she exults, I retrace my steps from Levallois-Perret to . . . where? Saint-Eustache? The Bourse?

Passemant's workshop, that's better.

I too inhabit a multiverse. *PsychMag* is just a planet among others. LSG is fun, but I'd rather leave him to Marianne. I zap him. To be honest, I add him to the flow of times and lives that compact, reabsorb, and cancel one another out in my personal instant. I disseminate in them. It's not that I forget him—I don't forget people, but from where I stand I see only masks. If there have to be masks, let them be as beautiful as possible. For what? For whom?

For Stan, obviously, the heart of my heart, my all. For Astro, who maintains my times suspended and connected. Truth is, I am available only for Stan; Theo knows it. The King is not of those instants.

"I'll be back, Marianne. Ciao, darling!"

"You're going back to Venice?"

"With Stan."

"Finally, without your Astro!" She's relieved.

"You're not with it at all! We'll be thinking of you. And keep an eye out on the ephedrine!"

22

HAPPINESS AND FIRE

With Émilie du Châtelet

N ivi is convinced Claude-Siméon is not one to be interested in Émilie. He can never have known of the *Dis-
course on Happiness* by Voltaire's friend, had he even
wished to, because the king's engineer passes away in 1769, and
Émilie's manuscript, held by Saint-Lambert, is published only
ten years later. He also will not know, though he could have,
her *Lessons in Physics*, dedicated to her son, the first part of
which will remain for centuries the clearest exposition of Leibniz's doctrine (in French, of course, and published during the
clockmaker's life). Nor will he read her translation of Newton's
Principia. Never mind, it will be read.

In contrast to the manic-depressive orphan Claude-Siméon
would have been if he had not been able to find his reality (or
lose himself) in stars and automatons, the four-years-younger
Émilie is persuaded that nature's only purpose is happiness.
While Newton and Huygens are the readings of the embroiderer's son, the Baron de Breteuil, Louis Nicolas Le Tonnelier, dispenses to his darling daughter an education of the most uncom-
mon rarity for people of the weaker sex at the time. Latin, Greek,
German, harpsichord, theater, dance, singing, okay fine, but also
calculus, algebra, geometry, and the sciences. Émilie, presented

at the court as expected but preferring to study, has to accept that her manly intelligence is worth a lot more than her womanly charms. She acts the extravagant. Much to the dismay of the ladies of Versailles, this learned lady collects shoes, dresses, jewelry, and lovers. Although she becomes Marquise du Châtelet through her marriage, she prefers mathematics to her three children, to such an extent that she devotes herself to Newton's work and undertakes to translate his *Principia Mathematica*.

"I Newtonize after a fashion," she disparages. Voltaire, in contrast, is dithyrambic: this Émilie will be his Minerva. It is she who dictates what he is going to write in his *Elements of the Philosophy of Newton*. She provokes jealousy in Mme du Deffand, one of Voltaire's later lovers, who writes about her, in ink mixed with bile: "Picture a woman tall and thin, no derriere, no hips, fat arms, fat legs, enormous feet; a very small head, a pinched face, a dark, mottled, red complexion, a flat mouth, teeth scattered and excessively rotten. Born without talents, she turned herself into a geometer to appear above other women, not realizing that singularity does not grant superiority. People have said she studied geometry to be able to understand her book." Mme de Créquy and Mme de Staal-Delaunay share this opinion. But the medal for vilification goes to Charles Collé, songwriter and *goguettier*.[1] When the philosopher dies in childbirth at forty-three, pregnant from her young lover Saint-Lambert, Collé says: "We have to hope that this is the last of the airs Mme du Châtelet will give herself. Really, to die in childbirth at her age is to do nothing the way others do."

---

1. The *goguettiers* were participants in or organizers of the *goguettes*, popular singing societies where people gathered regularly to perform songs.

Maybe. And too bad for the scandalmongers. Nivi prefers her to all her contemporaries because Émilie has the fire and believes happiness is possible. Happiness is a new idea in Europe—Saint-Just will say so later—and two versions of this experience already exist side by side at Versailles: Émilie's burning passion and Passemant's fine work. The captured infinite on one hand, the infinite expansion on the other. The infinite within oneself and the infinite without oneself. Émilie, who dies of love, and Claude-Siméon, who is consumed with driving in the screws of the hours, the minutes, the seconds, and the sixtieths of the second, up to 9999.

As for the modest artisan, proud just to be the one who divines and reproduces the rules of the universe conceived and implemented by the Great Architect, the mere thought of happiness, even an ordinary one, suffices to make his temples start hammering, and the turmoil yanks at the roots of his hair. Claude-Siméon does know he is not God. He is angry with himself for appropriating with such pride the *time* that God himself created, and he can only rid himself of this insolence through anger. But against whom? Against everyone, always! *All of you*, he thinks. All those who hamper him, who wage battles against him, directly sabotage him by not providing the conditions necessary for the equilibrium of his tools and telescopes, among other ultradelicate machinery. Their hypersensitivity, unimaginable for the common folk, suffers from those uneven floor planks, doors that slam shut, voices that puncture the eardrums, the crazy promiscuity. So Claude-Siméon fumes, his shame follows his rage, and then he ends up withdrawing into his shell.

Even his faithful Louise, who has taken charge of the embroidery workshop, sees him neither during daytime nor nighttime.

Louise-Françoise, his older daughter, and even Marie-Aubine, the younger daughter, who adore the music boxes fabricated by their father, no longer dare approach him. Obviously Claude-Siméon refuses to see the inquisitive people who bury him in advice and compliments and offer to publish his work. And what else! Hypocrites, robbers—worse, naïve people who harbor the vague desire of becoming famous thanks to him! Profiteers who hope people will be talking about them and ensure their posterity, at his expense . . .

Passemant cannot conceive of this mania that takes the place of philosophy for the majority of the French. Don't they have better things to do than be happy? To understand Newton, all you have to do is put his discoveries into practice. And become one with the harmony of his work, with its beauty. No need to seek within oneself or elsewhere: happiness is excellence. It's his clock 9999. And since God's laws are those of matter, the order of the world is the proof of God: it says so in the Psalms. Passemant heard this just today at Saint-Eustache: "The heavens are telling the glory of God." Naturally, Claude-Siméon understands such things as a man of science, how else? It's not worth taking the trouble to delve into the true cause of phenomena, even less so within human souls. A job well done replaces happiness, or rather displaces happiness onto the work. On the outside: the works, the works, the works!

Physics, astronomy, and clockmaking hardly need metaphysical hypotheses. The Cassinis have been saying it all along, on the whole, and that's enough for Claude-Siméon. He'll be content to reproduce divine laws. In so doing, does man become God? Passemant rejects such madness, but even so does not renounce it; he is convinced that nothing of a divine order can escape him. He wants to believe it, although . . . And yet, *that* will not escape the men who will succeed him. As a

consequence of which God will be reabsorbed into our calculating and clocklike humanity . . . The clockmaker knows he
will find inspired minds who will object that this future is not
so seductive. But reassuring, certainly. In any case, the man of
art hopes so, wants to believe it. Modestly, serenely. A certain
joy, and the migraine evaporates. It suffices to accept one's
limits.

We are all entrepreneurs, technicians, the more or less gifted
workforce of the Great Clockmaker. That's what he thinks. Is
this to say that man no longer invents anything? But people do
invent, they invent what is, what was, and what will be, by reproducing it. Neither split off nor propulsed, everything is there:
finished, but to be redone. The effort to calculate time replaces
enthusiasm—calm down, you men of the revolution! Since the
human engenders only what is reproducible and discovers only
to reproduce all the better. A true joy? But coupled with the effort to do well, do well without a break.

The inventor remembers only one thing from young Cassini's
speech: a strange and noble woman has written an essay about
the nature and propagation of a certain fire. Passemant doesn't
see what's so interesting about that. Nevertheless the astro-
nomic clockmaker wonders about it as he walks through Paris.
What exactly is this fire she is talking about? What red and
black force exerts its action on all of nature to the point of
consuming it? A universal Prometheus who both unites and
dissolves everything in the universe? Big Bang and expansion?
Assemblages and dissolutions of the universes? Unifying cohe-
sion that contains and connects body parts and at the same time
pulls them apart, dissociates them, rarefies them? This fire of
Émilie's clearly operates at the antipodes of his 9999 homunculus. Where Passemant *calculates* and *masters* time, the marquise

amplifies and *annihilates* it. Could this fire be what every self-respecting clockmaker considers as a sort of nothingness? Brilliant Émilie, who dares to think up the inverse of his clock! Hellfire . . . ?

Not a single member of the Academy would be in a position to imagine Mme du Châtelet as the only one to integrate Leibniz and his infinite identities into the attraction Newton discovered. Is Émilie already anticipating the boson and dark matter? Does she realize she is projecting her own passions onto her prophetic astrophysics?

Claude-Siméon doesn't want to see, any more than do the academicians, that this precursor of modern cosmology was inspired by the fires of her senses. Yet, learned and amorous, it's all the same for her. That's what Émilie says. Nivi is convinced of it, and too bad for those men and women who are hoping to find happiness in social networks. Or even worse, those who have the luxury of at last conceiving the child of a spermatozoid in a hospital in Belgium or Spain by means of a daily injection of the follicle-stimulating hormone Mister Gonal-f. The latest honeymoon for the third millennium . . .

23

DO NEW PATIENTS EXIST?

Don't you think it's a funny coincidence, these women in their thirties who have consulted me in the space of a month, all presenting the same symptom? A real epidemic!"

I am often asked if there are "new patients," ones different from those Freud analyzed. Marianne, of course, has the answer. She specializes in sleep therapy and hesitates to prescribe the new molecules to her clients, who can't sleep unless they are exhausted from tango marathons. Does this have anything to do with Émilie, with fire, with happiness? Maybe Gonal-f is not so far off. Be that as it may, I adapt; internal coups d'état often depend on technical progress: for the duration of a tango, patients endure them or try to avoid them.

"Oh yes, you're falling behind, dear girl, it's the latest fashion! My tango fans are in love with their DJ—or with the first virtuoso tango dancer they come upon, they get totally hooked . . . Result: gynecological catastrophe, professional disruption . . . In the end they appear in my office, asking me to make them get a good night's sleep at last."

My friend has stopped taking Prozac. She is doing Pilates, and she too has started tangoing, "but in moderation, you know me!"

Indeed: prudence. It was at the club that she met her patients. But that body-to-body languishing was not her forte. Marianne soon traded the dance floor for the floor mat, flourishing instead with the help of Ingrid, an athletic German who is attracting all the adepts of spiritual yoga you can count in the sixth arrondissement. Thanks to her, Marianne has better posture.

"I had become a real tortoise, Nivi, a bit like you, sorry . . . But much more than you, and you never said anything! Now I walk with my chest out, you see, no need for implants. A good thing, too, with all those charlatans! No, just a few muscles, and goodbye to guilt! We shall see what we shall see!"

Marianne transfigured: I have seen mauve lipstick color her lips, her dull uncombed hair transformed by a square-cut platinum blond hairdo, stiletto heels giving her style, miniskirts replacing her eternal jeans. But no man on the horizon—no woman, either, for that matter.

"What do you think about surrogate mothers?"

My silence must have been longer than usual; my friend blushes, doesn't wait for my reply, as per usual. "Don't worry, sweetie, I'm simply asking if it's a good subject for *PsychMag* right now, that's all."

Of course it's a good subject! There is no bad subject for *PsychMag*, nor any moment more favorable than another. Whether it's with Ulf or with the King, or anyone else. I dodge, I fill the airhole, I get tangled in the adjectives: intimacy is an untouchable zone. This is not the moment; it's so rarely the moment. I look at my watch. I'm in a hurry, you too; it's crazy how time is accelerating these days—call me, we'll talk when you want, as you know.

A few weeks later, *PsychMag* devotes an issue to assisted procreation, the early mother/infant bond, infancy, the baby's distress, sudden death of the nursing child, transitional spaces, the desire not to be a mother, the desire to be a mother . . . All under the guidance of Dr. Marianne Baruch, who received carte blanche from CEO Ulf Larson. Larson, minutely attending to the needs of LSG the King, devotes himself to the life of stars to increase the circulation, leaving serious subjects to the real specialists, like my best friend. For my part, I've been shelved, and I'm proud of it. I'm not complaining. Since the new leadership has to make its mark, contributions by Nivi Delisle, even modest, but always very serious, too serious, risk causing difficulties. It's out of the question to make a point of my difference and hence influence. Making a point of being gracious, I acquiesce to the globalization strategy, which after all leaves me to my dreamy escapades with Astro and Stan.

Once a month, the editors ask me to write about the "societal issues" pop psych is so preoccupied with, such as: "Does going digital mean a new Renaissance, or does it spell the end of Planet Gutenberg?" "Text messaging: writing or drug?" Or even more unbeatable: "What is left of *Homo sapiens* in blogs and social networks?" Inescapable but without interest, these meditations excite colleagues and other cultural animators. Whereas the Ulf-King couple, not knowing how to dispose of them, sends them off to "Chronicle of the Month by Nivi Delisle," reduced to the bare bones. Today I'm supposed to sound the depths of the Apocalypse by discussing the bankruptcy of reading: "What Is Reading? or, The End of the Civilization of the Book."

"That's the kind of thing people love, but very very concrete, and *fun*, please . . . ! Of course you can do it, you're the best!" Marianne really wants to be seductive, her new hobbyhorse: "to write is to seduce."

Maybe. Why not? As for reading . . . I have a new patient, a freelance journalist at France Culture, about forty, unmarried, BA in sociology, parents are doctors, originally from Lyon. "I ought to be a success"—but she's consulting me because she *can't read*. "Don't worry, I'm not illiterate. I read the books by the people I interview, editorials in the paper, letters I get in the mail, but each time I realize I don't know what I've read. Not a trace. The screen is empty. Flatline EEG. Is it serious, doctor? Is it an illness? A symptom? Do you have other patients like me?"

My analysands do not fail to ask the protective question: "Am I like the others?" If yes, then fine, even if it's mortal. *To be*, to be *with*, to belong, to *be one of.* Otherwise, panic! But it's not enough for them to "be one of": they quickly realize that they want to "be one of" in order to "get out" all the better, to claim the exception. I want to be the unique one of, the only one of!

Justine—let's call her Justine—manages to read only text messages. Two lines, not more, preferably with abbreviated words, not much grammar, a concrete message. Whereupon she shuts up.

"Concrete," I punctuate her silence.

"*Love u. Meet at 5. Buy sugar. Boss sick, stay home. 1500 wds for your column* . . . That's clear, isn't it? Info, useful words to set down a situation, a goal . . . They stick . . . No reasoning, no speeches . . . Those I don't retain, they slip by me, scatter . . . I'm scattered."

She's afraid, won't say anything else today.

As a teen, Justine liked to read novels. Can't anymore. Even films repel her: she founders in the unfolding of images, can't follow the plot; the sequence of events annoys her or puts her to sleep.

She and I are going to follow this thread together. To un-knit the anxiety and traverse the abyss that as a terrified little girl Justine dug between her body and words. To protect her-self? She doesn't know from whom, from what. She will try to say. Let's not be in a hurry. We will gently remove the screen that put the untamed, horrified child's fear to sleep without extinguishing it. We will then enter into the seeds of suppressed desire, in search of the unspeakable. "To go always higher, stronger, faster! To succeed!" That is exactly what dad and mom wanted. To the point of emptying everything out of Justine: senses, sensa-tions, times, all abolished, evacuated, struck down . . . We will reawaken the devitalized words . . .

Women are scary—too much, not enough, that depends; it's well known. But their fears? Our fears? Ungraspable, scarcely audible in the breath that separates words. These rebellious frights have an animal substance; they liken us to the beast's need for survival. Justine's terror refuses reading. But it can also seize hold of the written, transport us into it, and as a result we are seized, set fire, consumed for good.

It's not the same fear? True, Justine's panic and the quaking of Aubane, the Owl's assistant, are miles apart. A graceful tit with eyes as blue as the wings of the little bird, Aubane shud-ders at the slightest contact with our modern encumbrances and, panicked, takes shelter in the mystery of Versailles. But once there, the tit flits about, pecks at manuscripts intact for long years, makes her nest out of the precious fragments. Stan eventually finds her full of smiles, truly enchanted, the flutter-ing archivist of the Château.

"It's simple: absence of concentration. How do you expect young people to read if they can't pay attention? The learning-disability classrooms are full of teens like that. Your Justine is so banal! I mean, she's typical . . . Normal, if you prefer. For us it's the best! Her case lies at the heart of illiteracy . . . There's your article, hon, I can see it like I was there." Marianne encourages me with all her heart, but she's beside the point as always. "So 3,000 characters. Okay by you?"

I say yes, but I have my own opinion all the same. My paper will have an intimate quality; Larson and LSG will find it *too French*, but they'll let it go. They'll think I just have to have my fun, with my propensity for splitting hairs . . . Ah, these French shrinks, always on the other side of the mirror . . . !

"That's it, diversity, right, my dear Madame Delisle? The *multiverse*, if you don't mind my quoting you . . ."

My Swedish CEO has a globalized tolerance, perfectly fake. But he insists on a kiss on the cheeks, in the French manner.

I count on Marianne, my liaison, to continue in this job as a temp in the globalized psych vulgarization.

Bill Parker, Theo's colleague, originally from Seattle and on assignment at the Observatory in Paris, has just encountered Justine on her way out after her session. Parker, who is studying the mystery from before the Big Bang, thinks he has detected the existence of an impalpable numerical quantity, *information*, the prototype of God. The "tetragrammaton," he claims. I have a lot of affection for this ageless adolescent with the 1960s curly haircut à la Bob Dylan, occasional violinist, father of numerous children, including four with his sweet Mary, wife and lab colleague. This feminist of the last generation, as she describes herself, powerfully intelligent, doesn't talk a lot but loves to calculate data from the Planck satellite with her husband. Who is in love with her, with Paris, and with all the beautiful things in the world, among them the Leaning Tower of Pisa, which once sheltered Galileo; the north pole from which

the frozen astral sky can be observed; Passemant's clock, which
Stan showed him in Louis XV's residence; and not forgetting
the innumerable female students he meets throughout the world
and who succumb to his charm. Today it's the turn of the "beautiful redhead" leaving my office.

"Will you introduce me?"

Bill, true to form! With me he plays the part of the rigorous
and austere scientist: astrophysics is the only profession of value,
and psychoanalysis is latter-day magic. As a consequence, he
ignores my discipline and, to protect me from it, Professor
Parker addresses himself to Nivi Delisle only in her role as a
journalist. No way am I going to tell him that "the redhead"
was just leaving my couch. I shrug my shoulders, try a graceful
and dissuasive pout. It doesn't dissuade him; he insists. I end up
avoiding the question: I'm not sure my Justine and Bill are living in the same timeframe . . . Parker goes red, then his fury
descends upon me.

"Nivi, you don't know a thing, time is virtual, just like
money! It's a fiction that links bodies and physical systems to
each other." Could the professor be angry?

Time is money? That's it? Cosmology's latest brainwave? I'm
trying to make him laugh.

"Not in the usual sense, but in a way . . . No, you have to
forget time, I've already told you and repeated it, we're not there
anymore . . ." Is he really annoyed?

Events cancel each other out, agreed. Time no longer exists,
only catastrophes. But globalized citizens overcome them by
continuing to live all the same. And to earn your living, you
have to begin by reproducing life, don't you. Artificial repro-
duction has never been in better health: Bill can't disagree, can
he. I don't remind him that before earning his living, and while
earning it, he also made children—all over the place too, it's

public knowledge—because he was eager to perpetuate the duration that escapes him and that he goes looking for as far away as the galaxies.

All I say is: "Virtual time?"

With that I unleash his compassion. Phew! He even forgets my Justine. The professor as pedagogue is never more seductive. It's his ultimate weapon.

"Yes, and really, it's clear as day! Let's take an example. If a cup of coffee costs €1.50, fifty cups of coffee add up to a pair of shoes at €75, and you would need ten thousand cups of coffee to make a car at €15,000. You see? We link objects to each other by the intermediary of this *fictive value*, which is money. It has no value in and of itself; it only has value for placing things in relation. Well, it's the same thing with time. Time can dissolve into placing things in relation. Yes, it's true! We no longer need an abstract notion like 'global time'! Finished! It's enough to relate physical systems to one another."

Do I look incredulous? Parker pursues.

"Another example. The Earth rotates once per day, and the heart beats at seventy-five pulses per minute. That comes to 108,000 pulses per terrestrial rotation. Are you following me? Global time is resorbed into a series of specific measures placed in relation. We can thus summarize the workings of the universe by physical laws that act in an entity called 'Time' and connect everything to it without being concerned with the relations between those phenomena themselves—the heart and the Earth, the coffee and the shoes . . . We're not interested in their affairs."

The handsome Bill can certainly intoxicate! I'm willing to accept that there is no global time in the universe, but if you decompose it, can't certain of its elements serve as a clock for others? Time then emerges in atemporality. We are that part of a time structured by experience, where the correlation among elements of a fundamentally static world is elaborated. The silence of those infinite spaces no longer frightens us, Pascal! We measure, we calculate, we relate. Infinitely!

Lucky Bill! He sows to every wind, then settles down as a consummate expert on virtual worlds. He wins on all counts.

I forget nothing, neither his explanations nor Justine, the others, Stan, Theo. My vertical time crumbles. I do sense that a *depressed* person suspends his time: Claude-Siméon Passemant recovers from his father's death only by ejecting himself into Newton's global time, which he shuts up in his astronomical clock. The orphan Louis XV is haunted by grief for his assassinated parents; he denies it through sexual exploits, hunts, and feverish conquests. Global time is replaced by proper, singular times, memories, traumas. How many? Numerous.

Take the *Inferno*, its name is legion. The damned, the outlaws in the time-out-of-time of the unconscious. The *Purgatorio* follows. It is established when one strives to compress a mass of incommensurable existences; it's the recomposed family, the chimerical wager on cohabitation, it's the "living-together" of breakups and solitudes, jealousies to the death and toxic cultural diversions. *Paradiso*, finally: the loving ultratime of Astro and Nivi . . .

What else?

24

IN PRAISE OF ILLUSIONS

Nothing takes me farther from my patients than my scrupulous clockmaker Passemant, though the fiery Émilie is overtaking him. The inventor's "internal coups d'état" tear him away from the automaton spectacle, whereas the translator of Newton and Leibniz doesn't ask God for an order she can reproduce. She wants passion, even if it's destructive. However, the divine Émilie is not making me neglect my moony engineer. I'm just taking a side trip with her while keeping tabs on the somnambulistic pains of the hurried technician. In this era of triumphant technology, in which Passemant excels, I stake a claim to the incalculable and the useless, and I thrive on the *illusion* of happiness. Since *there is happiness* in divine purpose, it is not forbidden to be happy, says Émilie, the mathematician who is consumed by love.

But watch out: do not be satisfied with insipid contentments. Think about your health, Passemant, anticipate the malaise. You have my approval. Your family is a seatbelt. Your wife Louise is master of the ship. They attenuate the cephalalgia and often serve as an antidepressant, but not enough, not always. And yet, the principal matter is elsewhere, do you understand? Are you hot-blooded, Monsieur? You don't know? I, Nivi, am going to tell you. Listen carefully: it is vital not to reject a fiery temperament like Émilie's. And you have to get rid of the crippled souls—for they do exist, just as there are corrupted bodies. Bodies of men and bodies of women, obviously.

I take God, nature, and society into account, Mr. Engineer, just like you, but less than you. I believe I have the means, even if I am a woman. But whatever their ambitions, women are excluded from glory. My ambition is pretty healthy: I'm not ashamed of it, but the fact is, only study remains for us (as for you, right?) to *console a somewhat lofty soul for all the exclusions to which it finds itself condemned.* (I'm speaking to you with Émilie's words, no less.)

I do not dispatch happiness into the void, oh no! You expel it from yourself, and that's a mistake. Do you know why? To be happy, you have to be able to have illusions. You of course know all about it, since you fabricate music boxes that imitate flutes and harpsichords and even clocks that harness time for ten thousand years to come. But you don't have the courage to praise illusions. Either you think of yourself as all-powerful, and find that repugnant, or full of illusions, and that depresses you. In both cases you get headaches. Relax, Passemant!

Illusions are not mistakes. You who are an expert on optical illusions, you amuse the lords and ladies of Versailles by offering them the sky itself. It falls just as it is into their plates and floods the Hall of Mirrors. In this way you construct an illusion that does not make us see objects as they are but as we need to see them for our utility or our pleasure.

Now, in Versailles, utility *is* pleasure. Let me reassure you: there's no connection with deception. Watching puppet shows, I laugh too, maybe more than anyone else; I like to think it's Pulcinella who is speaking. What a joy also to see literary illusions make historical personalities—Greeks, Egyptians, Moors, gods—speak in alexandrine verses! And I adore opera. You don't go very often, but you adored it during your youth under the Regency. Such a spectacle of enchantment unifying everything, much greater than the pleasure that music or dance bring, you surely agree. Opera, yet another effective antidepressant. I advise you to try it!

I think I know what's holding you back, clockmaker. It's because you *fabricate* the illusion that you've lost the desire to *enjoy* it. You would have had to embody illusion, shelter it; it would have had to be your spouse, your alter ego. Believe me, my friend, you cannot instill an illusion any more than you can instill taste or passion; you just have to not attempt to neutralize them. Stop thinking about those gears your brain and your hands constructed, which will make music and time resonate for centuries. Producing the illusion is not enough: to enjoy it is an art, and this art is neither frivolous nor Machiavellian. I'm telling you because I know what I'm talking about. Differently from you, but no less.

As Émilie confided to Voltaire, it is imperative to convince yourself that happiness is not impossible in this life. How? By love, of course, my good man! Don't tell me you don't know love! Your mother, Marie-Madeleine, your Louise who protects you, your daughters: that's love. Don't look away, it's you I'm talking to. Love first! Especially! It's up to you to . . . begin again. And I promise you, you will no longer have that pain in your skull. Love is a commerce the illusion of which is never destroyed and whose *ardor is equal in the enjoyment and the deprivation of it.* Only in love will God, the gods, women, society itself, men too, appear to you as inevitable and necessary illusions. To be constructed for our utility and our pleasure. It's happiness, the happiness of illusion.

I know what you're going to say. Didn't Voltaire himself flee from that big old Love when he left Émilie so he would no longer be dependent on her? Or so he would be dependent on another woman instead—temporarily and relatively—or another man, and so on until death ensues? Okay. And so what? The passion of love places happiness in the dependency of others. In the plural.

Ah, shared tastes, that *sixth sense*, the most delicate, the most precious of all, for two people equally sensitive to happiness! *One is happy only because of vivid and pleasant sentiments: why forbid oneself the most vivid and the most pleasant of all?* Émilie will suffer from love, no doubt, die in any case from the fruit of her entrails left to her by the love of Saint-Lambert. She knows that was an illusion, but her desire for it remains. That's the price of the fire; you have to keep it going. She maintained it.

She obeyed her will, you know what that is. But this will in which she found her happiness wanted both the fire in the body, which Voltaire wasn't giving her anymore, and the fire of the mind, which she stoked until the end. Both together. It's the task of reason to engender happiness, and hers placed the fire above the risks incurred by the uterus of a woman of forty-three.

What can you do, clockmaker, death inheres in fire. The marquise-mathematician sensed it, was afraid of it, but didn't want to avoid it. It was an illusion, this new love. She knew it and, just like Voltaire, maintained her desire for it. But she was not duped, since she wrote: *there is no passion one cannot surmount when one has truly convinced oneself that it can only serve for our misfortune.*

The flame with its dark forces. Believe me, Newton and Leibniz and Saint-Lambert were her happiness, and they go together, my friend, I'll never stop saying it.

I'm talking to you about happiness, and you would be quite right to ask me what I think about unhappiness. The only true unhappiness is *the presence of an object that makes us lose the fruit of our reflections.* You might say the same, except that you reflect as a worker does, and the fruits of your reflections are machines. Misfortune for me, I say it without pretention, is being prevented from thinking.

And Émilie, all her life, avoided that misfortune. Did she kill herself for the fire that's called "love," "illusion," "happiness"? Or simply *thought*? As long as we support our existence in this matter that constitutes us, we have to try hard to make pleasure penetrate through all the gates of the soul. Illusion? Fire? Thought is included in them. Émilie's thought, in any case. Perhaps one can live a fire, that fire, only in a fiction, as Voltaire did, by writing a sort of total novel. Émilie the scientist did not push the Word to that point; she let herself be consumed by the illusion. Not too bad for a woman in a society regulated like an automaton—but what society isn't? Ah, the utility of fictions, Passemant, and pleasures too! Try it: you will not despair.

25

MARIANNE'S SILHOUETTE

Marianne's silhouette has thickened, unless I'm mistaken. We don't see each other enough: she's right to reproach me for it; we're growing apart. My friend is aging, like everyone else—like me, even if I pretend not to care about it. Did she give up on the Pilates? The tango marathon did not last, but it did serve to keep her physically fit . . . Or is Marianne pregnant?

"At last you've landed among humans! It's true that with her Astro, Nivi is happy only in the sky . . . Oh yes, darling, you should have guessed . . . I thought that *madam analyst* wasn't mentioning it out of delicacy, waiting for me to bring up the subject . . . Besides, you're always blowing in and out at Levallois-Perret, and you're so quick to get off the phone, when you're soaring among the supernovae, that I didn't know how to go about announcing it . . ."

Her eyes go misty, tears stream down her cheeks, lodge in the corners of her mouth. Marianne swallows them, makes excuses with a pinched smile; I clasp her in my arms. Her yellowish complexion, the vomiting, the fatigue.

"It's hard, you know, after all I'm past the age, well past . . ."

"Don't worry, nothing is simpler, maternity is right up my alley . . . Fabulous, you'll see! I'm with you. Not as far away as you think . . ."

I kiss her, I reassure her. I don't tell her stories. Each woman her own. When I was pregnant with Stan, Ugo and I were the happiest in the world. We would listen to Haydn and Stan would respond by dancing in my belly. I was bathing him while swimming at La Conche on the island; I talked to him about the herons and the swallows. I would gather pink seafoam salt and give it to the horses on the swamps at dawn or sunset. I would tell my son everything. I never had nausea. It was paradise. Afterward, with the daily worries, the three-person friction, the constraints that put a brake on desire and then extinguished it, we lost Ugo. Before leaving us for good, he took his distance, with that Italian cheeriness, innocent and cruel, that left Stan and me with a lot of bitterness. And with the certainty that everything is for the good in the best of all possible worlds as long as we love each other. Neither pathos nor tragedy. "My father lives in Italy." "He writes me." "He sometimes stops in Paris." "He travels a lot." "My mother's a shrink." "I have problems." "Life is difficult." "I'm different. Aren't you?"

For a long time, I thought Stan was reciting ready-made sentences echoing mine—well-learned lessons. People think so, unhappily; Marianne also, I presume. Now I know that Stan says only what he feels, what he lives, what he believes and thinks. Because for him, they go together: he looks for the exact word, the sound that makes sense. He and I have navigated under a good star thanks to Dr. Freud, and now Astro has joined our planet. Marianne can lean on me, as she well knows.

"Ulf helped me a lot. He's supporting me." That's all she'll say.

Was our CEO Ulf Larson the father? Or did he steer her toward the artificial paradises in Belgium, Spain, Norway? Marianne had written a long article about these new forms of motherhood for the special issue of *PsychMag.*

"Yes, with Loïc Sean, Ulf has been . . . He still is . . . They're really good friends." She forces herself to smile with her teeth unclenched. I think I'll believe her. I embrace her.

"We'll be with you too, Stan, Astro, and I. Girl or boy?"

"I don't want to know yet . . . It's so . . . surprising . . . I'm not saying abnormal . . . A sort of miracle . . . I hardly dare think about it . . . I'm waiting."

"We'll dare together, okay? Come on, I'm taking you to Café Marly . . . Shall we take in an exhibit?"

26

THE DREAM OF THE
PRIMORDIAL UNIVERSE

Two Journalists Without Borders savagely murdered in Africa. Like the whole nation, the profession shares in the families' grief. *PsychMag* joins in the emotion. The items run one after another on the TV, on the smartphone screens. Finally, hostages are liberated. Now all that remains are the tears, the barbarity. Several hundred high-school girls have just been kidnapped, valued at eight euros each by Boko Haram in Nigeria. Just now jihadists have cut off the head of the first Frenchman, after the American and English heads. But where are our ministers, our military, our drones, the UN, the IMF, and the rest?

The "red caps" destroy the "ecotax" portals and burn pyramids of cabbages to avenge the poverty of the Breton farmers. The gloom is affecting agro-alimentation, household appliances; the press is no longer taking in money, catalogue sales are dropping, the chicken, salmon, auto, and textiles industries are all *distressed* . . . The unemployment curve is not inverting, but at Saint-Germain-des-Prés they're putting up buffet tables with champagne and vermillion plates for this year's grand literary prizes . . . An airplane is about to take off using solar energy, tomorrow it will be Icarus . . . A beautiful Chinese woman, speaking for her government, mildly protests American espionage, whereas China has banked enough billions of dollars to topple the still leading world power . . .

"Lima is humid but without rain, and there are too few trees in bloom to bring light to this melancholy."

Astro has called me via Skype to describe the "City of the Kings" in the Andes, where he has observed, in a NASA lab, "enormous concentrations of galaxies separated by unimaginable voids, massive agglomerations witness to the birth of the seeds present in the primordial universe."

My ILY is now in the plane bringing him back from Peru. There is no longer any place on earth or in the sky where we cannot connect. Yet another security precaution that falls by the wayside. Like me, like you, Theo glances at the latest news, rarely mentions it, no longer comments. "We're not going to interpret the news, it's already old." On the other hand, every item of news becomes political for him "as long as we envisage it from the point of view of our strong interaction," he says—the interaction that keeps us from disintegrating and allows us to accede to an accretion of matter imbued with expanding energy called *love*. Why that word?

He insists on it. My Astro can't keep from going against the grain, and he reveals his new anarchist version: "There is no idea that love cannot eclipse.

"It's simple, Nivi. Love liberates information and energy, connects events, creates correlations among the elements of a perpetually evolving foam. Love, however different it may be— for Émilie, Claude-Siméon, Stan, also la Pompadour and even Louis XV, for the despairing unemployed, for those whose throats are cut by the jihadists and those who resist them, not forgetting the feeling you have for me—love makes singular times emerge from the depths of depression's atemporality. Oh yes, more and better than thought, love bears witness to the course of the world, this world that exists only because a bend occurred, a swerve that gave birth to visible matter, while our very experience ceaselessly appropriates the invisible. Only after this swerve do singular times emerge from ultratimes—rebeginnings, from these fictions that hold us in thrall. Everything lies in that swerve, remember it!"

How could I forget it? Your plane has landed; our hands, our eyes embrace for a long time. My time is not an unfurling of instants. My time is neither stopped nor present. It is an extreme time in which tension unfolds into a plural *now*. There everything holds together; all hold together. You also hold, yourself. Until everything is eclipsed in the reflections of emerging times, and new choices emerge in which I am reborn into infinite reliances.

Hand in hand. Bodies in proximity. Hand that holds and holds me upright. Touch, gift, contact, tact. *Now* states this reciprocal agreement, this strong interaction, better. Better than "love," too vague, too demanding, already condemned; better than "presence," which signals the approach but evokes neither the duality of the gift and the word nor the vital tenacity of *now*.

You are held by Stan, you upheld him, he held himself for you, and from now on he keeps to himself, with others and for others.

Hold yourself in me now, I hold myself in you.

Now does not say "*There is time*," which, with its impersonal "there is," gathers in and reassembles. No. *Now* is the pressure of the blood that rises and receives, its sonority preceding the voice. Without sounds, without communication, without words, neither I nor you. The expansion of the *now* transcends excitation, tenses it again and again, beyond pleasure.

One in the other, one enfolding the other, outside of ourselves, inseparable. The universe calmly stands still. At the instant of orgasm, bodies are fixed, eternal. The density of the burning osmosis keeps light agglutinated. We are the same spacetime beginning to bend, but barely. Until the brilliance of light emanates from Theo and Nivi and daylight dilates, splendorous torrent, a blinding and a cry.

Deep sleep.

Theo will sleep until the sun rises. I wake before dawn. Not really—I don't open my eyes; I live in the deep field of the dream.

Everyone is familiar with those dreams that come before dreams. Tortures or pleasures, neither words nor images, they abandon you upon waking, as if destroyed, without memories, shipwrecks aground at the edge of ordinary life. Nothing like the pulsation of the embrace that fulfills my night. No characters, no plot. Skin, breasts, and genitals all engorged, pains and joys; emptied, the embrace concentrates and dilates, then the rhythm subsides into wandering shadows, and a bursting, airy sonority abducts me. Poignant yet sovereign, Couperin's notes resonate in the dawn of time.

Leave this dream? I don't want to; I'm not able to. Because nobody inhabits that sleep. Not even me. Just masses of galaxies that pass by a milky way, are lost, stretch out into pink clouds, and end up descending upon the Louvre pyramid. A variable star pierces the dark matter like those white sculptures cutting through the shadowy lower sections of Café Marly, which we glance at when we kiss: an Egyptian queen, a Greek goddess, a decapitated head on the silver platter of the fleeing moon.

My cell phone rings: the Owl informs me that the attack at Versailles was actually aimed at Passemant's famous astronomical clock. I must be dreaming—how did she get my number?

It's my Astro's voice that makes me realize I have rejoined the day: "Nine o'clock . . . You're shivering, you left the window open . . . No, it's not raining. The springtime dew smells of greenery." Theo likes my perfume. "I don't understand why people get bored."

He doesn't close the window. Covers me with laughter and kisses. Didn't have the same dream—another one, but similar to mine, because our two pleasures take us to a time from before time, a world from before the world. And wake us up glowing with a radiance that does not pertain to quotidian measures, that no code or identifier can decipher.

"But that's because they don't know us yet!" Nivi replies, provocatively.

She dares to claim that the two sexes will not die separated, each in their own spaces. And that neither Madame Bovary, nor Madame de Renal, nor Albertine, nor Lolita, nor Molly Bloom, nor Colette told the story of that *now* where a woman and a man, each in their own spaces, can together lose themselves and encounter each other.

III
REBIRTH

27

DEATH IS NOT NEWS

A journalist famous for his investigations of the very private lives of stars has been found dead in his apartment on the rue du Pont-aux-Choux, near the Picasso Museum. Was it natural causes or a criminal act? At the present time, the demise of the Franco-British Loïc Sean Garret, known as LSG the King, remains unexplained, according to a source close to the police. An inquiry has been launched. Several leads are being considered, the most likely being connected to his profession. Did he perhaps use illegal phone taps? With whose assistance? One recalls the scabrous affair of the *News of the World*, known as *NoW*. Is the magazine that employed the King, *PsychMag*, a disguised tabloid? Who among the stars would have been angry about things to the point of committing the irreparable? Will multiple arrests follow?"

Death is not news if it does not cause a scandal—the media impose this law: they decide on the tempo, feed it with details.

"Homicide, suicide, hard sex. Wire taps and incestuous relations with the police. Show-biz, LSG-LSD, the Murdoch empire. Could Levallois-Perret, where the respectable *PsychMag* has its office, be to the Champs Élysées and boulevard Blanqui what the London Docklands are to the once honorable Fleet Street? It is not known how long it has been since LSG contacted his editorial staff."[1]

Am I dreaming, or is that France Info? The sleepy voice of the announcer buries the information under the threat of a market crash or a New York hurricane; then comes a report on the kamikazes blowing themselves up in Kabul, in Algiers, in Iraq; last is the death of a security guard in Paris.

Is it the start of the broadcast or the end of the story? So the world turns. I go back to sleep, then hang around for a while. Marianne's cell phone is on voicemail. I have some tea; it's ten o'clock. One more try: Marianne is still not answering: what's she doing? I rush to the office.

The police are already there: seals, searches, inquiries, depositions, everyone gets a turn. Ulf is livid, Marianne aghast. And me? I don't know the first thing about it.

The investigation is just beginning; no hypothesis is favored for the moment. But we are subjects supposed to know! And it's not over: we'll have to report to the police station. Supposedly, we are the sources, the witnesses, the accomplices—the suspects, while they're at it! Tension succeeds stupor; the team comes together and speaks with one voice—"we." No tears for the time being. "We are overwhelmed."

I gather my wits. All I need to do is call Rilsky, my friend— ex-friend—Northrop Rilsky, the most enigmatic of men devoted

---

1. Offices of the distinguished daily *Le Monde* are located on the boulevard Blanqui; the Champs Élysées are the site of *Le Figaro* and other newspapers. The Docklands scandal refers to the Murdoch style of journalism.

to criminality, his vocation. He'll know. Otherwise, after such a creepy business, our goose is cooked. That's it, I'll get him. Not right away, tonight, tomorrow, he'll be willing to see me, like before.

28

OVERDOSE

Police Chief Rilsky is not personally involved in the LSG matter. I had guessed as much. Paternalistic and undeniably provocative (that's his way of staying in love with me), Theo's uncle reminds me that I shouldn't neglect the importance of his responsibilities in the National Police hierarchy. No comparison to the fieldwork where our paths had crossed before. To satisfy my curiosity, though, he does what's needed to obtain "a few secret elements." Here's where we're at, my dear Nivi, he says.

"The autopsy done by our services confirmed the initial observations by the police: it was indeed a suicide. Loïc Sean Garret, the star reporter of your *PsychMag*, succumbed to an overdose. What reasons for his action (if you can talk about reason)? The dashing LSG, 'the King,' who covered the world of nightlife, often began his day with a rock star's breakfast: Jack Daniels and a line of coke. That's not all. To be at the top of his profession, demanding as he was, your diva had become accustomed to inviting fame-seeking therapists along on his nocturnal outings. When you powder your nose with such people, you end up uncovering intimate if not precious information about the private lives of people in the media, in cinema, in music

or television . . . You can see what I'm getting at: some of the
honorable protectors of our mental health are in danger of losing
their jobs. They sold information like raw material, like indus-
trial silicone or Mediator . . . We know that GlobalPsyNet and
PsyNetOne have already spent several million euros to stop judicial proceedings and avoid trials for the extortion of medical
secrets by various shrinks who were treating celebrities like
Zina, whom LSG was very close to . . . Ah, when dope—I
mean the spin doctor—has hold of us . . ."

Rilsky is jubilant. I remember the King's article on Zina. The
detailed account of her enforced sexual relations with her
brother and their abusive teacher at elementary school had provoked denials from the alleged sexual delinquent: "Do you have
any proof?" The King's reply, stating that a team of psycholo-
gists had gathered the needed evidence, had put an abrupt end
to the denials . . . His lapidary formula had brought fear. It
implied that LSG drew his information neither from Zina nor
from her brother—whom alcohol and drugs had rendered voluble, in the end—nor even from illegal phone taps. It was becoming clear that his principal source consisted only of the
confidences of certain shrinks. But since no one had sought to
bring accusations of professional malpractice, it seemed the matter had been buried.

I can hear Rilsky's appetite feeding on the supposed culpa-
bility of my colleagues. I don't point it out.

"The investigation is continuing . . . In the meantime, your
profession enjoys the benefits of the presumption of innocence,
needless to say. As for the phone taps, the King was not a rank
beginner: his lucrative relationship with Scotland Yard is well
known, and he thought he could continue the same little
games with us in Paris. We had him under surveillance . . . We

didn't put pressure on him until he attacked therapeutic deontology."

Northrop thinks he's surprising me. I let him have his triumph.

"LSG was paid for that; granted, it's common in the media, needless to say, except that he overshot the mark a bit—to the point of slinging mud on some good doctors. He may not look it, but your King was a clever manipulator. He got them to sing . . . oh, sorry, professional jargon. He got them to talk, like so many magpies . . . serious druggies . . . Their required reserve, the Hippocratic oath—what a joke! A disappointment, your dear colleagues, hmm? Psychiatrists with diplomas, plus the others who are their own authority, as they put it so wittily, imprudent people. Real suckers in the PR game . . . You know who I'm talking about? It's a hypothesis, an interesting lead . . . To be followed up . . ."

To think that all this emerged from that pathetic business about Zina! Not so petty after all. The secret services are interested in psychoanalysis! How long before an NSA lurks under the couch? Drug trafficking in the pharmaceutical labs—forgotten; from now on, it's the shrinks being wiretapped. And what if they flood the wiretaps with stories about cocaine maniacs' vices corrupting the community? Paranoid cops or puerile psychiatrists: which are more dangerous? Was Rilsky hiding a story from me about gangsters charged with eliminating their most naïve member, a rat, a squealer, LSG? Or was he expecting me to confirm his suspicions—but about what? Shrinks? Journalists? Power and the sensational transform man into a machine who no longer dreams but consumes artificial paradises, so . . . Surely Rilsky doesn't believe that the police are going to save morality?

LSG was just an actor; he had simply participated in a trans-plantation of Murdoch-type methods. The conception, the brains, was none other than Larson. But his global network, *our* network, covered him, and no one for the time being had an interest in proving anything . . . So we would be stuck with the underlings, and *PsychMag* as well as GlobalPsyNet, PsyNetOne, and so on would survive without Larson, sent back to Sweden.

As is often—or always—the case, I had guessed Rilsky's "se-crets" before he discovered them. I had my own intuitions. Which are not proofs, I admit. The police chief did not know that I was already informed about the departure of our CEO. By way of explanation, our sponsors had just eliminated his po-sition—perfectly normal in times of crisis. And since Guy Thibault, the editor-in-chief, was about to retire, it was logical to promote Marianne Baruch to the position of director of the publication. "You're in charge, no helicopter surveillance, you're the master of the ship, my dear little mommy," Larson con-gratulated Marianne before flying off to Uppsala.

"You see, they noticed that the 'French exception' exists, and it rejects any graft of models that maybe work elsewhere but turn out to be catastrophic for us." Marianne is already reason-ing like a director. "You weren't expecting it, I know . . . The nation is well and truly a reality, that's what you tell yourself, isn't it? With your dreams, your clocks at Versailles, your French follies . . . We haven't been French enough at *PsychMag*. Well, we will be, you can count on me!"

She announces her promotion like a highly strategic decision that I have to accept on the spot. I reassure her: I find it per-fectly well deserved.

"And also I'll be needing cash to have someone mind the baby, if I want to pursue my professional life . . . Obviously I want to! You have to agree: there's no turning down a salary increase, is there?"

Of course not. A little embarrassed, Marianne even has a consolation prize for me.

"Ulf is leaving Paris, as expected. As a result, his apartment is free. You adore the Lux—it's an unbelievable stroke of luck, isn't it?"

Larson had set up a nice little pied-à-terre in an old apartment building overlooking the Luxembourg Gardens, not far from the mansard I used to occupy during the time of the Vogels. I had never been to see it, but Marianne had not failed to connect it to my former love life.

"We can go see it when you like . . . Later! I have to run, got to get the baby's bedroom ready . . . It's a jewel, that apartment, you're going to love love love it."

29

ONCE AGAIN I HAVE BROKEN
WITH THE HUMAN RACE

For three whole days I have disappeared into my imagination. Absorbed by a tale in which I am searching for myself. I listen, I look, I read, I plant, I water, I cook, I converse. I direct (rarely), I raise, I educate, I write, I live. I try to make my surroundings live. My A? A lover, but more than that. Beside the point. A tutor for Stan, for lack of being a father like the others. "The secret of being boring is to say everything." I will not say everything.

The salt marshes in front of the garden are covered with pyramids of salt. It's summer; people are on vacation. Stan also, not me. Still and always this suspended time. Its luminous weightlessness, nowhere as palpable as in front of the steeple of Ars, which overlooks the ocean and gives me vertigo.

Astro has just left for I don't know what sky at one of those labs that don't have a name, just a series of capital letters. Is it infantile to open one's soul to an interstellar friend? Harkening to his cosmic babble, is it possible I find pleasure only in the calculations of a quantic James Bond whose returns I am on the lookout for, whereas he saved me from drowning the better to cut me off from the world? Little Nivi, a masochist? No more than Astro. Each of us is a searcher aspirated by our Grails. I, accessory to roses and souls; he, navigator of stars and dark matters. What relation? "There are no sexual relations." Fine. Ought I to write him, as did lovers of those times past: "Love me a little, it's only justice, loving you, as I think, tenderly." This rhetoric from the more-than-perfect past is not merely outdated; it is unavailable to us because it remains to be translated into our world as it is. One does not see its anguish, which may eventually be revealed and delivered in words. Astro plays with it and displays it, against, or in addition to, or without eroticism. He admits it, even if he doesn't say so using my words. Love is our traversal of anguish, like the happiness that emerges from grief.

Love exists so rarely that it has not changed since the time when lovers sought it in the sun and the stars. A sixth sense, a *mutual taste* (Émilie constantly brings me back to it) *that links two equally sensitive souls to happiness*. Like Theo and Nivi, persuaded that happiness is an illusion—tenacious and irrefragable—that *one should avoid if it makes us lose the fruit of our reflections*.

9999 heard the Newtonians, the Cartesians, the Leibnizians argue. Today my A's *instanton* is of interest only to hyperspecialists and a few peerless lovers, like us. Bloggers, indifferent, spend all their time on their iPads, get worked up over sordid little news items, or bet on the given name of the British royal baby: *It's a boy!* Fortunately, Facebook, Twitter, and other social networks repair these forsaken egos, unless they precipitate them into suicide. And the sands of August, pushed toward Singapore and other offshores, erase the traces of fiscal evasion.

Nivi contemplates the flotilla of shoveler ducks in front of the lavender, six just hatched and the two gray-chocolate-green parents. She thinks about the other side of Planck's Wall, where Theo is. "We are two in one, my Astro and I."

When Yuri Gagarin's historic flight shook up the planet, I was a quite young girl, discovering I was in love.

"Gagarin has brought the world together!" said Papa, always a believer.

"You're dreaming . . ." Mama, a convinced Darwinian and always pessimistic, gently objected.

I went dancing with Wlad, who was getting ready to take his baccalaureate exam, pressed against him as we did at the time, overheated teens fired up by totalitarian communism, ardently romantic. He kissed me for a long time, biting my tongue and my lips, in front of the door of my apartment building at 4 Saint Sophia Street in Sofia. Until the end of summer we danced and wept some more. After his exams, Wlad left for Dubno in Siberia to study astrophysical engineering and work on the future sputniks. We corresponded, a little. I never saw him again.

I delved into astronomy. I think I read everything one could find on the subject at the time. Papa and Mama were not communists: I was not admitted to study the hard sciences (secret defense) nor allowed to join my dancer in Siberia. All I could do was fall back on my inner core: languages, literature, writing. Psychology inevitably followed. All taking place against a backdrop of warming relations, the Six-Day War, May '68, the Yom Kippur War, Glasnost, Perestroika, Solidarity, the fall of the Wall, studies in Paris, avant-garde, modernity and postmodernity, Twin Towers, and the Clash of Civilizations . . . Until the sky once again fell on me: my Stan, my Astro, and along with them, Passemant's clock.

Chance? Miracle? Émilie, reconciling Newton with Leibniz, knew that a miracle is not an exception to natural laws but an event in nature itself. No Saint-Médard for her or for me; the supernatural is part of the natural order, which is not the order of the Divine Clockmaker but a perpetual shared engenderment of causes and effects with no other agent than Nature herself.

The Being? An infinite series of unpredictable events in which one derogates one law only to obey another. Mixed in with the law of understanding are the laws of enthusiasm, grace, love—fire, says Mme du Châtelet, Nivi's cult reference. And the laws of the unconscious, adds the disciple of Freud. Which changes everything. To convince yourself that you dominate the laws, you don't explain them, and you don't even reproduce them, as the excellent Passemant did. It is up to us to institute them. Certainly not to use culture to conquer nature, no, why would we?

Planck's Wall traverses each of us. I am a cone of light. The past infiltrates me and recontacts the future. The more I advance in space, the more I retreat in time. Traveling maintains youth. And my singularity is not an exception. No more than my encounter with Astro at the Phare des Baleines. Because *chance* is the very nature of the event. Émilie was convinced of it, but Astro proves it with his telescopes. He demonstrates, with the support of his calculations, that the probability of seeing elementary particles follow the Big Bang is infinitesimal. To be exact, it has a value in the 120th position after the decimal. It's the same probability, incredibly small, that made me meet my A in the waves of the Atlantic after having discovered Passemant's clock, thanks to Stan.

It was also that probability at work as I embraced Wlad, back in Gagarin's time. Gagarin, the first cosmonaut, was to crash near

Moscow a few years later, having lost control of his craft during a depressurization at altitude. Unless he was asphyxiated because of a badly closed ventilation panel during a training flight? Or had he already succumbed to alcoholism, his mummy continuing to orbit at the end of a failed secret space mission? Some claimed that Gagarin ended up in a psychiatric hospital. Toxic rumors? Or tragic events? They prefigure another miracle: the collapse of the Soviet empire. As for me, Nivi Delisle, I was to settle definitively in Voltaire's country, and at the Phare des Baleines for vacations.

What does a man want? To be free of his mother by making himself as desirable as she, if not more. To annex the father's desire. Jesus died on the cross, and in communion after communion, from host to host, Christians never stop tasting the fateful delights of his experience. Has *desirance* (that is the term for endless desire) truly changed its goals in replacing the father's place with science, the Big Bang, and the *instanton*? In my opinion it could not have done better.

A man's homosexuality and a woman's phallic aspirations are legal now; they have even become the norm. People want to be normal. Medically equipped rooms supervise coke, MDMA, ecstasy. No S/M ritual upsets the religious coteries anymore. Nauseating pissoirs, *Our Lady of the Flowers* or *The Naked Lunch*, neither *The Ticket That Exploded* nor Burroughs nor Genet. There are no longer any scandals. *Madame Bovary* and *The Flowers of Evil* figure in homeopathic doses on school curricula, and what does it matter if no one can read, since no one has anything to say about it either. At the same time, the smartphone, with a click, assures your full enjoyment, on a street corner or at home, if you'd rather. The Web makes everything available for everyone; nothing is surprising, astonishing, or frightening. Where in the world can *desirance* possibly have got to?

The legislator who decreed "marriage for everyone" must have faced the facts: *desirance* between a man and a woman is out of style. What becomes of the feminine of the man and the feminine of the woman in equalized-legalized love? The subtle Viennese doctor thought that female sexuality, an insuperable taboo, is never and will never be uncovered.

There remains one chance, a risk to take: meet body to body, outside oneself, in oneself. An interval, so delicate and so finely orchestrated that the ambient universe ceases to be flat. Fragile *desirance* bursting out like the very first light. So vulnerable that its value is written, Theo claims, with an interminable rosary of zeros: 0, decimal point, then 119 zeros behind it before arriving at the number 1:

0.000000000000000000000000000000000000000000000000
000000000000000000000000000000000000000000000000
0000000000000000000000001

A prodigious adjustment, it inaugurates the beginning of the expansion—from *nothing* to *us*, living speakers. "A value so close to one splits off from platitudes, and this infinitesimal split will have created the world inflating and expanding toward you and me."

My lunatic Theo doesn't renounce the mythology of love, and that's fine by me. Especially since he keeps his mythology sober, and it relays our fragile miracles.

30

A RAY OF ICY LIGHT

A ray of icy light penetrates the stained-glass windows of the chapel, a rosy arrow piercing the polar cold. Solitude. There's a freeze in Paris this winter, at La Salpêtrière more than anywhere else. At least the heating works; the country still has the means. Sterile drapes are in short supply, the staff is overworked, people have to bring their own medications because the central pharmacy no longer has any, nosocomial infections and errors proliferate, people are talking about two young men who were dropped from such a height that the necks of their femurs broke. "With the thirty-five-hour week and budget cuts, the hospital has become a powder keg again—explosive saltpeter, more precisely!" Professor de Latour, looking after Stan, tries to make me smile by trotting out this rather worn-out play on words that nobody finds funny.

Suffering with exhaustion, I don't comment. I take refuge under the towering occiput of the Saint-Louis chapel in La Salpêtrière; I pass by the stone phantoms of saints Thomas, Philip, and Mark. There's no chance of encountering any of the faithful in this now deserted refuge, the glacial vestige of a statue-incarnated faith. Frozen, I advance in the chiaroscuro that filters from the ceiling, a sleepwalker pierced by the ray of red light. I let myself be guided toward a mirage. And what do I see? My clockmaker! Him again!

"It's not possible, you here, Passemant? An obsession, I have to say . . . I thought you were at the court, in the King's Cabinet, Mr. Engineer . . . Weren't you supposed to present your clock this very evening, the clock that will see 9999, as you say?"

Claude-Siméon is having one of his bad days: feverish eyes, seems out of breath—did he run? His skin is not so much pale as colorless, oily. His long, golden-brown hair is dusty, matted down; he must have lost his hat. In the half shadows, the scarlet ray of light contours a rounded forehead, a straight nose, a receding chin, thin, clenched lips. I infer the skull; I imagine the brain that conceived and calculated the clock, then wedged it in the Beloved king's crotch. It's hard to get used to the idea that this is the same man. The shameless insolence of the inventor in love with his sovereign has pulled back today, has perhaps even disappeared, enclosed in this hunted specter. Nauseous grimaces have survived, but his sense of humor has disappeared. Fear remains, unless it's the hope that everything will crumble.

It's enough to make him feel like vomiting, he says, and he wants to see with his own eyes. Me too, that's convenient. I remind him that abjection is not at all pathological; it's common, always around. He is aware of it. But in this month of May 1750, it's gone beyond understanding. People are saying that a leprous prince needs to bathe in human blood to be cured.

"And since there is no purer blood than the blood of children, they are being seized in the streets and bled from their four veins and sacrificed."

"Are you sure? Who? Where?" I can't believe my ears.

"You think I'm delirious? Not at all. Listen: The minister of Paris, the Marquis d'Argenson himself, is worried about it, and he has said they're false rumors spread by people above the lower classes. Parliament is looking into the affair, with the magistrate Severt . . . Rumors like this have been common since the last century, but it's not by chance that all this mud is rising to the surface again. Children are being grabbed in the streets, right in Paris and elsewhere too, as I said . . . Traffic in fresh flesh headed to the colonies. Some is needed to populate the Mississippi, that's what they're saying . . . Or better yet, it's to offer young flesh, both boys and girls, to those *amateurs* you call pedophiles . . . Even the king himself is being accused, it's awful, you see . . . How far will people go?"

"Wait, who are we talking about? Yet another plot . . . Who are they, these people?"

The specter doesn't hear me, consumed with his nausea.

"People say Louis XV is a kind of Herod. But who can believe that? His Majesty is furious, you can imagine . . . 'I am going to show myself to this lowly populace,' that's what he says, and he should! What else can he do, there's no dealing with such cruel people, their criminal leaders . . . This whole business is unbelievable. You think it's unbelievable like I do, don't you?"

Claude-Siméon is looking for reassurance. The king's engineer is depressed because he is a perfectionist—given that he wants to calculate time down to the sixtieth of the second, how could he not be? At this very instant, on the 4th of February 1750, his astronomical clock is showing 12 hours, 32 minutes, 26 seconds, and 13 sixtieths of a second.

"Have you already seen my clock? Of course you've seen it. We are not yet in . . ."

He looks up, stares at me without looking at me, talks to himself. He is possessed.

No, he does not want to know what the world will look like on the 31st of December 9999 at 23:59:59:59, when his astronomical clock, given to His Majesty, will have chimed the last stroke of the year 9999. He's not interested in others; he finds them horrible, at least that's what he thinks. What's the point of knowing what they will have become in the year 10,000? He just wants to *possess* the flow of time—right this minute, in his mind, because such is the programming of the clock. The engineer, his king, and all Versailles are and will be there, present at that instant, as they are now at royal ceremonies; 9999 will have displaced them to that ultimate instant that opens the eleventh millennium. By the same token, the probable or improbable humanity from that distant epoch will at every moment be present at Versailles, at this clock that counts time and contains it for them, for this humanity united with Louis XV, la Poisson, Voltaire, Émilie, and Passemant himself, it goes without saying. All together!

"Stopping time is out of the question, it will continue its course to five digits, six, etc. 100,000, 1,000,000, who knows? Someone could redo this clock to infinity, if possible. Other electronic clockmakers will perpetuate the project. It doesn't matter . . ."

His frozen lips are drawn back in a crazy smile, his eyes widen, but he's not looking at me; he's picturing the clocks of the future. Such a perspective doesn't bother him at all. What he is interested in is to coincide with the passing of time, to live in an infinite now. Only then does he succeed in ridding himself of his nausea and his headache. The engineer of the king, the rival to la Pompadour, the incredible one.

One has to be scrupulous, and if Claude-Siméon is, it's because he is anguished. He is afraid that everything will collapse. He can see that nothing runs smoothly anymore; the kingdom is no longer what it was. The proof: these unbelievable stories, these circulating rumors claiming that Versailles will be burned. His Majesty installs troops on the Pont de Sèvres and the narrow passage at Meudon. He has a new route opened that skirts Paris on the west, running through Saint-Ouen. It's the "Highway of the Revolt," the mockers guffaw.

The astronomer looks for his hat, doesn't find it, affirms that those stories about the leprous prince are just gobbledygook. The revolt, however, is very real. Children disappear by the dozens, by the hundreds, from the streets of Paris and the General Hospital: La Salpêtrière, Bicêtre, La Pitié. Odd that Mme Nivi Delisle doesn't know this.

Claude-Siméon detests politics; the panics his contemporaries feed on don't concern him. But the revolt is building quite close to him. Young Millard, son of his clockmaker friend, was playing with two apprentice shoemakers on the rue Royale when he was kidnapped by the "beggars' archers" and unceremoniously pushed into the police inspector's carriage.[1] Claude-Siméon heard it from the boy's parents.

"Apparently an invalid witnessing the scene intervenes to defend those innocent boys. Mistreated in turn, he is arrested. The police chief, who knows the Millard family, is about to liberate these harmless youngsters when he notices that the

---

1. The "beggar's archers," or *archers de gueux*, were the king's archers charged with rounding up beggars.

order to round them up came from the lieutenant general of the police, Berryer in person. A friend of la Pompadour, Nivi—did you not know that, perhaps?"

I did not know that d'Argenson himself was in on the plan; maybe he was even the director of this dragnet. Young libertarian vagabonds and crooks, fine . . . But now they're arresting little kids. Why them?

Claude-Siméon feels he's going to be sick to his stomach just by thinking about it again here with me, under the frigid statue of St. Philip.

"To populate the Mississippi, Madam, those people were already helping themselves at the General Hospital. But why scoop them up right in the streets at present? Could it be because the hospital is no longer playing along and giving up their children?"

Now I understand. The Salpêtrière, at the time, is the dumping ground for everything in France that counts as superfluous bodies and souls. Women of dubious virtue—prostitutes and mendicants—are parked at the General Hospital, along with people without means, without names and addresses, without papers, without a home. Children are taken along with their mothers, from whom they are immediately separated, thus swelling the ranks of the "exposed" ones, as they call abandoned babies. Can you imagine? What can be done with these hordes of little boys and indocile, recalcitrant, gambling, blaspheming, and quarrelsome preadolescents? Passemant thinks they are entrusted to the Jansenist fathers charged with giving them an education. Those holy men begin by putting an end to dirtiness, drunkenness, and brigandage before teaching them reading, arithmetic, and, of course, prayer. Whereupon the engineer learns from the gazettes that a fake confraternity of devout men, composed of magistrates, noblemen, financiers, lawyers, bourgeois, formerly members of the Compagnie du Saint-Sacrement, now Jansenists, has gained total power over the hospital, its children, and the *convulsionnaires* shut up there as well! Catechism and writing do not prevent abuses. On the contrary. Everyone knows this, not you?

Skin piercings using pointed triangles, blows with sharpened spades, shooting pitons, logs, hammers, and swords, collective tramplings. Could the king's engineer be reading too much S/M literature? He recounts these tortures in detail; it seems he cares. Then calms down to tell me that the king himself wanted to reform the hospital because irrefutable evidence of dissipation and corruption had been reported to him. To eliminate Jansenism from La Salpêtrière, His Majesty names a new archbishop, Monsignor de Beaumont, who has the good idea of dismissing the former mother superior and naming another, Louise Urbine Robin, widow of de Moysan, his beautiful friend of thirty-eight who is nevertheless quite serious. Beaumont and the widow Moysan listen to the Jesuits, which does not displease the king. It's the beginning of the end. The hospital affair will have lasted nine years.

The specter is out of breath. Coughing fit. Long silence.

Oh yes: a scandal hidden from everyone in the sands of history.

"Didn't Voltaire himself talk about this affair? Without getting overly concerned about it, actually: 'Never has a smaller affair caused greater emotion.' Don't you agree? You are exaggerating, clockmaker; it's not worth going to pieces over."

Claude-Siméon finds me quite offhand about it. He is no more interested in politics than in people. This hospital affair is only the straw that breaks the camel's back of his disgust, nothing else. What disgust? "Are you asking me? But everything's falling apart, Nivi, can't you feel it? His Majesty first gets Parliament to capitulate for a short time. The judges rebel and refuse to apply the royal reforms, they disobey and censure the king . . . Like I'm telling you . . . Then they end up legislating in his place! Louis XV does not tolerate these remonstrances. It's an impasse."

Passemant asks me if we're not heading toward an overthrow of the monarchy. Already?

Parliament goes on strike. Sabotage of justice. But the people wait, and the country suffers from this manacled governance. All that remains for the monarch are his parliamentary sessions: Louis XV tells the strikers that their positions are now eliminated.

"As if by chance, it is precisely in 1757 that Damiens attempts to assassinate the beloved king. The same year I present a new 'parallelic machine'—on an axis parallel to the axis of the world—to observe the passage of Venus. Damiens will be drawn and quartered, did you know?"

Again this odor of terror . . . Did Louis XV understand the message?

"At first demoralized, finally soothed by la Pompadour, who governs him."

The king is suffering; it's public knowledge, my visitor confirms. And rethinks his decisions. One can no more reform the hospital than the financial markets. His Majesty capitulates. Parliament triumphs.

"Passemant, do you think the revolution is under way?"

"We haven't reached that point yet. Today Parliament is against the all-powerful church, run by the Jesuits and supported by the monarchy. Unless it's the church that humanizes the hospital by resisting the offensive, vocal, and ambitious magistracy, which is ready to cover over all sorts of corruption and fraud. Or perhaps the church participates in them?

His Majesty's astronomer doesn't quite know: he's not excluding any hypothesis; in his view everything's imaginable. But he does know that something is already broken.

31

REVOLUTIONS START LIKE THIS

Ever since the affaire of the Millard boy, Claude-Siméon is indignant. He has let himself be dragged along by the angry mob. Willy-nilly the inventor espouses this plebian rebellion. He hates promiscuity; his upset stomach returns. But he can't do anything about it: the crowd carries him along, everyone in it for himself; it's total chaos.

"Listen, at the Saint-Denis gate people are beating passersby whom they confuse with the child thieves. In the Croix Rouge neighborhood, in the Faubourg Saint-Germain, a policeman attempts to grab the son of a chauffeur, the throng goes after him, destroys the house where the predator has taken refuge. On the rue Saint-Honoré, the people seize Labbé . . . yes, yes, you know, the rat who keeps the child thieves informed . . . He is lapidated . . . Then, best of all, the insurgents invade the house of Berryer, the lieutenant general in person, oh yes, la Pompadour's friend!"

Here indignation conquers nausea.

"The pilot-fish of liberalism, that's what this royal mistress, this Poisson, is!" Passemant in triumph. "She has got her come-uppance, she has, oh yes! Infected by the king, the lovely lady suffers from a bad salpingitis; her bellyaches are of interest to the court . . . The doctors have forbidden her any commerce with His Majesty . . . Never mind, we needn't feel sorry for this woman. She will remain the *favorite* who directs the Parc-aux-Cerfs, which she created . . ."

The clockmaker is not an ingrate, far from it. He knows what he owes to la Pompadour since the presentation of the clock to His Majesty, not to mention the woman's numerous interventions with the king's ministers to facilitate his work. But with time and his growing proximity to the Beloved king, Claude-Siméon no longer can stand this body who distances the sovereign from his true passions. Does she protect the king, or does she prevent him from rising higher? This philosophical creature sings in tune, so much the better, but does not let her lover pursue his otherwise favorite and nobler occupations—science and study. At bottom Passemant has always hated his learned-lady rival. To spill his rancor, he takes advantage of the deserted chapel where we are.

"The people have forced her to return to Versailles, I swear, I saw her. This person goes to visit her daughter Alexandrine at the convent of the Assumption—why not, a mother like any other . . . Then goes to dine at the home of her friend the Marquis de Gontaud, rue de Richelieu . . . Bad luck: the rioters are gathered there."

Swept away by the tide of humanity, Passemant joins them. They lapidate Berryer's door; he escapes, takes shelter in the home of the chief judge, then hides in Versailles until the middle of the night before returning to his digs, escorted by two hundred cavalrymen.

"What's the connection with La Salpêtrière?"

"Oh it's obvious, Mme Delisle! If the hospital no longer delivers young flesh to fill up the colonies or satisfy the desires of certain depraved persons, all they can do now is round up children in the streets! Well, the royal attempt at reform coincides with the first kidnappings. Therefore they tried to destabilize the king, but he reacted . . . In vain, as I told you— Parliament sabotages him. Result: everything can only get worse."

Catastrophe appears to have seized the wanderer. Long silence. Then, with a calm voice, eyes cast on the stone floor: "The royal clock has broken down, madam. I tell it to you as I think it. We are left with the clock of the stars, which is infinite. I will have done what I could so the infinite would be now . . . And that *now* would be as long as possible . . ."

Engrossed in his phantasms as a repressed and anxious perfectionist, the astronomer is delirious. I've been familiar with this since my internships at Sainte-Anne, not to mention the few delirious patients that come by my couch. However, the times are troubled, and the historians themselves are still arguing about La Salpêtrière, the king, and the Jesuits.

My phantom is just a more or less artistic intellectual who thinks and invents. He believes only in time, lovingly invests in it. I point out to him that the poor are like him, except that the only astronomical clock they have is their work, their economies, and, most of the time, their children. To rob and rape their children is the worst offense because along with the children, it's their time that is stolen and violated. Their only recourse is to destroy everything. That is how revolutions begin, without our being able to see them coming: when people are dispossessed of their progeny, the only time that counts for them.

Claude-Siméon is sitting in front of the three saints. Head held high, speechless. His eyes are tearing. Poor nauseated genius, who thought the infinite world was within reach. Automatic, like the royal clock. I take him in my arms.

"Give me your hand, come, get up, sir! This Red March by the rioters is only a hors-d'oeuvre, wait for what's coming! Wipe your tears, come now, here, take this handkerchief. The Apocalypse does not exist, clockmaker. This revolt against real or imaginary pedophiles is just another system of time. An emergence, the prophetic sign of another desire. Go on, dream a little, it's nothing—nothing but an expansion, passions on their way."

All his limbs tremble. Eyes wide open but no longer with tears.

"You're afraid the rogues will break your 9999? No, my friend, the astronomical clock will not be damaged. There will always be enough men of taste to protect works of art: stop worrying yourself sick! You did not put time in a case; you had the genius to construct fleeing time. No one will break your 9999, because the unknown is unbreakable, you know perfectly well! Always to be begun again, always to be reinvented."

No trace of fear in his eyes now. A mad glimmer of hope, perhaps. Claude-Siméon Passemant comes to the chapel at La Salpêtrière to avoid going crazy, not to pray. He is only looking for how to live while time is escaping.

I'm wanting to tell him that we are afraid because we don't know how we will die. But that's not the question. Because we are dying all the time, here and now. As far as I'm concerned, I've always known it; I'm not afraid, so I don't need God or the hereafter. Does one have to be sick to perceive death inhabiting us? That it's in the process of slicing up the kingdom of the pleasure-seeking king?

"Did you need the Red March of the Parisians to come tell me that death tick-tocks with the elegant ambition of your

astronomical clock, you, the poor son of a German immigrant?
Not really, you have always known it. Come now, you're letting
politics affect you at this point?"

I have rarely been sick. I'm not often sick as I age. A child at
war's end, I must have sensed that things were cracking everywhere: government, family, education, languages, laws, parents, space and time included.

"Things crack all the time, Mr. Inventor! The Red March is
always more or less ongoing. Today, things are cracking more,
and Versailles trembles. Damiens the apprentice assassin is dis-
membered; you witnessed it. Another forty years or so and the
aristocrats will be on the chopping block. Then come colonial
wars, world wars, atomic wars. Melting glaciers, global warming, endemic crises . . . Be comforted, Passemant, the times re-
emerge, return, relink, and relaunch time. Once again there
will be 9,999 pulsations of love; it's Nivi who's telling you. How
I've figured that out? Well, partly thanks to you! Thanks to
your clock, which scans fleeing time: time that I don't enclose
and that doesn't enclose me . . . Go on, let go of my hand at last,
leave, go in peace!"

I say nothing else. I press him in my arms—my way of thank-
ing him.

I have so many things to do that the polar solitude of Paris
no longer impresses me. It melts with the shaft of light that
penetrates the chapel when I open the door to the Mazarin
nave.

Stan is waiting for me. He is no longer sick; we have some
plans.

32

HYPERCONNECTIVITY

Is the imagination *an organ for the enjoyment of beauty*? Certainly, but not only. Nivi invents a life for Claude-Siméon and transports it into hers. She invites Émilie and Pompadour to *PsychMag*, listens to Justine who can no longer read, but drifts in a cosmic time (inexistent, per Astro). She joins Stan in his comas, hears in them the ultrasounds of the salt marshes of Ré. She neither flees herself nor multiplies herself, however it may seem. Nivi makes herself a neobody in a neoreality.

From the outside, this imagination seems pure madness—as a shrink, she doesn't fail to realize it. But she experiences it in depth, like a metamorphosis. Nivi changes bodies because she changes time and space. Not species—neither parasite nor medium. Nivi reincarnates herself as inventor of a clock, as mathematician at the court of Versailles, as king infatuated with science and his philosopher *favorite*, as astrophysicist chaser of bosons. Transferred into their lives, she lives again.

Her imagination is her only organ of survival. Fragile equilibrium that, for the time being, does not collapse. Since Stan and Theo support her in their respective survivals.

Thus filtered, the psychic or physical coups d'état deploy as canvas, treatments, encounters, writing, continuous connections of threads. Nivi the spinner, the reliancer, the weaver, virtual cousin of the mercer Passemant, Nivi transmuted into a time traveler.

"Don't you think that hyperconnectivity and the change from the written to the screen, all that stuff, will completely change the way people think? And sexuality—I mean sexual *relations*." Marianne is not smiling. Gravely, my friend takes up philosophizing as a bluff, to justify her pregnancy or make me forget it.

What's the problem? In this matter as in others, the causes and effects are reciprocal and reversible. There is no problem, the answer precedes the question. I am convinced of it. But that's not all. If I'm participating in this cosmos as it appears in Theo's labs, then *who* am I in this fleeting, provisional time in expansion? *What* judgment or *what* morality translates it, translates me? Of *what* sex? No answers. Communicators and educators hold forth on the digital, the absence of authority, souls and sexes, but without retrospection, without any curiosity for neutrinos, the initial singularity, and cosmic inflation. I fear my new boss at *PsychMag* may be among them.

"I'll forgive you for being a moralist when you show me you are a better physicist."

My friend cannot know that I fished this sentence out of a collection of quotations from Sade; she hasn't read him. Me neither, actually, except in homeopathic doses as an antidote to the ambient, right-thinking, and unknowingly perverse intoxication—they go together. The philosopher of the boudoir, a libertine as we know, invited the *man* who moralizes to acquaint himself with the physical: in the first place, the physics of the body climaxing to the death and, definitively, the physics of matter. This little-known reflection agrees so well with my passion for physics of the extreme!

Today, the difference between men and women is getting blurred, for Marianne as for the "People" she feeds me on . . . I don't know from "People." For my part, I persist in thinking that a man and a woman do not have the same body and therefore not the same life. Especially if it's a life from a barely emergent time.

"Wait, can you explain that?" For once Marianne is listening to me. I plunge on.

"The mother and the child? Two bundles in expansion."

The new director at *PsychMag* couldn't care less about my interstellar flights of fancy, but on this she doesn't think I'm exaggerating; we understand each other. This is my way of telling her that there are a thousand and one ways to tear oneself away from the anxiety of sleepless nights, from the excitement of the tango, from the invigoration of Pilates. By being doubled: impregnated with the pleasures called physical that are the *woman's* in her—and why not the *mother's*, which she will be henceforth?

"Can you imagine the maternal languages that remain to be invented . . . The nameless perspectives to be named . . . You know, there are astrophysical animals, are you surprised? Stan's guinea pig, James, functions in nanoseconds. He receives our physical vibrations, which are also mental, but he doesn't know it. Like babies, children, mothers . . ."

I stop, annoyed at myself for digressing, stupidly. Marianne stares at the ground, then: "There are also those who can't stand themselves. They freeze, they drown, they kill . . . Whom? Themselves . . . Or because they are incapable of separating . . . We are incapable."

My friend is no longer in front of me. Tears slip out. She lets me into the obscurity she finds herself in.

Suddenly she continues, at top speed: "Well, a pregnancy makes people talk, I don't need to tell you. Our King, for example, do you know what he said to me before . . . before disappearing?" Her timbre trembles. "'You carry your maternity like Athena.' You see the type . . . Actually, he was very cultivated, that boy, it's a fact . . . Do you know what it means—you who know everything? Not too good for me, eh? A warrior, this virgin goddess, no connection with the ideal mother, unless I'm mistaken . . ."

What in the world do I know about this Greek pantheon, labyrinths and mazes . . . Nobody has done better at losing herself in it, and I am lost. As for guessing what LSG meant, that's another story, maybe the only one that the new director of *Psych-Mag* is interested in.

Athena the Wisdom-Virgin, Athena the mother protective of warriors and citizens—not a bad match for Marianne the militant, the woman of the mind. But Athena coveted by Zeus, escaping from permanent copulation inflicted by her celestial partner by spilling his semen into the entrails of Gaia, the Earth-Mother, thus turned into the first surrogate mother— that other Athena then welcomes and raises the child she did not carry . . . Alone in the task, she then becomes the adoptive mother . . . And in any biological maternity the female parent learns to adopt the coming stranger . . . All in all, it seems there is a little of both Athenas in Marianne . . . I'm rambling, I suspected as much . . . I tell her, gosh, I know nothing about it, but antiquity had identified various images of maternity. Ones that our modern cleverness separates and makes possible . . . One thing is certain: the *generating* parent becomes a *mother* when her child hears her speech and fulfills it.

"They were already shrinks, your Greeks?" Marianne doesn't trust me—she's right not to.

"I remember that Chronos calls Gaia 'mother' when he becomes capable of putting what she tells him into action: 'Mother, perhaps I could accomplish what you say—I pledge to do it.' You see, it's not enough to carry the child. The woman who makes herself heard, after giving birth or adopting, is a mother. That's it: our suicidal, parentless King sought the adoptive mother in you, the one who understands him and whom he understands. Okay?" Once more that mist in her eyes. "Wait, it's not your doing . . ."

I can see that my improvisations are embarrassing her. I continue.

"It's this globalization, dear, always, and right from the start! Globalized vulgarization, the pits! Mama welcomes her progeny and by being understood separates herself from it. There may be an adoptive mother—an Athena, if you like—in each of us. In you too!"

"Oh great! I've still got a long way to go!"

She pretends to pout, but I know her, my Marianne: inside she's triumphant.

The pain has not gone away. My skin is no longer twenty years old. My back bends; I feel death making his bed there. Death swells the veins in my hand; accelerates my heartbeats, which wake me during the night; clouds my eyesight, even behind recently adjusted glasses. No longer is death a stranger as in the past, at the time of my arrival in Paris, when I would hear myself speak a painless dialect masking the wound of a maternal tongue soon reduced to a skin of sorrow, dead skin. Like Colette, I don't like death. The fatal event that transports me is birth. As a consequence of awakening it every day with Stan and, with a bit of luck, with my analysands, birth provides the rhythm of my words, my voice, my senses, my sex organs. The suffering does not cease, but it becomes passage, a cry of delivery that expulses me out of myself and frees me, irrepressible departures.

Solitude here is no longer a threat. I like being inside the enclosure of my overpopulated isolation, where one scare remains: Stan's suffering. And his unacceptable, unimaginable loss at the end. My conditions, my flourishes aim to prevent this terror, this reality that catches up with me in dreams.

Tonight I glimpse a white room—hypermodern kitchen, infirmary, or waiting room in a luxurious clinic. The blinding light slices my pupils. In the abyss, on the other side of my cornea, in a burning spot in my brain, I see Stan as a child, always those comas. Infused, intubated, barely alive. A siren smashes the whiteness, it's actually Mahler. Howling trombones, the storm bursts with trumpets and muted horns, mass deflagrations, static horror, the hue and cry of the Earth replaces the Rite of Spring. Wild translation into music of a surge foreign to time.

The loudspeaker announces the alarm. We have to evacuate this building very fast. Atomic attack? Chemical attack? I don't move: it's only an absurd dream; I am going to stay with Stan until the end of life. Suddenly I jump, nerves and muscles tensed: leave, go out, flee this agony, far away! Neither quaking nor fear. We run away.

The scene changes. I am in my office in Ré: Astro is beside me; he's holding my hand. He looks like my father as seen on that old photo I showed to Theo yesterday. I was four then. We'll be all right. Necessarily, with Astro, there is no end, there will be no end. The end has already taken place, it inhabits me, it flares up in my neurons, which accelerate and disintegrate, it smothers my chest, thrills my heart. I join with it; I call it "coma," "alarm," "nuclear war," "death." I proffer these words to Astro. Then the end dilates in his hand squeezing mine; it dissolves in the billions of milky ways that people his world.

My throat relaxes, the blood flows back into my breasts and perks them up; they are calling for hugs, kisses, they receive them and like it. Poor elementary homunculi, they know only of women with breasts like washcloths or silicone prostheses that they don't even detect! And they do not understand that cares and curves cohabit, no more than they imagine that I participate in Stan and Theo and they in me. With Astro inside me or without him, whether he satisfies me and I do myself. Time, shortly lost, emerges now, a brilliance of me without me. It's my body beginning anew, I escape.

Here they are! Marianne arrives at the house with the bassinet, introduces her baby to me. "La bébée," to be exact.

"Indira, her name is Indira."

With a sweet pretty face like a Buddhist statuette, the child sleeps peacefully in vapors of tulle and lace. Perfect features, a matte complexion. Some resemblance with her redhead mom, visibly thinner. Amber-colored skin, the father's, no doubt. No comment. I rave about Indira's serene beauty, her entrenched calm, sign of good health. This little girl, Indira Baruch, will be a lively woman, we know it, we hope so. Our chatting wakes her up. Her great black eyes are not yet smiling; they only stare into emptiness. Very quickly she makes it known that it's time to nurse. Indira too is *now*. She will always be so in her mother's eyes, and perhaps in her lover's. With the history that precedes her and whatever may be her days and nights to come, her loves, her failures, her life. Now she keeps to herself, she keeps us, she links me to the expansion of worlds.

"I love you," says Stan, who adores babies.

I smile, looking directly at my redheaded Marianne, who cries no more. She learns to cry from the inside; she learns to be a mom.

33

COMMON INTENSITIES,
STRANGE INTIMACIES

The few memories of this period, with Passemant, Émilie, the Beloved or detested king, and all those people around them, are always more precise when they return. About these people, however, I know almost nothing. Scattered documents, snatches, fragments of conversations, letters, songs, looks that speak to me. And anxieties that rejoin me, trajectories that I've read or written. Common intensities against a backdrop of vacuity.

These encounters resemble those everyone has at various moments of life, chance meetings in train stations, libraries, beaches, lecture rooms, or in the pages of a book. Encounters in airports, for instance, especially abroad, give birth to strange intimacies. I am sure Claude-Siméon and I have always been taking the same airplane at La Guardia or Roissy. Or buses and metros to get to Paris, Versailles, Saint-Eustache.

Chaotic memories in series. They are engraved in my senses more than in my memory, and the present is the time when these shining moments vibrate in me. That's how it is for my encounter with a person who continues to intrigue her biographers: Jeanne-Antoinette Poisson, wife of d'Étiolles, better known under the name Marquise de Pompadour.

In 1750, when Claude-Siméon presents his priapic clock to Louis XV, the marquise has only just left the rooms attributed to the king's mistress, which she occupied on the third floor at Versailles, and has moved to the ground floor, where the princes of royal blood are housed.

La Pompadour has tuberculosis; she coughs up blood. She is overworked. "Scarcely do I have a minute to myself," she breathes to the engineer. Does she feel connected to Passemant through the coincidences of destiny? Because both of them, with their families of weavers or artisans, belong to the third estate? Or because her father, Poisson, the agent of the Pâris brothers, accused of fraud and condemned to be hanged, was obliged to seek exile for twenty years in Germany, where Claude-Siméon still has connections? Whatever the case may be, the *favorite* feels authorized to address the clockmaker.

"Aside from the contentment of being with the king, the rest is just a fabric of cruelty, platitudes, and misery," she blurts into his ear as she escapes.

Claude-Siméon thinks she looks unhealthy, as if sucked dry. I do too.

La Poisson complains of coughs, fevers, suffocation. Potions, aphrodisiacs, herbs—she's drugging herself. In vain. She's exhausted. They whisper that the king is henceforth so cold in the marquise's bed that he sleeps on the couch. La Pompadour remains the favorite nevertheless, the indestructible friend, the minister of culture. But not of research. Claude-Siméon's clock has invested the sovereign's heart, and now it's 9999 that lies near Louis XV. The man's penis will, however, always need a no less oiled and automatic clockwork, of which the marquise improvises herself as the irreplaceable engineer—and that will be the Parc-aux-Cerfs with its little mistresses.

There she is getting into her "flying chair." The king's technicians have fabricated an elevator that functions by means of a weight, so she can reach the third floor without fatigue. Always overworked, la Belle Jardinière constantly coughs up blood.[1]

Claude-Siméon seems embarrassed either to meet up with her or to avoid her. And embarrassed when I see him speaking to her. I don't know what these men and women of all classes can be doing in Versailles. After so many years of documentation, interpretation, revolutions, terrors, restorations, and diverse interests, I have no desire to know.

It was during a masked ball (was it at Versailles or in the Hôtel de Ville?) that the unforgettable *favorite*, at the time Mme d'Étiolles, twenty-four, young and pretty, was to win Louis's heart. The motley crowd—gardeners, florists, ridiculous doctors à la Molière, Chinamen, and Turks—welcomes a strange group: eight yew trees of paper and cloth pruned in the style of Le Nôtre's gardens, with holes for the eyes, make their entrance. Jeanne-Antoinette is disguised as a shepherdess, while one of the yew trees is none other than the still-Beloved monarch.

Passemant reminds me that la Pompadour frequents Marivaux, Montesquieu, Fontenelle, Crébillon; that she plays Molière but is better at singing. Her voice, full of gaiety, delights *le président* Hainault, and everyone thinks she's a great talent. The clockmaker is of the opinion that all this is of no importance because the king is interested only in science. That, in any case, is what my learned gentleman wants to believe.

---

1. The Marquise de Pompadour was called "la Belle Jardinière" by allusion to a 1754–1755 painting by Charles André Van Loo depicting her with a basket full of flowers; it is on view in the small dining room in the Petit Trianon, at the Palace of Versailles.

He is jealous; so is the court—which treats Jeanne-Antoinette like a working girl (a *grisette*). What a mistake! Louis finds solace with this bourgeois woman because she makes him feel his time: she's a sort of clock, but in the short term. She reassures him with her intelligence as a woman who knows not passion but the heartbeats of the senses and of words. She senses bodies, men, affairs; calculates the royal interest; adapts and cares. With grace and malice. The marquise is an exquisite composition that inflames her king, excites him as no female has been able to, more clock than the clock, yet he can never satisfy her. A real challenge.

For this male hunter, to love an intelligent woman (though not a genius) *is not a pederast's pleasure*, as Baudelaire will claim; it's quite simply unheard of. And much more useful than the company of the extravagant Émilie, who thinks for herself and believes in happiness. This Marquise du Châtelet is an adventurer, hardly one to solicit a position, a charge at the court—no, it's really not her thing, in no way. She consumes bodies and ideas for eternity, some rare wits claim. La Pompadour, on the contrary, settled comfortably in passing time, does not dominate. Jeanne-Antoinette disarms. Beginning with the queen herself, her entourage, and the royal children.

In a corner of a nighttime airport, I again meet up with this high society. Here's Marie Leszczynska: "Since he needs to have one, better it should be this one," she says about the *favorite*.

Claude-Siméon is not following my encounters. He persists in calculating the inclination of the mirrors in his telescopes. He is jealous, and he's right. As for me, I am sure that Louis the child, this eternal orphan sheltering under the sumptuous garments of a libertine sovereign, will always go bury his face in Jeanne-Antoinette's bosom to recount his uncertainties. Or mourn the death of his son the dauphin. And that he'll emerge with a smile on his lips after having shed his quantum of tears. Happy like in front of his clock.

I change the subject. "You're not reading the gazettes, Claude-Siméon? France is no longer recognizable—neither its land nor its seas, neither in verse nor in prose. It was already written during your lifetime. Everything is falling apart. The kingdom is nothing but an old power in decline—since when, though? You had sensed it as early as the Red Marches, the scandal at La Salpêtrière, I remember."

"And things are going from bad to worse! Every day we are threatened with land taxes, but no one knows how to set them up. They tax the air we breathe through increases in tobacco and letter delivery." Claude-Siméon waxes indignant.

"It seems the ministers are tumbling down one after the other, like the characters in your magic lanterns."

"Oh, you know of my music boxes? My daughters have a lot of fun with them . . ."

"Mozart is inspired by them . . ."

"Don't know him."

"Oh yes, his mother will be buried at the church in your parish, Saint-Eustache, like I'm telling you, next to La Pomme d'Or! I went there."

"How about that . . . Do you think? During this time, the French were being beaten to a pulp at the four corners of the earth."

"What difference does all that make to us, for the four days we have left to live?"

"You're talking like la Pompadour."

"No, like Madame du Deffand."

"Don't know her either."

"You are only a technician, my friend, in spite of your *extollers* and all your talent."

He knows it; he accepts it. Nevertheless he points out that he is not among those who are occupied with *killing time*, mutilating it, even decapitating it—which happens. Certainly not; he is one who listens to time, he hears it.

The train transporting me from the Montparnasse station to Versailles is not very full. Two black women with a happy baby. Another, veiled, with her husband beside her. And ten or so female cashiers preparing to take up their positions. Men whose professions I guess at: agents, tired, looking bored and boring. With Claude-Siméon, here we are now on the grand avenue leading to the Château.

Jeanne-Antoinette is walking toward us. Slim, easy, supple, elegant, taller than average. Impeccable oval face, light chestnut hair, fairly large eyes, perfect nose, charming mouth, the most beautiful skin in the world.

"Where does this charm come from?" I'm seduced.

"What charm?" The clockmaker's grumpy.

I talk to him about the marquise's eyes, their uncertain color. The infinitely varied but never clashing play of her features. Quite the mistress of her soul. I've read that, so it did exist. La Poisson was for a long time the canonic incarnation of beauty in the French manner. Revolution or no revolution, and still in our time. Well, before trash and antiglobalization . . . From now on, she is just a name, at best; do you think it still means anything to anyone here?

We are against the light, in shadow. Claude-Siméon appears to be calculating the distance between the source of the light blinding us and our eyes, struck by the sun. Suddenly: "They taught la Poisson everything. Except morality."

I knew it: he won't disarm in his rivalry with the *favorite*.

34

SCENES FROM LIFE AT COURT

This time it's Passemant who insists on meeting with me. He wants to entrust me with the memory of a few scenes of life at Versailles as he lived them. Why me? You shall see, he answers. Here is what remains from his final confidences. They begin with la Pompadour, the one he prefers; I can't help it.

Tuberose, cherry, hellebore embalm the Le Nôtre gardens, making one almost faint. The time is spring 1764, after a strangely harsh winter. The rumor has spread: the Clock is dead; time has stopped. Passemant is urgently called to the Clock Cabinet.

That sonorous pendulum had always bothered him, but today its silence is anguish. A brutal cessation of the metallic movement has suspended time. Could the homunculus be fatigued, prey to a mysterious lethargy? Or did it disobey the absolute fingers of the Great Clockmaker and give up the ghost as a sign of revolt?

After twenty years devoted to his eternal automaton, Claude-Siméon knows that's impossible, yet he is shaken by what some are characterizing as the "suicide of the Clock." Absurd scenario . . . Only ignorant courtesans would let themselves be duped . . . The engineer's heart is pounding as he opens the crystal door of the pagoda where the soul of Time lies. He puts his head into the belly of the robot.

Today Passemant is a haruspex—one of those Etruscan priests of ancient Italy who read the future in the viscera of sacrificed, disemboweled animals. Certain organs, generally the liver, gave them surer indices than the predictions of augury. Into the entrails of the machine the haruspex slips his soul, which is at the tips of his fingers; he unhooks the troublesome pendulum. Not to provide predictions of any sort but just to make the gearwork conform to science.

He begins with the routine gesture: using the key that hangs on the base, Claude-Siméon begins to wind the spring. It takes only three turns to convince the technician that although wound up, the spring is no longer functioning.

Then the clockmaker takes from his pocket a little tortoiseshell scraper with a steel blade and presses where it's needed. The gearwork makes a screech but stops dead. Alexandre Dumas will one day envision this kind of damage in the same location. So the breakdown is more serious. With the point of his scraper, Claude-Siméon goes digging in all the corners of the disemboweled prey's entrails, taking them apart piece by piece, spreading the screws and nuts out on the console.

Still the mystery of the damage escapes him; his anxiety increases, when all of a sudden his searching eyes light up. He has just discovered a set screw acting on a hairspring that has let go of the spring and stopped the driving wheel. It just needs tightening. The movement of time can resume. It resumes immediately.

With a smile on his lips, the astronomer contemplates the gear wheels with their fine points, sharp teeth that bite into even finer springs: the spring-loaded system of the chimes, fu-see, and chains, the motion system with double weight blocks. The gears return to their ponderous rotations, the axles turn in their ruby-lined holes, the music is heard once again—the frag-ile harmony of the mechanical shocks, the swinging of the pen-dulum, the shuddering of timbres, the movement of hands and wheels.

Calm now, the magician removes his head from the cage and stares at the escapement of the second hand. It fascinates him at each auscultation of 9999, sliding as it does on the seconds de-composed into sixtieths of seconds. It's like the quiver of pho-tons in quantic states, leaving only a few tiny wrinkles on the beam of time.

The marquise detests this installation. An automaton with the body of a man, which will strike the hour until the year 9999? Who will hear it inaugurate the eleventh millennium at the twelve strokes of midnight? The idea does not scare her; what's the use of asking such questions? No, it's the man who causes her anguish because she loves him, the one whom this clock of more than two meters—two meters, twenty-six centimeters, exactly—embodies.

Enclosed in glass, the head is the moving sphere that dominates the assembly. Turning around the Sun and one another are the planets of the Copernican system: Mercury, Venus, Mars, Jupiter, Saturn, and, of course, the Earth with the Moon. Each location on Earth sees the seasons pass—solstices, equinoxes, eclipses, the rising and the setting of the central star. Better than being at the head of a kingdom, this man is at the head of the universe.

The clockface is his heart, housed in a sensual chest all in ormolu. A crescent moon decorates his belly; his navel is dark-ened as night approaches and melancholy overtakes it.

But the omnipotence of this cosmic being, whose taste for power Jeanne-Antoinette shares, swings with the pendulum framed by the royal legs, perfectly *rocaille*, in the purest Louis XV style. While a lenticular pendant attached to the rod of assembled steel and copper captures the rays of the sun.

Today the marquise is alone in the laboratory known as the Petits Cabinets. Louis is engaged in his favorite occupation: riding to hounds, horns, and hollers. He adores venery, which fires up his blood—the pack of dogs chasing the stag, the fox, the roe deer, the hare. He rides a thoroughbred horse, gallops, ruses, jumps streams, is wild about the kill. Dagger or spear, flintlock shotgun if necessary, followed by cutting up the animal. And also the intoxication of the quarry. Then returning home and throwing himself upon her. Along with astronomy, venery is the only passion of the predator: the marquise knows it better than anyone.

She doesn't like the hunt; it's him she loves, his stature and his governance. She is involved in it, she governs with him, she almost governs him—not altogether, and yet . . .

Today, out of breath, shaken by coughs, tottering with anger and fear, she is going to hunt another beast: Passemant's astronomical clock. Her venery, her kill and her quarry, shotgun blast if necessary. With her left hand she holds her capuchin monkey, a companion more faithful than a dog, gentler than a baby. In her right she holds her fan. One suffocates at Versailles, the unbreathable court of plotters and poisoners. All's fair in war? Pompadour knows what to do. Jeanne-Antoinette Poisson, Mme Normand d'Étiolles, now Marquise de Pompadour and the *favorite*: she is a woman of wit. With a stroke of the fan she smashes the torpor; the little wing restores her breath: Madame adores winged creatures. She opens the door to the hidden staircase that leads to her lover's cabinet, where the mechanical monster reigns.

"You here, clockmaker? Well, you are certainly making yourself at home!"

The pallor of her face gives way to sudden anger. Being marquise and the *favorite* of His Majesty doesn't protect you from an internal coup d'état. The king cannot do without her, yet he is becoming detached, and the rounded charms of her bosom are now more attractive to Voltaire's pen. And as if that were not enough, certain people are still trying to poison la Poisson. She carries an antidote on her person and accepts drinks only from her devoted Nicole du Hausset, who keeps an eye on the cooking.[1] This M. de Voltaire, her favorite author, is an enchanter who thinks while laughing and laughs while thinking, he always pleases, and he persuades. A true sentinel of the state, whose tolerance, sparkling wit, and charity for the unfortunate Calas family correspond so well to the marquise's sentiments. Moreover, she does not hesitate to say so and to write it to all the people who count in the kingdom. However, the philosopher has the gall to call her "*grassouillette caillette pompadourette*," that is, "pudgy quaily pompadourette," on the pretext that he had seen her eat a good quail while forgetting the delicious Tokay wine she had served him on that occasion! So much for the "divine Cleopatra," "sincere and tender Pompadour," and "Pompadour, you beautify the court"! Nothing but poison everywhere, no sincerity.

The worst is this astronomical clock that the king is so taken with. And Jeanne-Antoinette did not fail to praise, to His Majesty, the perfection of the robot and the merits of the artisan. The marquise thinks, like those gentlemen of the *Encyclopédie*, that it

---

1. Nicole du Hausset was a faithful chambermaid and companion to Mme de Pompadour.

is important to defend the sciences. But what does this obscene sculpture have in common with such elevated ideas? An astronomical marvel, they say? More like a lubricious mannequin, a living insult to the royal mistress displayed as a spectacle for the centuries to come.

Ladies and gentlemen, you are invited to picture the enormous machine striking its 9,999 years multiplied by twelve months for each year, by thirty or thirty-one days for each month, by twenty-four hours for each day, by sixty minutes, by sixty seconds, then sixty sixtieths of a second! What woman could stand a muscle like that? Decorating that animal with all the gilded marquetry of the kingdom, draping it in scientific, apocalyptic, or astronomical speculations doesn't change a thing. Nothing can spare the impartial observer the outrage of the exhibition before them: a veritable attack on morality. This machine is the successful illustration—if one can call it that—of the dangerous visions that invade people's minds today. Some learned men among the most renowned even consider them natural; doesn't the respectable Buffon, for example, friend of the queen, profess that in love only the physical is good?

And if that were not enough, now here's an obscure mechanic who, after having seduced His Majesty with his astral calculations, shamelessly celebrates phallic power by making you think, without saying it but by showing it, that it governs the sun and all the stars. Really? This automaton preaches devotion to priapic desire: it does not celebrate time. Can it claim it's the same thing? Of course not! Frankly, it murders her love as a woman, which blossoms in words and song, in the theater of Reason and the stratagems of the state.

The king's mistress did try to be reconciled with God, to enter into the Capuchin order, to cultivate elevated sentiments and pure sensations . . . In the end she gave up . . . She even became the queen's sixteenth lady in waiting. She lived through the Lisbon earthquake . . . Today she is wasting away with diseased lungs . . . But don't go thinking la Pompadour is finished. Madame still finds the fire needed to organize a musical event at Fontainebleau for the following autumn, with that little Mozart on the harpsichord, the fabulous genius of eight, reserved to the queen alone with her daughters. She is killing herself with pathetic efforts to combine happiness with innocence, ready for anything so as not to leave the king.

Ready for anything—but this? Not this, no, no, 9,999 times no!

The haruspex was not expecting so much anger from la Pompadour. Is the insatiable organ, virile and massive, tearing open her vagina? Its infinite beats infect her entrails, make her uterus bleed, crush her lungs, tear apart her throat when she attempts to expulse it by spitting . . . In vain . . . Coughing fits and galloping fevers . . . Nothing can be done . . . The marquise is as powerless to rein him in as to satisfy him.

The capuchin monkey struggles under the hand that holds him tight; the fan no longer dissipates the heat that rises from the stomach to the cheeks, red under the tear-filled eyes.

Claude-Siméon tells her that he has come to rewind the clock, adjust a screw. Just a small detail. Soon there will be no need—the regulation will be done automatically, starting the following month. Mme de Pompadour has been so generous in supporting this work before His Majesty and his servants!

"You have exerted discernment in doing good because you judged for yourself. Believe me, Madame la Marquise, I have known no unprejudiced person who fails to render justice to your character. And the approval of people who know how to think is something, isn't it? Superior instruments are required for the progress of astronomy . . . Organisms that are so rare, so delicate . . ."

"Stop there. My poor man, what can you know of people who know how to think? And you call that delicate? *That? That?* Come now!" With a reproachful tone. "You are a handsome fellow also, I have already said so to Buffon . . . But worse than he . . . Worse than Buffon, and more physical yet, if that can be . . . !"

Simple coquetry or black fury, the marquise hits the engineer with her fan, which she then aims like a weapon against the naked torso of the clock. She fires into the head, points at the chest and her lover's pendulum—or her ex-lover's, still master of his mistress, who won't let him go, whatever may happen. A fury, a woman possessed.

Passemant staggers and loses his balance. He thinks there is no connection between this icon, who enchants so many people, and this bacchant taking on his masterpiece. She aims at her king, the Great Clockmaker himself, and the course of the stars, which the engineer has calculated all his nights long. With a stroke of her fan, this harpy is going to reduce the masterpiece to a pile of viscera, as thrown to a pack of hounds. This is no longer a marquise; it's an isolated wolf who dares to confront the antlers of a stag, the fangs of a big boar, the infinite correctness of 9999.

A fog hides the scene from his eyes; the gilding comes unglued from the ceiling: la Pompadour's rouge gets mixed in with it. Her convalescent face, thinner but willful, fades; the clock's lineaments flutter away; the astronomer can't make anything out. He cannot stand this shadow relentlessly hounding his work over and over. She might break the shot chain with her hunting rifle . . . Tear out the gold and the marquetry . . . And now her monkey, like a crazy lion cub, to finish, crumbles the precious installation of time that Passemant devised with all his love for a world that no longer exists.

But the clockmaker does not die. This martyr of Pompadourian revenge still breathes, though barely. The oxygen has gone to his head. He simply wants to stand between the marquise and 9999, but paralyzed with shame he once again has a terrible headache. And he loses consciousness.

At nightfall, as the valet of His Majesty opens the chamber, he finds the man prostrate beside his fabulous clock. Mme la Marquise de Pompadour's monkey is watching over him, crouching on the shoulder of this abandoned body, looking like an orphan as only monkeys can. No one knows what star guided him to escape from the *favorite*'s arms and take up residence at the foot of the astronomical clock.

About twenty days later, on Palm Sunday, Mme de Pompadour breathes her last in the Château, where only the princes of the blood have the right to die. "Our anxieties have come to an end, in the cruelest manner." This wordless thought gangrenes the king's mind. Consolation and agitation. In a hurricane of rain, elbows on the balcony of his chamber, Louis XV silently weeps for the cortege carrying the coffin of his mistress of twenty years who thought she had found love. Until the carriage turns the corner onto the avenue de Paris toward the crypt in the Capuchin convent. It seems she still lies in the cemetery of the convent, which has disappeared, compressed now under number 3, rue de la Paix.

Voltaire sincerely mourned her. A dreadful destiny, all the same, of love and hate. A woman's end is sad. So is the end of feelings.

Passemant will live another five years.

No one knows where his grave is.

Scarcely has he come to than the astronomer gets away from me and indulges his ill humor. He speaks ill to relax. More indignant than ever, the man defends himself, and so much the better: he will no longer have nausea and headaches, or less often. Let him express himself!

"Ah, there are lots of people at Versailles, Madam, I deplore it. People with ugly names, worse than la Poisson, who has already badly upset the social hierarchy—and how! The daughter of a former lackey who almost got hanged! . . . Wait, the best is yet to come! . . . La Bécu, so as not to name her, the apotheosis of disorder, la du Barry, you've got it. No, I won't say anything against her, against anybody at Versailles; I myself do not belong here. Many people think so, very exalted people. Oh yes, I noticed it to my detriment, quite recently; I was almost considered out of my place. They don't say so, but they think it, they do what's necessary, and I feel it, you can understand why. I belong to the secret garden, you see: the far side of the moon in the kingdom of Apollo. More threatening than libertine luxury, in the eyes of right-thinking people. My time is not theirs; actually it hasn't come yet, it will never come, it's an imaginary time, they suspect so, and it bothers them. Nothing to do with the bawdy songs and the insulting pamphlets. I don't want them, and I don't know them . . . Scenes at court, viewed from this angle, granted, do not concern me . . . Where was I?"

"You astonish me, clockmaker. Mme du Barry didn't come to Versailles until after the death of la Pompadour, when the Maréchal de Richelieu forced her acceptance against the wishes of the marquise's friend Choiseul. That was the very year of the

queen's death, something you can't know about—you are going
to give up the ghost the next year. But you're picking your words
out of the gazettes! And from the mouth of Marie-Antoinette
herself, who is obliged to welcome the new mistress of her
father-in-law . . . You live in 9999, fine, but still . . . You're inventing history, Claude-Siméon! How is that possible?"

"Let's be serious, Nivi. In certain situations, asking the question is better than answering it. I'm telling you. Sticking to
what the rumors are saying, it is true that while the royal mistresses were not vestal virgins, the fault is with the gods who
made them so beautiful. What can I say, I don't like protectors as I ought to; I distrust them, and Mme de Pompadour
first of all . . . She was too . . . too much in everything . . . too
much between His Majesty and me . . . I have already told you
what happened to me—her fan, her monkey . . . shortly before
her death . . . As for Jeanne du Barry, who surpasses her in
patronizing the arts, who gives commissions to Greuze, to
Fragonard . . . she's something else again, a pure scandal! But
the devout party defends her to annoy Choiseul, who hates
them . . . I have to face the facts: I am not of their world. How
can you expect me to think highly of this new beauty, who
claims to be a Vaubernier, from the name of her mother's lover?
Vaubernier was a very special monk: Brother Angel, what an
antonym! Mistress of the debauched Dubarry, known as "the
Roué," this creature marries the monk, can you imagine, with
the simple goal of being received at the court, thereby becoming the sister-in-law of her lover . . . That said, the lady is overly
gifted with talents and charms; she has the gall to send two
kisses to Voltaire—him again—who replies teasingly: 'Two is
too many by one, adorable Egeria, I would be dead from pleasure with the first.' I hate this farce, which is going to turn out
badly, but what to do? If I start talking like that, I objectively

pass into the camp of Marie-Antoinette, my king's daughter-in-law, who is going to be decapitated . . ."

Brief silence. He continues, meditative. Nivi is all ears: she senses that the phantom is going away. Could this be his testament?

"I thank the Great Clockmaker for having spared me the continuation of this story by making me meet my death two decades before the Revolution . . . I am dead, in fact; I'm not keeping it from you, whereas 9999 will survive . . . Adieu, Madame."

35

THEO HAS JUST LANDED

O n the waters of the Fier in front of my veranda at
Martray, the vessel *Nordé* (from the name of the wind
Astro likes better than all the others), when it deigns
to berth on my island, makes the white swan, my constant
friend, flee.

For years, this strange being ("Furthermore, is it really the
same one?" says my falsely indifferent A) has regularly alighted
in front of my computer on the other side of the low wall that
separates me from the water. From dawn until Venus rises, and
sometimes even at night, he is there, blended into the grasses
that border the arm of the sea and faithful sentinel to my in-
somnia. It happens that he changes hue, going from white to
black, but I know it is the same one, I know he is mine. He flies
away only when Theo arrives. "Nivi and her lover," jokes Stan,
gently possessive.

Today Theo does not take me out to sea in his *Nordé*. Moored
we are, and moored we remain. To sleep, to love, to talk, to say
nothing. Curfew, silence. Listening to the melodies for lute by
Edward Lord Herbert of Cherbury. Renaissance lute with ten
courses, to be eclipsed afterward by the French baroque. Chords
picked as with the guitar, arpeggios and tremolos, sarabandes.

The plucked strings vibrate dry, incisive sounds, then quiver and fold inward. Tender coolness, restrained panic, concerted assonances and dissonances. Intoxication, white like my swan.

Astro browses my books and notebooks, peers at my computer screen over my shoulder. I don't like that. I say nothing. He guesses, knows everything.

"You imagine a lot about this good fellow Passemant."

"I have the right, no? He's my character, after all! Besides, he read a lot, it's been proved. Fine library in his Louvre apartment, which he left after his death according to documents Aubane found in the Notarial Registry."

My glance leaves the screen of the Sony and rests on my swan, faithful to his post on the water across the way. He too is one of my characters, just like Passemant. I can certainly make them say and think what I want, at least what seems plausible to me.

Today I've found a name for this winged visitor, my courtly lover: Leibniz. The crook of his neck, the envelope of his arched wings incurve the train of the white cloud, hook it onto the light that deploys upon the shivers of the water. In this instant, my permanent migrant is an arabesque of reflections.

Does he have a body? At the intersection of the elements, his whiteness is a Japanese origami that, from fold to fold, decomposes and recomposes sky, earth, and water. A presence? An act, rather, all in movements and contours, feathers, wings, leaves, cloth, and draping. His reason is external to him, in the wind that brings him to me and takes him away. In the rays of the sun and the halo of the moon that bring him closer to me or distance him from me. Or else in the odors of the algae and the santolinas that announce the coming storm so he can fly off in time. In the slippery movements of the eel that tempts him and coils his gluttonous neck, then plunges him into the water.

Plastic, elastic, my swan sketches an affinity between the elements and the bodies; he reveals the gradation in everything. Like Émilie's Leibniz.

"If you want my opinion, Émilie is the one who is the heroine of that period." Astro intentionally teases me about my passion for the erotic clock: he knows that in fact I tend toward Émilie's fire; I go to it. "Her dissertation on happiness, okay . . . Did she even know happiness? On the other hand, her effort to reconcile Newton and Leibniz, hats off! I've already told you that quite a lot of people around me are really into that."

Émilie seduces him too, but Theo is modest, or rather serious. No one speculates in an astrophysics lab; they do scientific theory, nothing else. All the same, like Voltaire's Egeria, he thinks one should not banish the hypotheses of physics, but mechanics does not contain the true causes of phenomena, so physics cannot do without metaphysics. And when his science is upsetting the standard model my A is surprised to find echoes in Mme du Châtelet's pages because she considers time to be an imaginary notion, a useful fiction. To which only so-called successive and existent beings adhere. That's all, but it's not nothing.

"In fact, she read Leibniz's *Theodicy* and wondered if we wouldn't one day arrive at the prime elements that compose bodies." I'm simplifying.

"She imagines beings without extension, without matter, yet constituted by elements. By elementary particles, we say. Unless they are not particular objects but vibrating cords moving at velocities that can attain the speed of light. Just as a violin string can engender several harmonics, the modes of vibration of the superstring would correspond to the different possible particles. It's as if she were wondering about what *preceded* the Big Bang! We find a condensation of info in her work. She speaks of divine impulsion. Your Émilie says it with Leibniz's words: the sufficient cause of the succession of existants is outside their contingency. That would be the proof of God, equivalent to what for us is the time-out-of-time. 'He' *is*, but 'He' is outside of us, who exist only in time and space." Astro is translating Émilie's flights of fancy into his cosmological dialect: how to reconcile quantum physics with general relativity.

I'm listening. With Theo I pass from our iridescent senses to a now calming, now blinding clarity. And I look at my troubadour swan folding sky and earth onto the water.

"We are illusions, like time and space. But also points impacted by an infinite expansion. For Émilie, this force is divine, of a superior rationality, but not in contradiction to our reason. That's what she thinks, I believe." Astro does insist on pointing out what separates him from this fascinating precursor.

"The surpassing of reason authorized by reason. The unconscious?" I try to fit in my vocabulary.

"This woman wants to think what she cannot know." Astro prefers his basic philosophy to my Freud.

"And do you know why? I bet it's her passion for freedom that makes her choose this Leibnizian metaphysics rather than Voltaire's deism. Fair enough, don't you think, with respect to the former pleasure seeker who dropped her?" I make myself into the infinitesimal disciple of the divine Émilie.

"Which brings us back to our swan, your Leibniz." Astro's half serious. "Neither dissident nor revolutionary nor anarchic. Only passionate."

"Like Leibniz—and the swan, if you like—she folds the forces of desire into the order of existing things, and vice versa. Even in philosophizing she relies on enthusiasm, which leads to her death but also allows her to think of the inexistent." Nivi speaking.

"The infinite is unthinkable. A way of defying finitude other than by the birth from which she will die (and her baby will follow)." Astro is moved, for once.

"Pregnant at age forty-two . . . Can you imagine such a snub at nature, at medicine, at common sense! While still continuing her translation of Newton that Voltaire will publish! And which will remain authoritative until modern times . . . Émilie never finished beginning." Nivi sticks to historical facts.

"Nevertheless your Leibnizian is a monad mixing clear ideas with obscure representations that seem to escape her, as it were." Theo is critical but nonetheless admiring.

"Isn't God a 'capricious Worker who is determined without sufficient reason'?" Nivi returns to Leibnizian sources.

"Not a worker but a passionate researcher who operates within another order of reason, neither ordinary nor extraordinary. It's no longer a matter of understanding but of explaining how what resembles chance is in reality conforming to what today we call information that precedes us." Theo speaking of himself.

"By dint of frequenting its mysteries, this libertarian exceeds herself in the quantity of possible worlds . . . While putting herself in danger . . . Finitude put to death is passion, isn't it?" Nivi, grave, almost inaudible.

What are those two doing at the edge of the Fier d'Ars? Abstractions as flying buttresses against the appetites of desire? Cold follies, impenetrable allusions?

Far from separating them, as a hasty observer might have thought, each proposition here is a question that they both share, that echoes and rebounds in each of them. You're the one saying it, or is it I? To think together, not the same thing but the encounter of two ways of being. Their way of loving together.

"You're not calling him Swann, your swan?"

"No, Leibniz."

"I thought so, an admirer of your Teresa d'Avila too."

"The difference between Émilie and Teresa: the saint is thunderstruck by the divine. She prays to the Dome of the world and her church; she savors their messages with her five senses and all her flesh."

"God is invaginated inside Teresa; she unfolds His dwelling places inside herself with her art of pleasure and writing."

"Epileptic or enraptured, the *Madre* yields to streaming sensations, body and soul wound up like two entwined clocks."

"Look at her *Transverberation* by Bernini. Even though the luminous point is above our heads, the ecstasy reveals that the incarnation is a bodily tumult. The sculptor noticed that, and his marble draping palpitates like flesh."

"But Émilie? The same thing in concepts."

"Not the same experience, not the same being in the world. Émilie understands like a mathematician and presents like a philosopher what Teresa lives in her organs and recounts in letters, like a novelist."

"The fire of desire and the fire of reason, happiness and damnation, confront the folds of this soul of infinite density. Did she feel their singular harmony, as the saint did?"

"In thought, I believe. But with all her senses?"

"You're telling me that the theodicy of your Émilie completely separates itself from the Great Clockmaker who fascinated Passemant's time. He is the one who secretly governs modern minds when we extol social harmony, with the rights of man as key."

"Voltaire with the deists, the agnostics, or the atheists, everyone is content to ensure the Great Clockmaker's impersonation and service. We separate reason from faith and we lose the infinity of inner experience. Or what remains of it."

"Basically, the French Revolution occurs in the wake of the Voltaireans or, more concretely, in the movement of Passemant the Newtonian's clock."

"If you continue to spin out that metaphor, you will notice that the social contract, supposed to bring happiness on earth, was programmed from the start to become a universal timepiece—globalized, in the end, but perpetually needing repair."

"In search of unlocatable values that do not dissociate but definitively depend on the value of values: the Supreme Being."

"Newton's God, consisting of physics. In politics, the Supreme Being of evil spreads terror, becomes totalitarian . . . Among us postmoderns, we prefer to put him between parentheses, more or less evacuated."

"We are rescuers: we repair the endemic crisis of the incurable financial system, we announce the systematic flattening of our social systems . . ."

"Whereas the Leibnizian Émilie may be in advance of her lover in Cirey-sur-Blaise?"

"Oh yes! Because she concentrates on infinite fire and singular happiness. The automatons: overtaken! Long life to inaccessible and transversal spirals, inflections, symmetries and dissymmetries, spongy and cavernous worlds, continually variable curvatures, turbulences and new beginnings!"

"Émilie the baroque! If her body had been able to transfigure her science, if she had enjoyed the illusion, music boxes, love fiction, the flamboyant Émilie would have written novels. Or would have become a mystic Carmelite, after Teresa d'Avila and before Edith Stein."

"Certainly not! It's definitely because she is the way she is that she can anticipate dark energies!"

They will never finish rejoining and disjoining, those two, in time's states of emergency.

Leibniz the swan uncurls his neck. He stares fixedly at the geranium blooms on the low wall in front of the veranda. He approves. Not a single crease on the horizon.

The medieval steeple of the church at Ars hasn't heard of Teresa or Émilie. It stands out against the garnet sunset, quenching the stars and the dew that prepares to come.

36

VARIATIONS ON SUICIDE

What does the irreplaceable Rilsky have to tell me that I don't already know?

"Every suicide is unexplainable, isn't it? I'm not expecting you to explain it. This King was neither a beginner nor a *naïf*. Could he have taken everything seriously? Was he swayed by remorse over having violated medical secrecy, this holy of holies of modern times? Oddly, this type of young man possesses a severe superego. I'm speaking to a specialist." The police chief is thinking of the Zina case. Does he really believe it?

My old friend likes to be ironic, almost smug, when he wants to impress me. I don't bite.

"I won't kid about it—it's serious for me too. But is that a sufficient cause?" I temporarily abandon depth psychoanalysis and return us to the social, even societal, level.

"It seems he was intimate with the CEO, the great Ulf." The cop takes a further step.

"You're not telling me anything I didn't know. An affair among others. Perhaps more important for the CEO than for him, for little LSG."

It's clear the police chief hesitates to go further. But he does: "The King kept a journal. A fragile person, the way you like them. A shrink would have done him good."

I wait.

"We have the journal, okay, and a voice recording. LSG was furious at the world, particularly against the world he belonged to, which systematically violates the privacy of stars and ordinary citizens. He was getting ready to denounce everything, and denounce himself. A real *outing*, in the end!"

"You mean someone suicided him to keep him quiet?"

"It's a hypothesis. Personally, I can't believe that GlobalPsyNet and its branches are mafioso to that extent . . . You're only amateurs, needless to say . . . Maybe you're right . . . Anyway! The Levallois-Perret scandal has nothing to do with the Docklands scandal in London . . . no! You are much too small to make the truth come out."

I wait some more.

"You know who Indira's father is?"

The Purloined Letter! Rilsky as Edgar Allan Poe! I should have thought of it. Of course! Marianne won't say anything. It's nobody's business. Maybe Indira's, one day? But is it possible to say everything? Shrinks have different opinions on this, as on the rest. I'm annoyed at myself for having been so closed, so impermeable. I'm stupefied and have a hard time not showing it. The police chief hastens to come to my aid.

"I haven't read the file, but it's likely. At least the King actively participated in it. Adding that to the rest, the man ended up cracking . . . A sort of suicide by society, but suicide all the same. However, he could also have been suicided . . . For less than that."

I remember Marianne was abrupt, stubbornly close-lipped. This suicide is an additional burden on her. Or a relief in her lioness's solitude. Are hardness and harshness the appendices to contempt?

Indira will need a family. She has a few more or less distant cousins; Marianne introduced me to some of them. Not forgetting Nivi, Stan, Astro: we will love her. If Marianne and Indira even let us. "So goes the world," Stan will say.

As for Theo, he says nothing. Or rather, he changes the subject by shrugging his shoulders, meaning: there is no answer, since a suicide is not a question. The fact is, it comes only when there are no more questions.

Still absorbed in Émilie's reflections on fire, he shoots in passing: "People didn't fail to say that Émilie's pregnancy, at her age and at that time, was a suicide, or even a sort of rootless happiness. A delivery."

On the matter of happiness, I'd be glad to see the apartment freed by Larson overlooking the Lux.

IV

THE THEFT OF
THE CLOCK

37

9999 HAS BEEN STOLEN

That's the last straw! Did you see the headline from AFP? The astronomical clock at Versailles has been stolen. Oh yes, darling, yours, the only, the unique, the clock from the King's Cabinet! Unbelievable but true, what can I say. After all the fuss about this hotbed of science and curiosities, it seems. There are no safe places any more in this country of retirees, everyone knows that, why should Versailles be the exception to the rule? I have to confess it's really pretty cheeky. 'Your clock, France, is out the window!'"

Consulting the other headlines on her computer, Marianne exults but pretends to sympathize with my supposed sorrow, or my stupefaction, which is worse: "I'd say they really had to be after that jewel of yours to elude the cameras, the guards, the guides, the curators, that armada of 'Culture for All' supported by our taxes . . . But your national treasure must have been guarded to the max! Wow, they did it! *Well done! Congratulations!*" she says in English—the only way she can show how impressed she is.

She's right, I don't know where my head is. This is enormous. What can I do? Not much . . . So I "invent myself absent," as Astro says when I'm in shock. Paralyzed. Why should I, Nivi

Delisle, feel concerned when I hear that the fabulous clock by the engineer So-and-So has flown away to land in a vault in Qatar or China? It's never been mine, this "Fabulous Clock," and I don't want it. It's the clock that possesses me; I belong to it, in a sense, much more than it belongs to me. With Stan, we are *of* the clock. We dream about it. We invent it, we place and displace it. Marianne may realize that. She's annoying me the better to console me, as usual.

"This is serious, actually!" I say, to cut off the detective's catechism she's improvised. Waste of effort: she charges ahead.

"You know the robbers could not have worked alone. I mean it's not enough to get into the Château, which is only child's play . . . At least I suppose . . . You have to infiltrate the staff . . . Are you following me? . . . Better, you have to be one of them . . . Don't you think? You aren't listening . . . Nivi, are you okay? You should see yourself . . . You know everything about this clock, isn't that enough? Anyone can see it when they want, it's printed in all the catalogues, art books and others, they have even filmed it from all sides . . . So with this theft we're not losing much, okay, it's true . . ."

I don't even raise an eyebrow. She can minimize it if she wants, but this robbery is an event. Marianne isn't letting go, however.

"Besides, was that the real king's clock on exhibit there in front of the world's tourists, including you and Stan? Excuse me . . . Maybe it was just a model . . . Suppose the robbers only stole a copy? That'd be a good one! The real one is probably sleeping somewhere in the reserves of the Banque de France . . . But then why all this buzz at AFP?" Marianne reasons, skeptical.

"Buzz or not, the stolen clock deserves better than a brief item . . ." I am disappointed.

"You poor thing, you're not with it at all! No one's heard of your adored automaton! A few enthusiasts, nuts about former glories and . . . sorry, I'm not forgetting the rare connoisseurs, like Astro and you . . ." If there's a chance to put her foot in it, Marianne never misses: she's not joking; she says what she thinks and thinks what she says. I give up!

Who, in fact, could take the risk of committing the robbery of such a precious object? Not enormous, to be sure: 226 centimeters tall, but still, it's the size of a significant piece of furniture . . . A *true* enthusiast? A supersnob clockmaker, a fanatic of royal antiquities? Not likely. Not a single French person is capable of such madness today. A lover of astronomy, a spiritual person hooked on the stars, a Rosicrucian? No, that type of visionary crank is not enterprising enough, not courageous enough.

Marianne's got me going. Or maybe an astrophysicist seeking precursors, an archeologist of the prehistory of current cosmologies? Why not? But a scientific vocation is not sufficient for someone to commit such an act: there would also have to be a special passion, an abnormal refinement, indeed, courage . . . No . . . There is only one person in the world who possesses all these qualities: Astro, so as not to name him . . . Marianne doesn't think about it for a billionth of a second, no surprise . . . Nivi does! She starts to think . . . Not impossible, but absurd . . . Pure speculation. An upswelling of jealousy, of baseness? To be rejected right away! No likelihood, besides . . . Astro is in Chile now. Yes, but he could have accomplices. Stupid. Let's get rid of this idea . . . What else?

"Look, another headline: 'Three men wearing caps with their faces hidden by scarves burst into the King's Cabinet, where there were several people. Threatening with automatic pistols or AK-47s—witnesses differed—they carried off the famous object.'" Marianne sounds serious: this business looks like a real crime.

I have not forgotten the fire and the bomb alert during our visit to the Château with Stan . . . That was when? A false alarm? Are you kidding . . . What if that was already a test, a preparation for this theft they would supposedly accomplish one day or another?

"Listen to this! Are you listening? 'It's reported the police are on the track of a network of traffickers in ancient objects, museum thieves, including certain French people working for the Emirates. The latter, not content to own soccer and the Champs Élysées, are becoming antiquarians.' Why not? 'Art history schools are flourishing in Dubai. In view of the future Louvre in Abu Dhabi . . .' Skipping ahead: 'Their best students work in the great museums of Paris, London, New York . . . The Emirati are on the watch, constantly. We lend them our skills, as mentors and partners . . .' And how! Wait, wait, the best: 'The Emirate takes its place on the cultural stage, it's preparing for after-oil . . .' Oh yes! That's it!" Marianne has just discovered *the* track.

The Owl! I can see her as if I had just met her this instant. That woman was not just a guide: she was an experienced curator who didn't simply take tourists around but palled around with foreign students. I did notice . . . What were they saying on the terrace of the Marly?

These thoughts, which bring parasites into my brain like flies overexcited by approaching storms, don't fool me. What does the Owl have to do with this? An agent of some Qatari mafia or other would not let herself be seen with the members of her network in the café at the Louvre . . . Or maybe she would, on the contrary . . . And so what would that prove?

"A bit of advice, if you don't mind: you shouldn't talk about this with Stan, he could be very unhappy." Marianne looking for someone more unhappy than I am.

"Don't worry." I stick to my guns. "Stan must already know about it; he follows everything that circulates on the Web about this subject . . . Must have seen the news on TV about the clock . . . If another blow is added to 9999, I don't think he suffers, on the contrary . . . Stan is all memory and all virtual."

Marianne does not understand. She must think I'm a bad mother.

Best to talk about it with Rilsky.

38

BEAUTY SPOTS

What is beauty? Hybrid, rare, strange. Or whorled, a moiré of shady-clear, sweet-bitter, slow-fast. For Astro, beauty is called Venice: he only needs to arrive at the slab covering Monteverdi's sepulcher in the Chiesa dei Frari and stay there for hours with his eyes riveted on the eternal rose that a secret hand deposits on the marble.

"Your eye makes a summer for me in my soul." Ronsard's poem comes to mind as soon as I arrive on the Grand Canal. Renaissance and baroque palaces, gondolas and gulls, all my senses dazzled, fulfilled, borne to the pinnacle of life, which only the churches of Venice attain. I had to know the Serenissima to formulate my religion: beauty, the soul becoming visible like a flower in the summer's light.

Stan has no trouble letting himself be initiated: his gaze "incorporates." We enjoy only one painting per day. Narrow streets and canals impregnate our skins and absorb them. When we have passed body and soul into the eye of the beautiful, it is time to go back up to the terrace of the studio we have rented. Cormorants alight beside us—are they newly arrived from Ré? They're again going to break the breakfast dishes. The *vaporettos* pass each other down below; the church bells, in regular rhythms, make the ocher air of June iridescent.

We've just escaped from the crowds of tourists inundating Saint Mark's Square. They are not Japanese. Chinese, I suppose, content to buy tiny souvenirs from the displays, without photographing anything. "I've even recognized a few words in Mandarin," Stan ventures, having temporarily abandoned his passion for 9999. From now on, he says he's *hooked* on foreign languages, in particular the language that sings in his headphones, which provide a refuge he likes. With his absolute pitch, he is going to make rapid progress, Astro prognosticates.

As for me, I empty myself of passing time, my eyes full of Titian.

I don't really succeed. The globalized wave that grabbed us a while ago, in front of the Campanile, is still oppressive. Stan and I are not of that world. These fake travelers do not inhale the scents of the city, the colors, the lines, the lights, the years incrusted in the stones, the bells ringing the celebrations, nothing. They don't listen to the summer disseminated by the ruby-red sun at some billions of light years from another galaxy that my Astro is studying I don't know where. They are in a hurry to buy, to shout, to eat, to telephone, to leave. To fabricate memories, to save them. It's just an impression, a sensation that separates me from them, distances me. I am ashamed: I should be sometimes.

"What can they be thinking of . . . ?" It happens that Stan formulates my ideas.

His voice suspends the noise. He absorbs my states like a sponge, is even able to formulate them. We hear the beauty that surrounds us and makes a summer in our soul.

"Do you remember the Universal Exposition in Shanghai?"

Our two synchronized antennas capture the same thing, even in that dreary Expo of a world without a world that we visited at the other end of the world.

Immense plain strewn with more or less massive cubes, open doors of reunited nations. Blasé visitors enter and leave these containers filled with local expertise. Millions of dollars or euros gobbled up, globalization exhibits itself: the cultures of Latin America, Africa, Asia, Europe, limited to their memory of dead matter. Did Big Brother disappear? He continues to run rampant, in secret. The experience yields to the *process*, as they say: labyrinth, programs, schedules, rows of entities conserved for absolutely nothing, as far as the eye can see.

The guide's whistle returns the Sichuan peasants to their coach. Here they provide for the transportation of groups, not of individuals: "No individuals," the man with the whistle warns us, in English. He finds our situation amusing—what a crazy idea to travel so far without a tour operator!

I try to appease him: we are a group, just a *little group*, since we are two. The whistle becomes optimistic; he finds us an interpreter sporting the same smile but even broader. "A taxi stand is situated at the other end of the Expo. To get there, it's a bit of a trot . . . The equivalent of the fifth arrondissement in Paris!" She has been there. "The most charming of all the Parisian arrondissements . . . do you know it?" And how! No connection to the Long March . . . I thank them: *xièxie* in Chinese.

That night in Shanghai, looking for the exit among the multicultural bric-a-brac, I thought I understood Edith Stein. While Nazism was infesting the world, the philosopher abandoned philosophy to become a Carmelite, then let herself be immolated in Auschwitz: bear witness, engrave a memory, save her people, for later, for ever. Sublime Edith. Too heroic, too melancholy for Nivi the swimmer, the mother courage. What to do, then? Row against the current?

"Can we go see the clock again? They've put on a big exhibit about science at Versailles."

Stan always finds the solution, even in the dusty kingdom of cultural diversity. I am sick and tired of crisscrossing globalization; I would be glad to stand once and for all in the Clock Cabinet. I would lean on Apollo's window and dream all of history in the present, here and now.

39

SUPERLUMINAL SPEED

Astro bombards my Blackberry with a series of photos of Einstein. The last one shows the famous genius at the blackboard solving an equation about the density of the Milky Way. His moustache is tousled; his overheated eye pulsates in my direction. Astro's own lab is bubbling over: he announces the astonishing news.

"Superluminal neutrinos surpass the speed of light by sixty nanoseconds (sixty billionths of a second)! Do you understand? Six kilometers per second faster than light! Was Einstein mistaken? That's question number one. There are no others. With this we are at the very heart of things, aren't we? I remind you that every second, sixty-five billion neutrinos emitted by the Sun pass through every square centimeter of the Earth's surface, including you and me. And that only one in ten thousand billion of these particles is intercepted by an atom of our planet, potentially by you and me. But we're going to grab it, damn it all! ILY."

All the labs in the world are ecstatic. From the CERN in Geneva, to the Gran Sasso in Italy, along with the international experiment Opera, the APC (AstroParticule et Cosmologie) at the Denis Diderot University, not forgetting the Vatican

Observatory on the Alban Hills near Rome and the United States, in Arizona, where Theo is. The lives of particles illuminate the lives of stars and vice versa. But this news upsets everything! We'll have to revise the theory of relativity. Or at least find some clever way to twin it with these new facts, which let us glimpse another matter beyond the supposedly impassable limits of the universe as Einstein defined them!

And what if they are wrong?

"Of course we can be wrong," Theo continues, "mistakes are part of research, some even open new avenues of research, permit unexpected discoveries."

My A accepts uncertainty: he's passionate about enigmas, seeks astonishment, delights in surprises.

Fine. Why not? But what will that change for the rest of us? How does this concern us, you, Theo, me, Nivi, the anesthetized crowds at the Universal Exposition at Shanghai, Justine who doesn't know how to read, Marianne with her baby by no one knows who, the motorcycle cops on strike at la Concorde? These superluminal species and their nanoseconds are of interest to no one. The little world of utopians who had put God in the Big Bang or the Big Crunch will not hesitate to locate Him from now on in the superluminal neutrino. Couldn't this new discovery that transcends matter and all existence be the physical proof of the *miracle*? As rare as genius or ecstasy? As improbable as Eternal Life?

No. Astro is not into that fiction. Quite simply, neutrinos, for him, evoke the rapidity of our agreements.

"Think about it a bit: our thoughts, sensations, excitations traverse the density of the earth's crust and the randomness of timepieces and unite us in a few dozen nanoseconds. I'm not making this up! We only have to think about one another to touch each other and reach pleasure at luminal, maybe superluminal, speed.

Is it banal, when we love each other? No, it's rare. It's unique. It's us. An experience we write as 'ILY' both dematerializes us and materializes us. Superluminal Nivi and Theo adjust their incompatible diversities nevertheless correlated by that power of desire that the ancients called love."

He writes me this e-mail the same day they realize their calculations are incorrect. The miracle matter does not exist. Not yet! It's of no importance! Let's continue our research! As a consolation or an inextinguishable desire for exploration, Theo lands like a lover on our planet. Do I believe it? Does Astro believe it? He looks for new words. All lovers do. Each love is incommensurable, without comparison or qualification. Unless it's by stellar, quantic, utopian words. What does it matter: they are ours; they carry us at six kilometers per second faster than light. Tomorrow other neutrinos will exhibit an even greater celerity, just wait and see.

Astro's buddies will tell him he's reversed into poetry, no connection with astrophysics. They don't know that metaphors are seeds of language launched at top speed, neutrinos that interpenetrate and separate at a speed no "Double Chooz" (that is, particle accelerator) has yet detected. It's in process. No one knows about it. But we two hold the key to love, the vibration of time. The encounter is instantaneous. Pleasure also. A sort of particular reason: the raison d'être.

40

INESTIMABLE TROPHY

The Owl is not involved. Poor woman! I don't know why I keep harping on her. "Analyze it," Astro sneers. On the other hand, a cluster of presumptions weighs on Aubane Dechartre. Rilsky interrogates me in depth, acting casual (I know him). It seems the brains of the gang is the brother of my informer, Thibault Dechartre, an antiquarian in the Gulf affiliated with certain sovereign families in the region.

The sideways glance of the police chief signifies his confidence, which doesn't prevent him from arguing his point: "Needless to say, Nivi, the Persian Gulf has always been a stopping point for travelers, through the centuries. Which is to say, a den of traffickers. People have been talking about it much too much ever since the French government lent its support for the creation of a universal museum there. Mind-blowing! An aerial vessel in the sand. Flanked by hotels, restaurants, gardens, with a microclimate as well, because the action takes place on a little island, if you can imagine, Saadiyat, connected to the capital by a sort of dike. The construction site is colossal! Oh yes, Abu Dhabi is no longer reduced to its stadiums or its seven-hundred-meter towers . . . Earthquake, new epoch? Let's go! . . . And since heat devours the place, we help them protect the accumulated treasures ranging from high antiquity to the twentieth century. The fiber-reinforced white concrete of the site will be topped by a superb dome in pierced steel that filters the sun in a rainfall of light. Magical, isn't it? The architect's magic projects only 2 or 3 percent of solar light; imagine the investment! All our museums, our cleverest art patrons, are keeping an eye out. Naturally Versailles is among the sources. *Our* sources, the ones *we* entrust them with. You have no idea, my dear, how many petrodollars are flowing in this furnace! And imaginations that consequently catch fire!"

Ergo, a guy like Thibault Dechartre will not let this business pass him by—the great upheaval taking place, in a word. He's in on it! A true expert, this fellow, who lets nothing faze him. The police chief knows what he's talking about. Does Islam constitute an obstacle? Don't believe it! That pendulous member of 9999? Those people aren't fooled. And for good reason: the Louvre label was lent to them for thirty years in exchange for four hundred million euros, to which are added twenty-five million for the sponsorship. It's not enough, but that's not the point. Because in the wings—let's be clear about this, the police chief is only talking about offstage—shady areas exist. They always do: I ought to know that . . .

What's his point? Here my voluble friend returns to his pose as a not so much aloof as perfidiously mysterious detective.

Aubane's brother is often seen at the Hypnosis Café during his stops in Paris. Substances and alcohol.

"Which means?"

"We're on it."

"Dechartre's lawyer maintains there is nothing in the file that accuses his client." I'm repeating information that Marianne takes pleasure in transferring to me minute by minute.

"That's his job."

Infiltration of security through the intermediary of Aubane, who doesn't suspect a thing—white as snow. The guards are bribed, and the object is exfiltrated on a day when, as if by chance, there is construction going on in that particular wing. One more large crate being moved out of the Château is not too remarkable if the aforementioned security is duly paid to be distracted for the time needed. Rilsky seems sure of his scenario. To be verified. But there's a problem.

"The object has evaporated. No one is claiming the robbery, needless to say. The nutcase who gives himself the gift of the royal clock at home, so he can contemplate it at will—you can imagine, that marvel, all set to strike midnight before the year 10,000, just for him—or for her—that creature is not in any hurry to make himself known *urbi et orbi*. Of course not. He has all the time in the world!" Rilsky, ecstatic.

"You're telling me that the robbery was not committed by an institution, a museum or whatever, possibly with an eye to bargain or blackmail, but by an individual, by *someone*? *Primo*: I sort of suspected as much, poor little me who knows nothing about it but at least as much as you." Nivi never tires of teasing him; good old Rilsky, who doesn't like to remember that she has often been a much more perspicacious detective than his own staff. "*Secundo*: there's no chance of seeing the clock again at Versailles, is that it? The enthusiast wants it for himself alone. And his booty will remain a secret trophy until the end of time. Unless the eventual heirs of the ultrarich thief decide differently. One day, why not, and even . . . Or, *tertio*: the clock on exhibit was a fake . . ." I try to think.

"It was certified, not fake!" Rilsky is full of pride: at least one thing is settled. "As for the ultrarich fellow, that's not saying much. In your opinion, what does a masterpiece like that fetch today? Knowing that at least half, if not three-quarters, has to be distributed to the team of operatives who laid hands on your Passemant."

"No idea. Cezanne's *The Card Players* went for . . . how much? 191 million euros, I think, paid in cash by Qatar. An absolute record! As for the auctions of the Picassos at Sotheby's, not my department . . . The last two paintings sold by his grand-daughter Marina came to something like 19.7 million, if I'm not mistaken. But Passemant . . . I'm stumped!"

"According to our experts, not less than 100 million, objectively speaking. Not so sure, in my opinion . . . Since it's not an object of speculation like the paintings you like . . . Well, let's say 50 million!" Rilsky doesn't know any more than I.

Marianne does not agree at all. "One million at the very most, I tell you, not even . . . That's already too much . . . All right, two, to please Nivi . . . What? . . . It's simple, really, if there's no market, there's no value, right?"

She's right. But not in this exact case. Hence the theft. Unlike Sotheby's, the value of the Passemant includes risk value: foil the security, transport, hide, sell, hide again. An enormous part of the operation that only the police chief and his "experts" can evaluate. Which implies, at the top of the chain, someone somewhere. An obsessional who imagines the Hall of Mirrors, marquises and wigs, Beloved or not-loved-at-all king, a last minuet before the guillotine, and a whole world of scientists who know how to measure the sky and the earth, who gravitate around him and his courtesans . . . A megaspectacle . . . Priceless!

I stop projecting myself into the affair. After all, I know nothing about the thief . . . I'm giving myself a headache . . . And why not? Rilsky himself is not far from saying you have to be crazy to steal such an unsellable object. That's not exactly my thinking, but okay . . . Furthermore, the police chief suspects nothing of my affinity with Passemant . . .

I just answer that the thing is priceless. Such a spread, between 100 and 1 million—something's wrong, someone's wrong. Or else the thieves come from another planet. The police chief is totally in agreement with me.

"I'll tell you what I think. The guy behind this heist is necessarily a foreigner. To be infatuated with such an item at Versailles—you won't find anyone in France for that. On this point there is no doubt . . . Moreover, the associates of the elegant Dechartre who piloted the affair are pros. They disarmed the identification chip installed in the clock—child's play. But to get the booty out of the Château without getting caught, construction or no construction, they have to have accomplices, and they succeeded . . . What doesn't make sense is the export . . . 9999 will never make it past any border! Otherwise we'd have to despair of our surveillance programs, which go over everything that moves on the planet with a fine-toothed comb. I'm speaking now of Interpol . . . My dear friend, it's not only the e-mails from the Élysée Palace or the White House that are under surveillance through the Internet and other providers of electronic services, I'm not telling you anything new . . . The fact is that as of today we have lost track of the object. But nothing proves that it has left the Hexagon . . . All our customs stations have been given its description, and the external boundaries of the Schengen Area are bolted shut, triple locked. Red alert, needless to say!"

41

SIGNED, PASSEMANT

Astro was not in Chile. Or actually, after a single week spent at the European Central Observatory at Vitacura, not far from Santiago, he had precipitously left his telescope to shut himself in at the Notarial Registry of the National Archives in Paris. Nivi's passion for his improbable relative, the homonymous Passemant, had amused him at first, then annoyed him. Until that night in Vitacura when he changed his mind while studying the birth of a new planet resembling the Earth.

Theo was in the process of confirming the discovery made by his colleagues at the SETI Institute of the NASA Ames Research Center: Kepler-186f, an exoplanet of a size comparable to ours, on which water could be present. Could life exist in those parts? "It's only a matter of time before we know if our galaxy contains a multitude of planets similar to ours or if we are an exception," he wrote to Nivi.

Was he, Theo Passemant, an exception to the norm? This question, however banal, had until then never crossed his mind. An avalanche of reasoning, of implacable logic, was to follow, determining him at last to take an interest in the notorious clockmaker. He'd had enough of hearing her speak of the "clock by the same name." He wanted to find out for himself, more than by Nivi and if necessary in spite of her.

Theo's father, Jean Passemant, had never shown any taste for family trees. So a vague ancestor may have had his moment of glory at Versailles, what's the big deal? "It was May '68, a little before, a little after, nobody saw things that way, your father didn't either," his mother would repeat unceasingly, and Theo understood her. He had always understood her . . . until that day.

The Passemants, it seems, finished after the marriages of the two daughters of the king's engineer. The Olliviers and the Nicolets—with the name of a brother-in-law and his associate—apparently took over the business, the haberdashery and the clockmaking included . . . How those two held together, go figure!

Not so simple, according to Uncle Rilsky. We lose track of the Passemants, alias Ollivier-Nicolet, after the Terror. Probably too assimilated with the royalists, their massively decapitated clientele. The guillotine for them too, after all—why not? Someone might have bought the studio and taken the name Passemant. Was it a distant grandson or a cousin wanting to revive the royal and astronomical memory after the Revolution by taking the inventor's signature? Or simply a partner of this peerless man? A visionary, a lover of secret memories? Or—pure coincidence—a homonym?

In the plane returning from Santiago to Paris, Astro doesn't really think about it. He just has to go see, follow this in-sane, imperious impulse. The registry abounds in insignificant details—like so many not entirely dead stars. A refuge, also.

Theo is not looking for a family tree. Not even an origin. According to Nivi, the push to find one's origins is an antidepressant.

He has no need of that, of course. His case has nothing to do with melancholy. He is in search of a story. A narrative. The encounter with Nivi has revealed to him that love can be narrated: it tells the before, the instant, the after, all three crisscrossed in an endless *now* that holds those who love together. Who say they love each other. A story of attraction and extension. Expansion of luminous energies and dark energies. Theo Passemant has been a point without extension until now, containing all virtual matters and energies. Today and for the rest of his life, he needs to tell himself a story. With Nivi and thanks to her, he has to *happen*—where his father was, where plausible, possible Passemants were. Become accustomed to them, mix in with them, live their lives. A living planet, an Earth all for him, for Theo.

The Notarial Registry at the Archives puts a multitude of raw facts at his disposal. They pile up on his table: now he's an archivist. Letters exchanged between Passemant and Tournehem; the dimensions of the workshop the engineer is going to ask for in the Louvre, which he obtains thanks to the authorization of Louis XV; the inventory of his possessions after his death . . . No narrative; he, Theo, is the one who will construct the narrative. The necessarily subjective portrait, the documentary of this fellow who preceded him, Theo will have to invent. His fiction. A loyal, and in that sense legal, fiction. "The father is a legal fiction." "Of the only engenderer or engendered"— someone has already said that . . .

Theo scans a document, a revelation: at twenty-five, Claude-Siméon makes the acquaintance of Cassini, the illustrious discoverer of the great red spot on Jupiter and of the speed of rotation of Mars and Venus . . . In his lab at the Paris-Diderot University, Theo receives a photo of the Earth with the Moon at its right, photographed from Saturn by the Cassini probe.

A jewel, this probe, which for the first time precisely measures the distance from the Earth to the Sun . . . Cassini, the *extoller* of Passemant, no less . . .

Better yet: various anonymous correspondences with the director general of buildings, the omnipresent Marquis de Tournehem, and with the secretary of state Maurepas, from which it emerges that His Majesty frequently orders the construction of telescopes and other magnifying lenses from Passemant, whom he meets with to have them explained to him . . . His Majesty does not tire of receiving the inventor, just as he converses with Buffon, Cassini (him again), and, as frequently, the geographer Joseph-Nicolas Delisle. Fascinating— Nivi will be jealous, and let's not even talk about Bill Parker: he'll be invading all the labs.

Astro would like to steal this little pile of documents from the spring of 1752, the most novelistic of all. A nice little gift for Nivi. "I had the honor of seeing the Marquise de Pompadour at Belleville, and she told me to go see the Garde des Sceaux on her behalf, M. de Machault d'Arnouville, and that she had given him my proposal . . ."; "Today I present my clock to the king in the presence of the marquise . . ."; "I explained my difficulties to Mme la Marquise de Pompadour . . ."; "I had the honor of seeing Mme la Marquise de Pompadour last Monday at Choisy . . ." *She told me, I present in her presence . . . , I explained . . . , I had the honor of seeing . . .* Astro counts: the clockmaker saw the *favorite* at least three times. Three *attested* times. Certainly much more, in reality. Why doesn't history teach us such things, this intimacy of the greats and the nongreats? Around telescopes, automatons, 9999. Of no interest? It is for Astro.

The year 1755: Passemant has several meetings with the king to present him with new instruments of his invention. For example, the rotational watch, "made in such a way that one can see all of the mechanism that formerly was hidden." Those people wanted to *see* the mechanics. *See everything.* The Hall of Mirrors and the other side of the mirror. Once the formerly hidden technique is revealed, no miracle remains, no secret either.

Soufflot himself takes part in this engineering activity. Soufflot, like the famous street that leads to the Pantheon. Jacques-Germain Soufflot, comptroller of the king's buildings, asks the superintendent, the Marquis de Marigny, to intervene to facilitate the construction work at Passemant's lodgings in the Louvre . . .

The year 1759: additional meetings with Louis XV to present a new barometer, a telescope, a new magnifying lens.

Numerous orders. And successes . . . Astro photographs them with his iPhone—a sort of theft, actually. Could it be forbidden? Probably, probably not, whatever! An agent in the room supervises, but it doesn't matter . . .

The most precious of captures: this signature by the presumed ancestor. Astro captures it too, in all its variants, here, there, at the bottom of all the documents the registry holds. He sets it as the wallpaper on his computer, his tablet, his iPhone: PASSEMANT.

A breathing impulse, controlled, traced, flying, spiraled, gracious, vibrant. The handwriting of the visionary technician is both sure of itself and dreamy. The hand that held that pen could have been the hand of a tailor or a gardener, a mason or a pastry chef. *His* hand—Theo imagines it slender but hard, slicing, sculpting, fashioning into meticulous automatons the calculations of an organized brain and the beatings of a burning heart. It grips passing time, the starry sky; it embraces love of

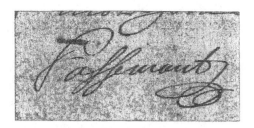

the king and the coming apocalypse. Spins the visible and pal-
pates the invisible that inhabits and incarnates it.

The armless body exhibiting an oversized member between
its legs is truly the body of the desired sovereign. Fine, he holds
the power! But the hand has nothing to do with it: reserved,
secret, the hand thinks.

To be continued. Astro will return tomorrow.

In the cold illumination of the reading room, Theo perceives
Passemant, who's a bit bent over as he stands and walks. As a
result of living hunched over his automatons, he displays a
modest air, but without a trace of hypocrisy. If he hugs the
walls and mirrors of Versailles, if he moves with many respectful and almost shameful bows, it's hardly so as to obtain more
space more "loudly," as the "little duke" said about another
royal servant. It's so the great nobles of the time, led by Le Normand de Tournehem, can ensure the conditions and the sums
they *owe* (the engineer is convinced of it) to his telescopes, to
science itself—to the stars, in short. A duty that these gentlemen of the court do not ignore, in their perfect wisdom. It is
nevertheless important to remind them of it, according to cus-
tom. So that from the very depths of their souls these Excellen-
cies, and His Majesty at their head, may participate in the
beauty and the light disseminated by the poor automatons that

only transit through his hands. According to the only order that remains and will remain: the universal order of the Great Clockmaker.

Claude-Siméon approaches, his speech slow, weighty, with a careful pronunciation, as if his impeccable French were a foreign language. His bows are just as slow and deep and his manner always respectful but sparkling with audacity, if not insolence. His sentences string along, composed with care; no pride, scorn, or derision, even less humility.

Never at ease, but always laconic, with a large memory. Split between observation, calculations of the stars, and the assembly of his machines, which is his way of collecting his thoughts, this ancestor prays little, perhaps hardly ever. Neither a philosopher nor an atheist, and though basically quite pleasant, amusing, and good, he can become uncivil to the point of not seeing anyone. He does, however, learn about everything the Château is occupied with, including the gazettes that arrived two or three months earlier, in order to draw benefits for his machines, which he considers capable of bringing the sky to the court and to the entire world here below. By the will of His Majesty, who plays the game with his habitual seriousness, a sort of solemn and sad humor. As for himself, Passemant never thinks about it, and by his own admission he is incapable of governing his own home.

"Can the hand of an artisan hold time? The answer is yes." Astro tweets this sibylline message to Nivi. She wonders what it can possibly mean. She thinks he's in a dilating universe, at 380,000 years after its creation, unless he's on Kepler-186f . . .

42

THE KING IS NAKED; OR, THE
BEGINNING OF AN END

Leaving the Notarial Registry, Theo Passemant is no longer quite sure that the documents he has procured about la Pompadour will arouse Nivi's curiosity. The marquise in no way seems an icon of the second sex, even if she posed for La Tour with the fourth volume of the *Encyclopédie* standing on her table. As for Nivi, always concerned about women's rights, she is not a typical feminist. Quite obviously, she prefers the Versailles of the little people with their unrecognized works, like the king's clockmaker, to the Versailles of the *favorites*. Neither Pompadour nor du Barry: Theo has never heard her mention these women, who are nevertheless exceptional. The fact is Nivi has eyes only for 9999.

The improvised archivist avoids the smile of that charming Mlle Aubane, whom Nivi introduced to him. What was her last name? Never mind. He'll take the rue des Francs-Bourgeois to the place des Vosges. Having escaped the penumbra of the archives and the twinkling of satellite screens, Astro lets himself dissolve in the white sun of August, nestles in it seeking protection, roams about in this past time that he has come to enjoy in a deserted Paris.

The name of the marquise written by the pen of a Passemant can only be impressive for another Passemant, Theo, who wasn't "well versed" in Versailles. Or so little—in school, where history was already beginning to disappear from the program. A smidgeon of general culture all the same, buried under the technological excellence of MIT. It happens that the Cassini satellite, managed by NASA with the ESA, sometimes puts itself into "safe mode" because of cosmic radiation; then, while waiting for the electronics experts to start it up again, Professor Passemant's doctoral students kill time by probing the life and works of the famous *extoller* of the clockmaker. Among them are two Canadian specimens, Jeffrey and Tom, more ignorant but more curious about the matter than the French.

This jolly pair has found everything on Google and YouTube: a silent film by Lubitsch, another by Sacha Guitry or Christian-Jaque, up to the most recent TV productions, with the sole intent of transferring their bounty onto the professor's iPad. A bevy of charming actresses resuscitates the royal mistresses, brilliant in the picture, insignificant and boring in the sound. Louis XIV more like a sovereign; Louis XV frankly pathetic; nothing on Cassini or the other scientists. Astro wastes no time zapping this dinosaurish reconstruction and sends the two apprentice historians to the expo that has just opened in Versailles about the science and the curiosities of the Château. They should obtain serious documentation and establish and maintain a good bib of scientific works about the period (beginning with the catalogue of the abovementioned exposition). And, why not, about the *favorites* on whom their juvenile attention had focused.

After a month, the professor receives a voluminous file devoted primarily to Cassini and copiously accompanied by complements on the two Egerias of Louis XV, la Pompadour and la du Barry. Which Theo just flips through, laughing with the Canadian schoolboys, but which he'll have to read one day, maybe?

As soon as possible.

Interminable, this rue des Francs-Bourgeois. Shops, cafes, art galleries, all or almost all closed, smaller crowds than usual, but still and always the tourists.

When Claude-Siméon wrote to Jeanne-Antoinette Poisson, Marquise de Pompadour, whom was he addressing? A commoner like him, having succeeded nine thousand nine hundred ninety-nine billion times better than he? Socially, of course, but had she at least made a success of her life? That's another matter. A screw, a lens, a nut from the royal machine made woman. She transmits, communicates, governs. She manages, in the modern sense of the term. Estimating the work-value that truly born aristocrats and even certain *parvenus* hardly appreciate, in those distant times.

It's important, even exceptional, honestly, and Passemant will use this woman with gratitude and humility while separating himself from this frivolous world that he otherwise serves. Detesting it, basically, but without knowing it: neither protest nor criticism, even less rebellion. The engineer keeps himself apart from the role-playing and the power he knows to be inexistent. La Pompadour knows it too, devoting herself body and soul to make it exist, this power. She wants to believe in it, and her intelligence suffers to see that it's only a utopia. Even if it means perpetuating the illusion, desiring it, at best reinforcing it, if possible. As for the astronomer clockmaker, he is annoyed with himself at being taken for a courtesan. In some respects, in fact, his role is not very different, if one thinks only of the spectacle at the court when the king exhibited the clock. And if one forgets that Passemant is not there on that parquet floor, under those ceilings, but rather in the flight of time, in the cosmic expansion of which politicians have no idea when they are courtesans—and without exception they all are. Trapped by the play of powers and masks. Stuck in the social contract, like it or not.

Similar and complicit, or enemies and incompatible, the *favorite* and the engineer. Like the politics of the spectacle and applied research in our time—Theo knows all about it!

"A bit of a king"—Theo's ancestral homonym cannot not know about it, since all Paris talks about it; the gazettes snicker, subjugated. Jeanne-Antoinette Poisson sings, dances, rides, does acid engraving and fine stone engraving, recites poetry as she was taught by Crébillon in person. She produces *Tartuffe*, plays Dorine, unleashes the devout cabal, who take her for a target.[1] Astro doesn't know it, but Claude-Siméon sees it clearly: the torments of his mind slacken his flesh; his penis is cold.

And yet la Poisson continues to display the most beautiful skin in the world, which augments the brilliance of her expression. Her eyes, especially, of uncertain colors—neither brown nor blue—give her, it seems, the irresistible charm of a mobile soul, nonetheless mistress of itself, so that all the features of her face express an elusive mischievousness. The lieutenant of the hunt, faithful to the royal escapes, notices this, fascinated by this person who "marks the nuance," he thinks, "between the ultimate degree of elegance and the initial degree of nobility." That's nicely put: between two regimes, la Pompadour is

---

1. In Molière's play *Tartuffe* (1664–1669), the portrayal of the impostor Tartuffe angered the devout cabal. Dorine was the bawdy, free-speaking servant of the household.

consumed and excels. D'Argenson, on the other hand, finds the marquise "without features," "ugly"—but those two hardly like each other, and he will be canned. As for Luynes and his dignity, he can't stand the hard loquacity of the royal mistress when she speaks of a cousin who is a nun as an "agreeable tool," even an "instrument."

Theo has no difficulty imagining Jeanne-Antoinette using the same sort of language about the astronomer clockmaker of the king. He's quite amused by it, and it's easy, at a distance, he admits: those people were shamelessly cruel—a lost art.

All the same, the legend makes of the *favorite* a skillful politician, a diplomat always respectful toward Marie Leszczynska, even though the queen's clan does not spare her supreme humiliations. Then la Pompadour strikes back by launching into a song: "At last, he is in my power . . . He seems to be made for love"—which distresses the royal spouse and children.

All kinds of stories can be learned in the naphthalene of the National Archives, miserable anecdotes that carry little weight in the face of what Astro retains from the documents gathered by his two Zebulons, Tom and Jeffrey. It was a good thing he shook them up. Definitively, the jealous populace detests la Poisson. They count up her expenditures: seven million? Much worse: "the heaviest burden of France," the lampoons guffaw.

Step by step, Professor Passemant comes to the same point. A war of nerves must have played out between the mistress and the astronomer. La Pompadour against 9999? Under the eyes of the king, in the body of the king, head and crotch included, between brain and pendulum? Is it conceivable?

Expert in pleasure and in judgment, la Poisson-Pompadour does not serve power any more than she does it disserve. She does much better: she exposes its intimate mechanisms, its public dependencies. The king is naked, and Astro understands, at this place des Vosges where he has just arrived, that in spite of what fables and tales recount, nowhere was this better known than at Versailles. Yes, "the king is naked." The French are in advance of others when they succeed in making a spectacle of this truth. And he, the hunter of gravitational waves, had to go underground to figure that out!

Does a man grow in majesty when he unveils the hidden mechanisms of his pleasures and his authority, in the image of those rotational watches that Claude-Siméon constructed for his sovereign? Not sure. It's not because he entrusts his pleasures and his decisions to the *favorites* that power doesn't abuse the feminine sex. Theo is in agreement with this. Except that by displaying the political power of eroticism like that, the man at the summit of the state is not only revealing the wellspring of power; he lets it be understood that women can have their part in it. Also. In some situations. On the condition of preparing their pleasures and their knowledge in it.

Along the way, Astro is surprised to realize that the politico-erotic avatars of the royal French clock are only marking the start of the beginning of the end of the occidental male. And of Power with a capital *P*, the one the Terror is going to decapitate. But that survives as a necessary though unsustainable illusion in all regimes, be they democratic. Even women are seeking it: many are those who submit to it; others exert it like men.

Is it really worth guillotining to understand that the re-composition of authority is not done with strokes of the ax and the pick? It is already under way in this war-and-peace of the sexes openly performed in the Le Nôtre gardens and be-tween the Mansart walls. War-and-peace that continues thanks to revolutions, then feminism, ART, surrogacy, stem cells, artificial uteruses, and other such clonings. Even Astro finds himself at a loss: biology is moving as fast as cosmology, if not faster.

The *ancien régime* is far behind us; marriage is available for all; certain men and women prefer to veil their faces, while others want to be everything and have everything . . . Here are the new Egerias of the globalized transhumance: they run in the Marais in the summer, they advance, they are in a hurry, they jostle one another. A swarm of laughing gulls: saleswomen, shoppers, hairdressers, researchers; they fly toward 9999 and beyond, they have won . . .

This doesn't mean the occidental male has lost: Astro is far from envisaging such a defeat. However, the question remains: this *humanitude* capable of shivering in expansion until 9999 and being dazzled by la Pompadour was missing something. But what? Ordinary lives are more difficult than the techniques, the knowledge, the philosophies, the revolutions. Those people needed new love connections. That's what he thinks, stupidly, pretentiously. And they still need them so that the quantum states of the two sexes may agree. Quite simply, discreetly.

43

WHAT IF HE'S THE ONE!

What's going on with Astro? His e-mails are becoming rare, elliptical; even Nivi can't understand a thing about them. Could he be depressed? But about what? He's not the type. Rather, he's absorbed in computerizing the baby universe, 3,000 degrees centigrade of hot matter made of microscopic particles, boiling magma of electrons and protons from which not a single grain of light can emerge. No wonder he communicates by ellipses!

That's how she prefers to see things. It's worrying. Or not, because the silences allow one to imagine. They force the imagination. They invite it. That's the reason why neither Astro nor Nivi have wanted to utilize one of those geolocation applications that certain consumers love. What's the difference if he's in the Andes, in Antarctica, in Haute-Provence, or in Geneva? Astro and Nivi are "inoperable," as Proust says, speaking of a love of Swann inseparable from his desires. And from those of the narrator.

A silence, too, around the theft of the famous clock. The news deflated as quickly as it exploded. General indifference: Nivi was expecting it. The proof, Theo himself: "I see!" as his only comment on the e-mail announcing the incredible event.

"In our period of austerity, no one is interested in Versailles."
Does Marianne hope to console Nivi or hurt her? Both.

Whereupon Aubane Dechartre, whom Stan ran into at the
Marly, tells her she saw Theo Passemant at the National Archives. That gentleman seemed to be in a great hurry. A simple
hello out of pure courtesy. Does he really remember the assistant curator of Versailles, met briefly in Mme Delisle's consulting room?

Nivi pays no attention to these imbecilic rumors. Astro is in
Santiago; Aubane must be mistaken. She would do well to occupy herself with the archives she's in charge of.

All the same, an idea takes hold of the psychology editorialist. Another one. The hypothesis may well be absurd, but it remains viral. It propagates by multiplication, takes advantage of
the fragility of the host and imposes itself virulently in all circumstances—as much when she struggles to listen to her patients as when she works for GlobalPsyNet or loses herself
wandering around the streets of Paris . . .

It's not because Astro has been avoiding her lately that she is
going to suspect him of having something to do with the
theft of Passemant's masterpiece. Nor because he has apparently come to Paris without telling her, as the little Dechartre
woman claims. Nor out of jealousy. She's not one to be jealous.
In no case. Nobody. Never! And why would she be now, and
furthermore of Astro? Astro whose preference for a celestial
object, a star, an emerging planet, a particle soup is the only
thing that can surpass her, Nivi (other than his mother, Irene,
or some vague double of that indelible infantile passion, but
that's another story, a really old one).

No, the origin of this viral and virulent idea is simple: if Nivi
were in Astro's place, if she even were Astro, she would like to

live in proximity to that now stolen being. Visitors looking at 9999 admire an extravagant automaton, or the vestiges of former grandeur, or even a witness to non-passing Time. But that's not the case with Theo, who, two and a half centuries after Passemant, has gone infinitely farther, from Big Bang to Big Bang, in cosmic expansion.

Some people lose the sense of human time when it inspires neither curiosity nor temptation, and they take themselves for bosons. Others close themselves up in the finiteness of our death-in-life and do not dare to transpose quantic and gravitational pulsations into their love life. Could it be because these internal coups d'état ceaselessly remind them of infinite rebounds resulting in death to oneself? Which make one live, live again, survive? Nivi believes that the android 9999 could actually be a point of reference and that as a result Theo himself could have, should have envisaged it like that. Even more: 9999 is a safeguard. A sort of third-generation neuroleptic capable of returning us to human scale, of tamping down the abstract ardor of science, to moderate excesses.

9999 in the body of a man . . . Proust was the last to see humans with the sovereign eyes of an inhabitant or a visitor at Versailles. His *In Search of Lost Time* proves it. The giants standing on their stilts, which bring regained time to a close, are hideous, verbal responses to the astronomical clock. At least that's how Nivi sees them. Unlikely that Theo didn't think of it. The Guermantes, Palamède de Charlus, Mme Verdurin, Swann, Albertine, the narrator himself—all are sensitive clocks excessively, simultaneously reaching to distant eras in time. Body-times not only occupying space but having accumulated time.

Today there are no sovereign bodies. The photo of the Big Bang, calculations and interpretations of what precedes it or follows it, those gravitational waves that forever fashioned the universe at the instant of its very first billionths of billionths of billionths of billionths of a second of existence—none of this can be held in a box; no model can possibly represent it. Try to imagine what that photo would look like . . . taken by a satellite like Hubble, if Astro wanted to give it human form. Certainly not like Louis XV, nor like the giant penis, nor like the dancer's leg. But who? Obama, Sarko, Lula, Ban Ki-moon, Mandela, Netanyahu, Hollande, Pope Francis, Bin Laden? Just asking the question makes one grasp its absurdity. No human form today can contain the present knowledge about time and space, no more than to embody it. Writers, scientists, artists, and musicians are no more capable of embodying it than world leaders. However, since a 3D photo contains knowledge of another temporality, the idea of integrating it into human life is tempting. It arouses the imaginary, the passions. The social animal being by nature successive, it does not wish to know in what expansion it is living. It says to itself that life is already complicated enough without that; it does not imagine that other vital experiences could be possible—precisely in expansion. Not in a box, nor even in sequences.

The man-machine still exists; it is serviceable, and the robot 9999 is one of its both most ambitious and most charming versions. If Nivi were Astro, she would install Passemant's clock beside a telescope or a screen to demonstrate what we are not, or are no longer, and what we do not want to know.

Our accelerated discoveries do not make of us individuals who are sure of themselves and omnipotent but imaginations that surpass the human in the human. Dante said *transumanar*. To *transumanar* in human bodies and codes. Passemant himself knows perfectly well how to pose limits, measure distances, meditate separations, calculate appearances/disappearances.

His totem is the homunculus, the astronomical clock. But there are now artisanal and increasingly learned engineers who tame deliriums and comas, rebirths, pain, and happiness. Below 10^{-33} centimeters, where trajectories no longer exist, each observer, each object, possesses its own time. Superimposition of different, ungraspable, counterintuitive, but real times. To *transumanar* escapes us from the finite and makes the unknown emerge. No one other than Theo could have joined or brought together side by side a screen from the Hubble or from Planck, which transmits 300 million years after the Big Bang, and the 9,999 years of Passemant in human form.

So, Theo as gentleman thief? Why not? And 9999 his anti-madness manual?

44

AUBANE WOULD HAVE
PREFERRED TO EVAPORATE

At the Château no one has seen the Owl's assistant since this implausible theft was announced on the eight o'clock news on France 2. Not even her hierarchical superior.

The fact that her brother was mixed up in this burglary demonstrated the absence of professional probity in Aubane herself, since it was through her supposed intermediary that Thibault had formed a friendship—oh so suspect!—with certain staff members presently under judicial review. At least that's what Aubane believed, and she thought that everyone had the same opinion about this horrid affair—beginning with the law. The young woman had been interrogated like the others, and more than the others, it goes without saying, but this inquiry had taken such a mean turn that she had been left speechless—nothing but futile and irrepressible tears, a sort of stunned shock.

She was ashamed, but beyond that, she literally collapsed at the thought that Thibault could have done that to her, his only sister, whom he claimed to love, his one and only love, he would say, which she had always believed. And for good reason: this elegant, distinguished, and well-known Parisian antiquarian was not known to have a girlfriend, and at past forty wasn't even married. Since childhood the brother and sister had shared the same tastes, the same sense of perfection, a reciprocal, almost spiritual passion. And now comes this ignominy—there is no other word for it—enough to hide her head in shame.

No news from Thibault. He could have sent word, said he was sorry, because it was a frankly criminal act, and Aubane wants her brother to refute these suspicions or at least explain himself. Nothing. The presumed guilty party has suddenly cut off relations with the family. The Dechartres' lawyer is no longer on the case. He claims Thibault fired him and chose an international expert; all he is doing now is shielding poor Aubane, hoping to prove her innocence. Aubane is afraid that on the pretext of protecting her they will hide disagreeable truths from her, infantilizing her. She who knows Passemant's clock better than anyone! Not to mention the inventor himself, the illustrious stranger, including thieves who likely don't know a thing about his life or his work, she would bet . . .

Only at the Château does the matter still make for chatter. Elsewhere, people were interested a little, a lot, not so much, less and less, not at all. Now it's over. Radio silence. The system is a spectacle in which Aubane inevitably has a part, at her humble level . . . All those visitors who come to look, what do they see? A brouhaha, body to body, the need to be together, to jostle one another in front of the myths, nothing more, or only rarely: Mme Delisle, for instance, such a subtle person . . . The system does not need 9999, oh no. This showcase of images, instant and toxic, is in its essence impermeable to mystery, to the sublime. Louis XV's misbehaviors, that's one thing, but what could he have been thinking more than two centuries ago? His clock, its last stroke of midnight before the year 10,000: people don't give a damn; they don't have the time; no one has the time anymore, today. Even the Owl, usually protective, isn't calling her assistant anymore . . . Today she finally decides to do so.

"There's news. You don't know about it? It's on the net. Go look . . . Yes, do, it's worth the trouble . . . A new development . . . Unheard of, I swear . . . It's hard to understand much about it, I hope it's not another PR stunt, there are so many . . . Internet surfers are all on it, we had to expect that, there's lots of tweeting already . . . They're likely to take an interest in us in high places—I'm not talking about the Château, no: much higher . . . This affair has become political . . . You'll see, click on WRE.fr for World Radical Ecologist, section France . . . No connection? Oh yes, there are always links, you have to believe it . . ."

The stiff voice becomes maternal again. As the Owl can sometimes be. In contrast to Aubane's mother, who never was.

The little sparrow couldn't believe it. Did Thibault succeed in exfiltrating 9999 to sell it to a superrich lover of French eternities in Dubai? Or was that hypothesis a decoy, worse, a trap that swallowed up Police Chief Rilsky himself? Could Thibault have orchestrated this staging to divert attention, allow the thieves to gain the time they needed to deploy another strategy, the real one, revealed only today yet at work from the start?

Whatever the case may be, according to WRE.fr (at the Château they pronounce *à l'américaine*), the French branch of this powerful NGO network found a spectacular means, one not lacking in audacity, for pressuring the French authorities to close nuclear-power stations! No joke! Beginning with the most dangerous, according to them: Fessenheim, Flamanville, Gravelines, Bugey, Blayais, Tricastin. How?

"We have sequestered 9999 in order to sound the alarm. We will return the astronomical clock to its rightful owner on the condition that the French government promises to close the most dangerous atomic power plants in the country within a month from today. If not, 9999 will be deposited and sold in a secure location. The price of this sale, which we hope will be considerable, will finance our militant actions on behalf of a radical ecology. Upon the expiration of the announced time, lacking a favorable response to our demands for the closing of Fessenheim, Flamanville, Gravelines, Bugey, Blayais, Tricastin, we will proceed to the auction with our supporters throughout the world, and 9999 will not return to its place in the cabinet of King Louis XV at Versailles." A communiqué from WRE.fr.

People should have thought of it. They steal the clock that symbolizes the infinite desire to live, to survive, to preserve the earth and its inhabitants, the universe itself. They point a finger at those irresponsible politicians and those industrial-financial mafioso giants that are destroying the planet well before the last stroke of the clock resonates on December 31, 9999. An atomic apocalypse during the lifetime of 9999 is being readied, good people! Up in arms!

Aubane doesn't understand a thing about what's going on, even less than the Owl. What she can grasp nevertheless is that Thibault works, has worked, or will work for this WRE (not to put too fine a point on it). A senseless thing by madmen. Hardly a militant fiber can be found in Aubane, and she has never suspected Thibault of having one either. But her brother has always had a life of his own: she knew it but didn't think about it much; unlike her, Thibault did not share everything with her. Whom does he see? At the Emirates, the royal families—to be expected. But in Paris? At the Hypnosis Café, the Baron, the

Montana, the Carmen? "I'm not taking you along, little sister, you're not mad at me are you, angel? Not interesting for you, I know . . . Later . . ." That's what he said when he went out. How could she answer, since he had already decided everything, whereas she would have liked to be with him too, follow him? But Aubane did not dare, and visibly Thibault had no desire for it . . . She would close the door and return to her monitor with the scanned archives.

With that communique, the affair of the theft takes a much more serious turn. The Owl is right. The clock will again be on the TV during prime time for the eight o'clock news on TF1. An eco action, durable politics. Well played, if Thibault is in on it, not bad at all! Otherwise, let them find another guilty party; we are innocent, and so much the better!

Aubane takes a shower, puts on some pretty makeup—why not a garnet lipstick, like for big occasions—and reappears at the Château.

45

JEALOUSY? WHAT JEALOUSY?

Nivi is incapable of it. Just as she is incapable of feeling hatred. "You don't know how to hate," her mother would say in a reproachful tone. This kind of naivety that excludes distrust is a handicap.

"Too bad. I prefer delayed disappointments to the smallness of hearts," was the girl's reply from her stock of moralizing quotations.

It does, however, happen that a woman or a man spoils her illusion with absolute stealth. Waste, bitterness. But the aggravation that follows is nothing like a catastrophe. Not even an annoyance. Nivi is never annoyed. Eventually it could even be a relief. Because from the start the wound itself is doubled by curiosity: how can they, what do they do to take pleasure in that?

And the certainty returns, the ancient certainty that the will refuses but that survives at the bottom, muted: *Nothing is everything. Everything is nothing.*

Melancholy superiority? Infantile defense? A dose of confidence also, but in what? In oneself? Which "self"? No fixed identity—other than the one attested by the passport—but a mosaic of "selves" that do not break into pieces. On the contrary: a tenacious mosaic that endures. More or less. Why?

Marianne, novice shrink riffling through the pink pages of the *Larousse Freudien*, does not fail to bring up the basic explanation: "Darling, you have always been sustained by another illusion, *the* illusion: Papa loves you better than anything! I know that's it. I dare you to disagree . . . !"[1]

Thanks to her analysands, Nivi has got beyond that stage: Marianne should know that. Stan and Astro help her with this too. She is convinced that jealousy is just a return of the disillusion as a demolition of the self, a bitter yearning disguised as a sickly sweet hatred. Ultimately jealousy betrays a simple lack of imagination. It suffices to avoid autarchy. No ecstatic reclusion. Links, dreams, blossomings . . . Until that admissible affinity happens: Astro's surprise in the waters of the Fier. A permanent and fragile adjustment, to be maintained permanently. By recomposing everything that happens, the weight of needs, desires, yearnings, the mythology of fidelity, among others, and the even stickier mythology of infidelity.

What a crazy idea to enclose fidelity in a box, to chain it! Links are played like a jazz *vocalese*, the text espousing the melody and the rules of life adapting as much as possible to the beat of the senses, morality to the attraction of skins and the passions of the sex organs, prohibitions to climaxing like death. Swing, bebop, soul . . . Until the jazz vocalese meets its Louis Armstrong and frees itself from the text, morality, words. Bursts apart into scat, disseminates into timbres, ground-up syllables, insane exactness, the entire body between cadenced

---

1. The *pages roses* of the famous Petit Larousse dictionary contained foreign words and phrases; Kristeva here invents a Freudian Larousse.

glottis and ear, the musicked delirium! Images, intrigues, impasses—all exhausted . . .

You can also play it more coldly, more chastely, like serial music. Then you break conventional harmony by a rigorous succession of tones, and as a result of modulations you arrive at a total absence of reference points. Dangerous? Up to you to adjust the melody of the timbres.

Jealous people are the bachelors of the art because they have only the imagination of the possessed/possessing, in other words, an absence of inventiveness, it's been said. But Nivi finds that's not saying enough. The jealous person doesn't risk composing his life in scats, series, modulations without reference points . . . He's lacking the ear—and especially the tact.

More tact than Passemant needed, although he was a peerless tactile humanoid, to refine his 9999. A jewel of precision—no surprise they stole it! That's not much worse than if 9999 remained stashed away in a lab in Seattle—and why not in Antarctica? The ultimate hiding place! Unknown on the Internet, just a warning . . . Invisible witness to this old species that was still *transumanar*ing in human form not so long ago.

To be sure, but Nivi is not Theo. Even supposing he could ramble on like her—which is not out of the question, but still . . . —Astro is above all a scientist. Nothing says he might have participated in the theft . . . Perhaps he merely approved of the project of sequestering the object?

Where in god's name could that damned clock have got to?

46

CONSPIRACY FOR A CAUSE

Theo Passemant? May I have a few minutes of your time? On behalf of Dobbel-you-are-ee-dot-eff-are . . . I would like to meet with you . . . It's about the theft of the clock, the Passemant clock . . . Exactly . . ."

"Excuse me for interrupting, sir, but I don't see how I can help you. I am not a clockmaker; I know nothing about the century of Louis XV and even less about Interpol, I'm afraid . . . As for my family name . . ."

"We know about it. But I'm seeking advice from the astro-physicist. I know, the connection is not obvious, but, that's just it, I would like to explain myself, it's important . . . really!"

The voice insists. Theo is so rarely in Paris, he has lost contact with reality and ends up accepting. They will meet at the P'tit Café, next to campus. "Not far from your lab, very discreet, the manager is one of us. Tuesday? OK! Name your time."

The man looks like a teacher or a middle manager, maybe he's a journalist. T-shirt under a jean jacket, glasses.

"Pierre Faure, from WRE.fr."

He doesn't pretend that the name Passemant didn't intrigue them. He seeks eye contact with Astro, who stares at his coffee.

"We're not expecting secret information about the inventor of the clock, let me reassure you!"

Although the subject interests them—interests him even, personally—that's not their problem, not our problem for the moment. Astro takes note, thanks. The other man hurries to make his point.

"You have certainly seen that the theft of 9999 is part of a militant action."

As for being "part of" it, Astro reminds him that it is in fact the central object! But speaking of militant action, "You're joking! A pretty word to designate what is really nothing but a heist." Small smile, eyes slightly raised from the coffee cup.

"The objective consists in alerting opinion and forcing the authorities to close the nuclear-power stations." Faure continues without paying attention to the qualms of his interlocutor.

Astro congratulates him: "Bravo."

The other man concludes, "For the benefit of renewable energy . . ."

"That's debatable, but what can I do? Is this a conspiracy?" Astro: hostile or threatening?

"There's little time, you understand. We can't wait until 9999. Besides, at our rate of pollution (and I'm not even talking about the nuclear risk that is our major preoccupation at present), everything suggests the Earth won't last until then." WRE.fr, serious.

"That's a hypothesis." Astro has managed to slip in a doubt; the man doesn't flinch.

Faure lets him know that the authorities are standing firm, will certainly not move in the good direction.

"The deadline we gave for a favorable response comes in a few days; we are going to launch a global request for gifts to 'buy'—in quotes, of course—Passemant's work."

"Passemant's work": that is indeed how Faure describes the clock. Duly noted. A symbolic purchase, in fact: it consists of intensifying the fight. Imposing it on public opinion, on TV screens, on the media, and on the Internet—that's where it will play out, agreed?

Astro agrees. The man repeats that it's a matter of time. So they logically thought about his lab: "Your lab . . . In this new phase of the action, we need to store 9999 in a safe place, to entrust it to the researchers involved in reflecting on time— that makes sense, doesn't it? And who can keep it hidden. *In secret.*" He insists. "That way we will have our hands free to run the collection of funds in his name in all security—in the name of 9999, you understand . . . Nothing could be more indicated or more serious than your lab!"

Astro shakes his head as if he's reflecting. He tells Faure that the idea, quite surprising—but that's his intent, after all—is not bad in itself . . . He has to admit, however, that he is a little puzzled by this affair, actually a lot. Between Seattle, the Andes, and the Harvard-Smithsonian Center for Astrophysics Studies, it's hard to follow . . . As for the lab, he regrets having to disagree, but people have strange ideas about labs. Those sorts of places are much more open than it would seem. A safe place? Not what you think! More like a store window. Might as well put 9999 at an intersection. You cannot imagine all those teams busy deciphering the data from a telescope like the Hubble, more than eleven tons rotating in the sky . . . Or like the one from the ESA, the Planck space observatory launched by the Ariane 5 . . . We have completed the collection of the data, but we haven't finished interpreting them . . . Not to mention the European space telescope Gaia, recently launched from Kourou in Guiana, a "galaxy surveyor" whose mission is to chart a 3D atlas of the Milky Way . . . Do you realize? All those minds focused on the time-out-of-time and those simmering postdocs speculating about the invisible. No no, some hiding place!

Astro can see he is not convincing his companion. Tries to be more precise, admits he no longer works in the great AIM lab—Astrophysics, Instrumentation, and Modeling, with MAXI telescopes and satellites orbiting the Earth and Saturn, gigantic digital simulations on supercomputers. Is that really what Mr. Faure is looking for? No, Astro is now at LUTH— yes, more musical, if you like, more obscure, in any case: Laboratory Universe and Theories, connected to AIM. But the work there is more meditative, if you see what I mean . . .

WRE.fr looks annoyed; he can't leave the stammering professor. Astro likewise: these ecology nuts are really passionate, impassioned . . . But he does give him the name and the contact information of a young colleague. She has just wrapped up her thesis on "Time as Illusion," let's call it that, to simplify. A subject that will surely interest WRE.fr, since it connects to your concerns, dear sir . . . A remarkable person, an ecologist so committed that she can have only one idea in mind: to help you out . . . Don't hesitate!

It happens that the wife of the messenger studied physics and had taken courses and attended lectures by Professor Theo Passemant . . . "Exceptional! You have the reputation of a great scientist . . . your diplomas, your awards . . . but also of a man of progress and probity, not so common. So naturally we turned to you, Professor." A timid grimace; shouldn't overdo it. "This action has to be ultrasecret, you'll have understood, we couldn't entrust it to just anyone. Will you promise to keep this all to yourself?"

"No problem. You can count on it. My compliments to your wife."

The other man will transmit his wishes; his wife teaches in a high school, science exists at all levels, doesn't it, they take small steps . . . The man leaves, crestfallen, disappointed.

47

TOGETHER AGAIN

The King and His Clockmaker

Theo has left WRE.fr to his concerns; he's still tracking his Passemant at the Notarial Registry. Strange phantom, here he is . . . Astro glimpses him.

They are together again, the king and his clockmaker, in the council chamber henceforth called the Clock Cabinet. Claude-Siméon shuffles in, gangling; his open physiognomy speaks of nothing but gentleness and goodness under the banal appearance of an artisan with the eyes of a distracted child. He behaves so modestly and so well that the king appreciates him more and more, and the clockmaker finds himself protected from the courtesans instead of being mocked, as happens often to newcomers unknown to the town. Amusing and useful, this Passemant. He provides His Majesty with a new product from his workshop: pocket lenses. The king likes him; it's perfectly normal.

Louis is also amused, like a kid. "Obviously, nothing can stop the artfulness of science . . . We creatures are of an age you defy, Passemant . . . How far will your technique go? Is it a gift of God or of the devil?"

Two years separate Claude-Siméon from his death, and the king of France has seven more years to live. On this October

2, 1765, the engineer has come to propose to His Majesty another vision from his dreams—not celestial this time but maritime.

"Another one of your original ideas, my good man. Will you never age, then?"

"A seaport in Paris, Majesty. It's possible. Your Paris cannot do without a port on the Atlantic."

"A port? Do you mean a maritime port? Where are you finding a sea in Paris, my friend? You see big, I know; is it your magnifiers that turn the Seine into an ocean?"

The sovereign seems not very surprised to discover that his clockmaker has ventured into a science he did not suspect him to possess. On the other hand, he doubts that the project is timely. Okay to scrutinize the stars and calculate the days that pass, but to implant a maritime port on the Seine, opposite the Louvre! Though the idea is several centuries old, and Louis approves it, basically, the times, alas, do not lend themselves to it . . . Now? With these crises, these attacks . . . These illnesses, these deaths . . . No way, no means . . .

"You're not with Apollo anymore, Passemant? You abandon us for Neptune? This is a pharaonic vision you have brought me, in your drafts!"

Claude-Siméon persists. First, it's doable. "Look, Sire: these canals, these dams, these locks, these sheltered basins. The Seine is navigable along a large part of its course: Troyes, Paris, Rouen, Le Havre. As Your Majesty well knows, its present appearance dates from almost twelve thousand years before us, and its minimal incline has brought about multiple deep meanders. The tide can be felt for about a hundred kilometers, as far as Poses. Those tidal bores are well known; in Normandy they call them "bars." We are going to do everything over, Majesty. Your engineers, your technicians, your workers will dig further, widen, canalize. It's perfectly doable, I swear! A seaport in the capital, on the Seine as you see it in Paris. That is what the Great Sovereign of Europe that you are needs, and the people will applaud!"

"Maybe. Do you think . . . ? It's very costly, such a job . . . The coffers are empty, my good man, everyone knows that. Would Parliament agree?"

"Indispensable, Sire. Everything on earth will play out on the sea before man learns how to conquer the sky. The English have understood this; they are ahead of us. They conquer America, India. The naval power is England. London is a great port; Paris should be, could be."

Louis XV is not insensitive to this rivalry, but do we still have the means? Isn't it already too late? What will the council say? However sovereign he may be, a man cannot do everything in the face of people's remonstrances. Not everyone can be pharaoh.

"We will think about it, Passemant. The idea is grandiose. Will I see it realized one day?"

He holds him in his arms for a long moment. Strokes his body. Then saddens, and releases him like a wounded stag handed over to the kill. The engineer withdraws, dubitative, already heartsick. The project will remain in its boxes and with it his vision of France. Time plays in favor of the English, Passemant has always known it, alas. Too bad. If that is the will of the Great Clockmaker . . .

A century later, the port of Paris will become the port of Gennevilliers, then take its current form thanks to works undertaken after World War II. The first French river port, the second in Europe. In the meantime, the British fleet will have carried the English language to all the continents. A few charming

Bateaux-Mouches will cruise the Seine in Paris, a delicious tourist consolation.

Passemant will know nothing about it.

He withdraws, more stooped than ever, convinced that no one will remember his "pharaonic" ambition, as His Majesty was so kind to call it. No one, except obviously the astronomical clock, which will bear witness until 9999 and after all sorts of apocalypses.

Except Astro, too, who has momentarily abandoned his telescopes to scrutinize the past with a magnifying glass.

48

BEEHIVE

My library is a real beehive. Files pile up on the shelves and in my PC's memory. Close-fitting alveoli, frail equilibrium that maintains me. Each in its more or less regular hexagon stocks the pollen I gather and the honey I draw from it.

Each file is an irreducible binnacle. There I lodge, shelter, make tame. The alveolus becomes my home, and I start over: next choice, new passion. Through their incredible union, I am fragmented, plural, polymorph. No "me" survives this tourney. My heart, my brain, all my organs diffract and recompose in the heart of the beehive. I observe my documents, read them on the screen of my computer: without a doubt the beehive works and makes me live. Through me and without me. I escape from myself, and a sort of swarm rebuilds, rebuilds me.

I'm not hallucinating: the proof is all there; notes and documents compose me in a cubist portrait, as Stan insists. I consult Google: "The human being is a beehive of beings." Could that be me, that being? Nothing less! Others rustle in my head, aggravate my tachycardia, take my breath away. I put myself in their place, argue with them; they flee, I retrieve them. No surprise I don't exist.

My former friends no longer call me. They consider me dead, I think. They are not wrong. When I left La Salpêtrière after Stan came back to life, I was the one left for dead. Another alveolus of the beehive then fills with the honey of Passemant, whom we will go see together, at 9999's, when they have arrested the thief. La Pompadour comes along, a beautiful mortal delighted to escape the frigidity of her bronchitis. Until Marianne, alias Dr. Baruch, comes and makes me laugh with her one-quarter-Indian "bébée."

Am I really alone, too alone? If Astro asks me, it's because he loves me. He knows that Nivi is not dead. She is, however, in a certain way, but reincarnated in the rustling of her beehive.

"What would you say if I told you I am a survivor?"

He doesn't answer. He has already told me that there are no graves in beehives, even though statistics are showing that bees are becoming more and more rare. In his opinion I would do better to count on him. He keeps an eye out for me. It's already huge that he says so, and thinks it. All the same, nothing replaces the beehive.

49

WHERE WERE YOU?

So you weren't in Santiago? You prefer the Notarial Registry now?"

Theo knows how to lie like nobody else. Caught *in flagrante delicto*, he neither blushes nor shuts up but literally disappears, buried under a placid mask of insignificance. Man as erasure! How is that possible? Since he does ten times as many logical operations per second than most gifted people, Astro knows that his lie has been, is, and will be discovered. He has therefore prepared not 9,999 disavowals, justifications, or denials but the parry of an expressionless face. Better: expression without a face. The labs are fooled: a natural innocence. Not Nivi. No, this blank glibness isn't in the least neutral, only a sort of eclipse that in no way covers the incandescent, explosive star.

"Me? Someone must have confused me with one of those defenders of nature who ripped off 9999 and don't know what to do with it. Unless they took me for a Qatari who's taking aim at Versailles after having taken over soccer? Do I look like a Qatari?"

He's not making me laugh. Nor is he smiling. He knows I know. Men (certain men), quite frankly, do not have the same reactions as women (certain women); can't change that. Me, I never forget, and I don't hide from anyone, all the less from Theo, that it was he, Theo, who made me listen to *Juditha triumphans* by the Red Priest of Venice. I like Vivaldi's cruelty, or *Das Augenlicht* by Webern. Among others. It was he who taught me to find the Vivaldi motifs in Bach's clavier and those of Bach in the crisscrossed cells of the atonal Viennese. Never has it occurred to me to forget, to keep quiet, or to deny that I owe him what I owe him. I write it even when, for instance in *Psych-Mag*, I celebrate the feminine genius of Judith triumphant, transported by an ecstatic tornado like my baroque Teresa.

I have no need to hide that it was Theo who opened this world for me after having fished me out of the waters of the Fier d'Ars. Why won't he admit that he is following in my footsteps in the kingdom of Claude-Siméon? If he has barricaded himself incognito in the archives with the inventor of 9999, isn't it so he can better join me where I'm looking for him, in my own way, through his hypothetical and homonymous ancestor? Without making a big deal about it, discreetly, with modesty?

Yes, let's talk about discretion! My Astro wants to keep *his* Passemant to himself. After all, it's his family name! I am unrelated—I should mind my own business. I won't say anything. Fine. Let him take initiatives the way he wants to, all alone; to each our route.

Unless my theft scenario, apparently absurd, is not so absurd as all that? Those ecologists who admit having staged the heist . . . Why does Astro tell me that Aubane could have taken him for one of them, at the archives? Couldn't he be an accomplice of those guys from WRE.fr? Perhaps they contacted him, unless it was the other way around . . . Could it have been his idea? You can't be just anybody to conjure up such a project. Could Astro be in on the thing from the start? Why not, it fits . . . Not very likely, however. Astro as a green militant? No. Tell me another!

Although Nivi lacks distrust, that's not it. No . . . Which doesn't prevent him from having joined them at the next stage, or the present phase, when they're trying to hide 9999 to make the government yield. Maybe that's it.

If that's it, he won't say a thing. Nor will Nivi.

I look for Leibniz the swan out front, beyond my computer screen, while Theo listens to "Straight, No Chaser," by Thelonious Monk—*my* Melodious Thonk, says he—royal bone structure, dissonant and melodic.

"He's not alone today, your friend." Astro joins me, sees what I see; I know he thinks what I think. "A flotilla of six black Leibnizes accompany him."

"A sign the wind is changing. Nature is healthy around here."

"Let's keep an eye on events, then."

50

WHAT THE PRESS WASN'T
SAYING

The judicial police had taken their time before making the fact public, and since an overdose, in and of itself, doesn't mobilize the investigative media, the press merely revealed, quite late, that an unexpected object was found near LSG's inert body. Or rather that LSG's cadaver was lying at the foot of the stolen trophy that the police were desperately seeking.

So the investigation was going to pick up again. How could 9999 have landed there? What connection with the presumed suicide of the journalist—unless it was a murder by overdose? The announcement of this "detail," which it wasn't, did not fail to reignite the almost extinguished interest, on the Internet and in public opinion, for this theft of a national treasure.

Bizarrely (or not), colleagues and friends of the King at *PsychMag*, though surprised, even impressed, did not seem to be particularly astonished, even less shocked. Was it because the discovery of the cadaver had already plunged them into deep sadness? And because the investigation, aiming its projectors at first on this atypical—to say the least—journalism (embodied in the "recruit to the Murdoch press," as some newspapers called it), had provoked a scandal that besmirched the editorial board itself, and a brooding insensitivity had succeeded so many wounds? Or perhaps, for reasons that no one could express, the presence of 9999 beside Loïc Sean did not seem either extraordinary or really unexpected, in the end? The question eating at everyone was not to know why the King had hidden Passemant's work but why this revelation came so late. Why were they only now announcing this major fact, "a case within the case"?

Duly interviewed, Police Chief Rilsky took questions with his habitual discretion: waffling and professional prudence. In substance, he argued that the two-stage communication was justified by the requirements of a complex investigation involving two tracks: the one about the journalist, a demonic character who had imported into the national press morals foreign to our customs, to the point of undermining the honor of his profession as well as medical deontology itself; and the one about the theft with violence and premeditation, though without infraction or victims, of a national treasure with no direct connection to the cadaver. It had therefore seemed more prudent to investigate each of the two panels of this doubly sinister scandal carefully so as to be able to grasp precisely its connection with the presence of the stolen object in the apartment of the presumed suicide. Several elements remained to be elucidated. For the present, Rilsky was nevertheless in a position to summarize the broad outlines of the criminal scenario or, rather, *scenarios*.

People listened with growing unease: don't these "arguments" apply to all matters that are sensitive in different though necessary ways? What are they hiding from us? What don't they want to know?

Let's return to the unfolding of events.

In the beginning, the supposed brains of the seizure, Thibault Dechartre, undertakes to steal 9999 on behalf of a prince in the Gulf. Art schools prosper in the region, the taste for antiquities develops, several young women and men from wealthy families in the region and other emerging powers frequent the École du Louvre, take a passionate interest in Versailles. That's in our interest; we encourage them. The brain's networks manage to penetrate the Château (we are making progress in identifying the accomplices), but they do not succeed in exfiltrating the booty. What to do with this cumbersome 9999?

That is when, at the Hypnosis Café and the Baron, with the help of controlled substances, the brain ends up confiding in friends (it's a hypothesis), and together they conduct what will be the second phase of the operation, a scenario the police chief proposes to call the "green scenario." These people know other people who know others, eventually including this phantom WRE.fr that floats around the net. We have identified some of them, difficult to corner; it's a fluid milieu. Sort of a "Green Brigades," needless to say clandestine, a "soft" version of the "Red Brigades" (apparently, I insist on apparently) in which the previous generation was compromised. Committed individuals, dreamers, evildoers as well, from their point of view quite honest—believers, basically.

They cannot let such a coup pass, and they decide to utilize it for a good cause. Harass the government, be done with the nuclear-power stations, no less . . . It's make or break . . . So those people attempt to put 9999 in a secure location while they mobilize public opinion, scientists, artists, that whole world of petitioners, before the expiration of their "ultimatum." The idea sounds clever, but it doesn't hold water. Scientists aren't risking it. Theo isn't either, in case Nivi needs reassurance—Rilsky confirms this, not Theo, no, never on his life! Fleeting contacts, perhaps, attempted approaches, one can imagine, but *there are no experts* with a reputation at this infantile phase of the operation, we are in agreement.

However, since LSG knows all the milieus and frequents the same nightclubs as the "Green Brigades," alias WRE.fr, the latter take advantage of his generosity. Rilsky doesn't think he's taking much of a risk in proposing the hypothesis that LSG is extremely flattered by their confidence in him. A nervous man, seeking recognition, eager for assimilation, or better: of an unlikely nobility. The weak link, in a nutshell.

We are now in phase three of the scenario, the most personal and, as always in those cases, the muddiest, the police chief believes. The diary of this atypical journalist (the first investigation had already completely covered that subject) apparently suggests the man was taken in. Rilsky has not read the pages of this diary; the psychology unit of the police is taking care of it, and Nivi will not necessarily share his opinion . . . Sticking to what appears certain at present, it seems LSG was attached to 9999 to the point of devoting a sort of cult to it. The clock had apparently become his fetish, his brother, the much desired friend. A passion, in any case, to which this delicate heart devotes pages and pages of his very personal notebook. It could not be more intimate . . .

Until the moment when the deadline of the ultimatum arrives. The "Green Brigades" no longer know how to manage their prey. LSG is afraid they will take back his friend and return it to its Versailles prison. Or worse, the journalist fears that the attention paid in France and the rest of the world to the cause and to the theft having multiplied by a thousand the monetary value of the automaton, the oil barons and the International Greens will find the means to pay new accomplices. These accomplices would finally find a way to unbolt the borders and exfiltrate the masterpiece to Qatar, where the fabulous clock would only see its value in the stock market grow, with time, for the sole pleasure of its superwealthy proprietor and without any hope of its regaining the Hexagon. The King minutely details his anguish in his diary. He cracks. A state of abandon submerges him, adding to the professional error committed in the Zina affair and to the departure of his friend and protector Larson. Needless to say, the police chief is not forgetting the turbulent existence of the individual in question, his antecedents as an orphan, an expatriate, and the rest . . .

"Is that enough to kill yourself?" The question remains. Rilsky tests me, but he must have his own idea.

Nivi thinks that Marianne is totally absorbed by Indira. Dr. Baruch perfectly assumes the obligations of mother and father within their little single-parent family. And even if LSG had helped her achieve her assisted maternity in one way or another, it had never been a question of seeking child support from him. On this Marianne has always been clear. Loïc Sean is an exceptionally gifted human being, she adores him, that's not a mystery for anyone, she was saying it again just recently before the discovery of the cadaver. So there was no reason there to kill himself.

"Besides, why talk of suicide?" Marianne is indignant. "The media thrive on the pathetic, we know that, but on the part of the police I was expecting more prudence. Loïc Sean may simply have overdone the dose, in a state of euphoria, or perhaps in a somewhat more pronounced state of depression, but with the sole purpose of feeling good."

Nivi doesn't have any idea. An overdose is an unconscious suicide, all the same. Maybe. Maybe not. She prefers to think that basically LSG, who loved the "royal language" French, truly fell in love with 9999, in love like never before, never as much. She'd have to read the diary if it's legally possible—and if the family of the defunct authorizes it; relatives must exist somewhere. Whatever that may be, she has her conviction:

LSG had reached a degree of solitude and passion such that he could not stand the idea of living apart from 9999. Therefore, by dying at its feet, his cadaver would be found beside the stolen work. That would be the end of the green scenario. And Passemant will return to Versailles. That's what the King wishes. Why?

Well, because then 9999 will stay in France. Where LSG caught sight of it for the first time, in the Château that enchanted him, whose provocative installations he loved. "You understand, Nivi," he said, "Versailles was a baroque installation, and now it's modern. Yes it is! I love the modern when it is baroque. Not you, I know you. But me, I'm baroque, don't you think? That useless luxury, the 'accursed share,' the debauchery of beauty, they have to be burned! Those people of Versailles burned the decors of their enchanted islands, can you imagine, they burned themselves to survive!"

And he laughed like a madman.

"One never knows why someone kills themselves." Nivi, alluding to the rose, comments that suicide has no why. "However, in dying with the astronomical clock's tick-tock for a lullaby, our King returns Passemant to us. Well, that's what he wanted: that 9999 remain in France, in Versailles. I believe it; I am sure of it. Not to be visited, catalogued, studied, evaluated, sold, utilized, sequestered, calculated, stolen, and so on. For love. That's all. The most fragile among us was the most seriously in love. He offered us his limitless love for 9999. Do you find that ridiculous? Not I. His world had become too harsh: he couldn't take it anymore; he was happy to give us the present. That's what I think. Not a suicide—he simply undid the theft. A gift."

Rilsky must think I'm delirious. "Nivi's into literature," he says. Though with fondness, as often in my presence, but he's deeply skeptical. The investigation is going to progress with or without a "cause." Whether the cause is green or red, there is criminal offense, there is premeditation, there is corruption, and there is the death of a man. A trial will therefore ensue. Can one speak of a crime? We'll see, but a certain number of the guilty parties, and they won't be minor ones, will be severely punished, as the law demands. At least that's what they're saying.

"Could psychoanalysis have saved him?" The police chief still doesn't understand a thing. Or is he making fun of Nivi—which amounts to the same thing?

She thinks LSG found the "point" where one can "delight in the good without being angry at the opposite evil." The secret of perpetual motion according to Pascal. Except that for him, it was a *final* point. Can one live when one has touched that point?

51

PARADISE IS AT THE LUX

D id you listen to the video by the American astronauts? When you have looked at the Earth from space and you return, you realize that Earth is the Garden of Eden!"

Pure Astro, transmitting his euphoria to me from the Gran Sasso National Laboratory in the Abruzzi—or maybe he is at the Fermilab near Chicago?

Voltaire had no need to be an American astronaut to know that Paradise is here: here where he was, in person. More precise, the Sage of Ferney, and more original than my A's colleagues. I understand him. Eden stretches out beneath my windows: it's the Luxembourg Gardens. With Stan, Astro, Marianne, and her new hypercomposed microfamily. With Rilsky and the cadaver of the King, Claude-Siméon and his 9,999 years, the Beloved then abhorred king, Émilie on fire and la Pompadour as rival to the Clock, Cassini and Saint-Eustache, La Salpêtrière and the Louvre, my veranda facing the Fier d'Ars . . .

The anticyclone has a lock on Europe, the tropical summer repulses autumn into Siberia, and the bees that have survived the pesticides continue to make honey around the queens of

France turned into statues along the paths that lead to the basins with their model sailboats.

In contrast to what I had imagined in the past, I did not commit murder to take over the Vogels' apartment. I look with their eyes—they who taught me to embrace the memory of France in this most logical, most childlike of gardens, most French of all. I am at home at my window on the sixth floor above the Lux. I have not forgotten. GlobalPsyNet, PsyNetOne, and *PsychMag*, my home ports, resist austerity. Suicides and business are still making the front pages. Indira has escaped Ulf and the King. The stars continue to reveal their secrets to Theo Passemant, my Astro. He follows me by e-mail; I accompany him by iPhone, the Latitude application complemented by Starwalk. The laughable cosmology of the ignorant: fine by me, I adore it.

With each beat of my heart I know what star is above the park, what other star is in my A's thoughts. Here, now. Pluto pulses in the heel of Serpentarius, blinding brilliance that eclipses the Moon. Tactile, surreal, more than cosmic and perfectly vegetal, I rejoin Astro through this miniature app Latitude. My Theo is not afraid of being located, at least not by me; he lets me follow him in his interstellar displacement, from lab to lab, whatever the continent. He knows I know where he is when he makes love to me in thought in the Abruzzi or in the very heart of the Andes, at five billion years after the Big Bang or at the other end of the expansion accelerating toward the glacial void. Astro over there is with me here and now, above the linden trees. In the compact time of the encounter that has no need to speak of itself, written ILY.

Yes, Paradise is at the Lux. If there are humans only on our planet, if France is more rural even than the rice paddies of China, if Claude-Siméon Passemant's clock and my Theo's neutrons inhabit my senses, then . . . Separations are appeased in voyages, crimes are illuminated by analysis, sorrow suspends the hours. But desire extends memory, and time escapes—both above and below, mobile condensation, continuous present, incommensurable.

I am not awake; simply I'm not sleeping—it's not the same thing. At dusk, the fabric of this limbo envelops my internal coups d'état and transports me toward Émilie translating Leibniz in the fire of the pregnancy that will cause her death; summons up Passemant's workshop in the Louvre; caresses Louis XV's legs enclosing his astronomical clock; protects Stan, who is teaching Indira to read; slips between Astro's fingers writing to me from the neighborhood of a supernova; slicks his penis possessing me all night long. This limbo is a nameless novel, color of black silk, taste of coffee and cherries, with the speed of lightning and the repose of a dream above the Lux.

I slip into a spray of water and into a ray of light shining in the distance on the Sacré-Coeur, on the horizon of my garden. I tremble under the chestnut tree pruned in a straight line, and I am extinguished in the feathers of the dead pigeon on the gravel that my steps trample. I follow the scarlet geraniums and the swings. The bronze of the lion, the horse, the tortoise bathed by the fountain, and Astro's eye screwed onto his telescope. The owl-headed guide who leads tourists at Versailles, the foreign students at the Marly, the King, the Parc-aux-Cerfs, and Rilsky. Ugo the toxic and Stan who speaks in haikus. I? Who? Dust of stars. Programmed by neurons that I reprogram in reverse by means of words, of vagabond meanings, of abolished and re-emergent time.

Me and my neurons. Fourteen billion. And their thousand billion nerve connections. Thousands of billions of cells of two hundred different types, 10 percent immortal, the others constantly renewed. We observe ourselves. We test ourselves. Who knows whom? The molecules have the first word; should they let go of me, the trip is over. But it suffices for my hormones to hold on and for me to take my beehive off its hinges. They are not annoyed with me: they demand tact, I try, I search, I recompose, and they come along in my wake, mine, ours. My pleasure is good for them. Sleeping neurons, hormones, cells, and particles awaken, reproduce, are vitalized, I get away from them; they let me get away again. Another race, a new life. Till breath ends, no more ILY.

52

SILENCE AND POEM

No word from Astro. I've lost the sense of time, as we know, but this time the break is too brutal and the absence too long. Although my paradise counts vast firmaments of winter, this is not normal. Usually he calls me morning, noon, and night, except when he is exploring a superluminal neutrino or conspiring in the Passemant archives. I generally answer within seconds, me too. But the unpredictable can happen. And it does.

I am in my Atlantic refuge. The storm has blown all the barrels of salt from the salt marshes against the windows of my veranda. Leibniz terrified and swept away, electricity and networks off, Nivi alone against the flood, darkness, cold. I was away from my smartphone for a long time and didn't get Theo's barrage of texts until much later, too late. A dozen "Are you there?" "Are you there?" "Are you there?" cut off by a furious "Ciao!"

Men are cruel babies—you don't have to be a shrink to know that. All men, but not Theo? But he is! It's enough to make you laugh and cry. Surely he heard the news about the storm: it was reported around the world; he must have understood that I was overwhelmed, and surely he must have worried, not being able to reach me. He could have tried to call Stan or Marianne or

the city hall or the police station or the fire station or whatever . . . But no, I had to be there, I had to reply "present," always present for him, reassure him—otherwise, panic . . . Poor
paralyzed darling! Oh, not that at all, much worse: a predator . . . Except that there is no prey, there never was . . . A sort
of love, this too: an unbearable state of abandon, the trap of
having been mistaken: she doesn't love me, women are all alike,
never again . . . I can picture the scene he might have imagined
for himself high under the heavens, at the Gran Sasso for
example.

Since then, radio silence, neither telephone nor e-mail—
unreachable. No matter that I call, try to explain, elaborate, make
myself understood—nothing. Disappearance of Theo. He
sulks and drops me. He plays dead . . . I take back my calls, my
messages; I'm angry. I could have been gravely disaster-stricken,
or drowned, you don't want to know how I am, what happened,
not important. "It's nothing, a woman who's drowning . . ." It's
cruel to keep quiet like that, it's killing me! Are you okay?
What's going on? A disaster, something serious at the lab or in
the cosmic background radiation? No answer.

After all, billions of men and women on earth are separating
at this very moment; the storm is nothing like an event. On the
other hand, echoing the Portuguese nun who finds that she
loves the love she still has more than the lieutenant who has
abandoned her, I realize that Theo's absence causes me less anguish than his mute pain. Compacted into a smashing silence,
his pain smashes me in turn. I hurt from not hearing him say
that he hurts without me.

Nothing . . . Still nothing . . . This silence from Theo . . . It's
not normal, even according to his own logic, his time that
doesn't exist and his intermittent appearances. No, it's not normal at all!

"Normal? Am I dreaming? If Astro were normal, he wouldn't love you, and you wouldn't love him either." Stan makes fun of me, with the same words I repeat to myself silently—but pathetically.

"Instead of worrying yourself sick, you should call one of those acronyms your lover hides under: ANGST, AIM, LUTH, and all the rest!" Marianne wants to calm me down by making me face the absurd; I confess I find this sort of tenderness exasperating at times. "Look, if there had been anything serious, his colleagues would have alerted you. Nothing fatal, so let it go, I'm telling you! From working day and night, or rather at night, with the stars, that man doesn't just forget you. He forgets himself. Maybe he finds that amusing, after all . . ."

Obviously they understand nothing about our affair.

But what affair? Does it make any sense?

It's not because he fished me out with his boat that I take Astro for the Savior. And while his ancestor Passemant projects himself to the year 9999, I only count the internal coups d'état up to 9,999 (and more, with affinities) by sounding my survivals with Stan and my A. We are *islanded*, Theo and I, the way others are landed, in the insane disunite of skin-to-skin, wounded blood and hearts, I breathed in by him, he by me. Each excluded from the other yet joined, reciprocal, thoughts facing thoughts that sometimes screech or scream, and cheer. Solitary beginnings that meet, unmask, dismember one another. And try to remain luminous, musical, swarmed, austere, outside the earth.

Could this be the first time in the world? Could we be a species of strange humanoids convinced *there is no solution*? Because the expansion of the world-happiness, of the world-unhappiness, is, was, and will be infinite? A way, perhaps the only way, of consuming death. Not the death that strikes once and for all, that science promises at age 150: future seniors equipped with hearts and other computerized organs, vigilant so that artificial uteruses and clever cloning programs do not overpopulate a planet already overloaded with the aged. No, I'm talking about the death that sizzles every nanosecond in Émilie's fire, the death permanently at work in life.

Astro's ellipses instill emptiness in my paradise and remind me that death, my own death, is a decisive part of the experience. Since those same suspensions teach me not to count on anything or anyone, not even Theo ("Are you there? Ciao!"), but to transmute the emptiness into rebounds, I no longer live as if we were born to die. Given we're born, let's innovate. Each in our own way, unpredictable and unique, ephemeral but sharable. Neither hope nor responsibility, it's only a game. A sort of paradise, all the same.

Whereupon here's Astro appearing on my screens again. After this long abyss of how much time? Two years, six months, three weeks, two days, six hours? I don't know, I don't want to know. He's in China. How could he escape?

The Chinese send taikonauts to the Moon, soon a busload of Sichuanese following in the footsteps of Apollo and Neil Armstrong! After Bordeaux wines, Ile de Ré salt, Airbus, African minerals, luxury industries, digitization, cinema, and other details, the Middle Kingdom wants to compete on the international market for space technology. About time. Too weak to worry the powers already in place, China launches scientific and educational partnerships with the European Space Agency, after the American contracts, which are imperative, and above all the old friends in Russia. Thus, from Beijing or Shanghai (it makes no difference to me: I delete the Latitude app), Astro lands by e-mail in my Lux paradise. But like a poet, for a change: "Our China: close/distant, small/immense, fragile/indestructible link. And breath fills the void."

That's all. I was no longer expecting it. Exactly what I needed. For the moment, Astro spares me the hypertechnical exploits of his sophisticated mission; I ask for nothing more. Not the shadow of an excuse—let it go. The ellipses confirm the pure Theo style: the spontaneous concision and gift with which he associates me: "*Our* China." Right away I approve the first-person plural.

Then I reread and decide that this prose poem is much more than a Taoist painting on silk launched as a tweet by my specialist in chaotic inflation, a yin/yang connoisseur of binary thought and a practitioner of the transcendental respiration of yoga. These ciphered flashes describe Theo *and* Nivi. Together? "Our China": necessarily, that is *us*, fragile/indestructible. I receive, let's say, a declaration of love; it matters little if that was the revenant's intention or not. What's written is written; each word overflows with a meaning that expands me, and I find I was unjust, earlier, in going over the behavior of its author with a fine-toothed comb.

Whether he eclipses or not, plays dead, capricious, predatory, or independent, basically I have never doubted that Theo exists and will exist for me in him, for him in me. The unknown space is he, the solid point around which my burning moments regroup, my transfigured hells and purgatories. A stranger among strangers, confirming my own strangeness, placing it in play like the others. So let him remain unusual! A chance, in fact, a harbor of grace for our solitary departures, these new lives for Nivi, transports and transfers, leaden echoes and golden echoes. He, the chosen silence, our disunite.

53

ROSE LAURELS

Quite young, I liked to hide in the garden among the rose laurels (oleanders) bordering the roses and peonies. A flowerbed of blooming forest decorated the wall of the property; I would hide in its vegetal light. The dew moistened my hair, the dirt crunched under my sandals, I would rub my cheeks against the polished leaves, the minute petals, silken drops of blood more welcoming than the royal flesh of the barbed rose bushes, less odorous than the toxic peonies. I felt time live. Was I three, four? The garden brought itself to me; I ran to it. It yellowed in autumn, was covered in snow in the winter. I awaited spring and until the end of summer perfumed myself in the green stems and the chocolate branches. A little rounded button, swollen with wind and water, I grew rosier from day to day in the warmth of the rains. I absorbed the rhythm of the laurels; I was one of them. A brown then wine-red bud, I became raspberry and opened into bundles of scarlet stars saluting the sun. I disappeared for good.

"Where has Nivi gone? Has anyone seen Nivi?"

Grandmother pretended not to know where I was, and the adults played along: no one would find my hiding place. Only Mama understood: "Leave her, she's taking her time."

The butterflies, confusing me with this peaceful blossoming, would land on my open arms, stop palpitating, and I would count the instants of their sleep according to the beating of my little girl's heart. I was butterfly, bee, pearl of dew, pollen, petal, twig. So that's what time is: rhythmic metamorphoses, luminous, volatile enclosure.

The magic ended one day during school holidays. I had already grown when I discovered that the red bundles had disappeared from the fresh bearer of my secrets. A huge burst of laughter shook my stupor. My cousin and her friends were filling the basin of the little fountain with the cut heads of my rose laurels. They were preparing a gigantic floral installation.

"That's so stupid!" Mama declared, sickened by this modern art that arrived at our house in the form of a cemetery of faded petals.

Grandmother asked that the massacre of the laurels be severely punished and the guilty girls denied the beach.

I didn't say anything. At the time the idea did not occur to me that this devastation could be part of a war long smoldering and declared by cowards against my secretive person.

"They'll grow back next year, don't worry!" snickered the little pests.

I didn't believe them. I no longer went to flower with the rose laurels. Only the golden memory of the words inhabits me now: rose laurels. The foliage unrolls only in my throat; their waves of sound often bathe my nights. They amplify the slightest noise in Stan's bedroom and abruptly wake me, butterfly held in the hollow of a vermillion calyx in a forest of dreams.

"Everything's okay, Mama, I'm cured now," murmurs Stan, curled under his comforter.

It's no use: I have trouble flowing into the sap of my laurels, where I sense time trembles. Sometimes it stops; sometimes it runs at top speed.

But the garden still brings itself to me, and I still bring myself to it. Is it the garden's time I am seeking in the stars with Astro? In this nature said to be still that ILY revives?

Today, nothing calms me better than to take care of the garden. Then the floral rhythm from when I was three returns, and I water the citronella geraniums with fresh water, in the rockery at the edge of the ocean, in front of the Ars steeple.

Theo is in a state of grace such as I have never known for him. He returns from Antarctica, where his Harvard colleagues' telescope, BICEP2, has just captured primordial gravitational waves, the oldest traces of our world. These extremely tenuous representations of the background vibration of the universe are said to offer irrefutable proof of cosmic inflation.

"I never would have believed I would live this moment! The world inflated like a balloon at a prodigious speed! In a thousandth of a billionth of a billionth of a second, all the points of the universe located at millions of light years apart from one another! Can you imagine? The confirmation we were lacking of the scenario called 'eternal inflation,' you know . . . Which postulates the permanent creation of the universe . . . Which reduces the Big Bang to a simple stage in the multiplicity of infinite new developments—some giving birth to all sorts of possible universes . . . some already known, others in the process of being born . . . With this, cosmology is moving farther away from metaphysics!" He couldn't be happier. "We proceed by demonstrations, you understand . . . Demonstrations! Fascinatingly varied multiverses are more than possible: they are . . . they are taking shape . . . Isn't it wonderful?"

He doesn't wait for my opinion; I don't have one. "Permanent creation" is good for me: start out differently, *be* differently, not once and for all, evolve with time while adapting to circumstances . . . What could be better?

Astro marvels: that's enough for us; they'll have to confirm in the lab, but a new era has begun for sure.

Whereupon Stan bursts in: "Hi Theo, you landing? Things are moving like mad in the sky, it's a scoop!"

"You said it, *mousquetaire*! And you? Better and better, I see. One for all, all for one!"

The two men have created a code, like for a partly secret "brotherhood," to show Nivi she isn't everything. And also to impress her. With three principles. *Primo*: As abstentionists and strikers, indebted and indignant, humans are unraveling. Never mind, France is resistant, take heart, you d'Artagnans! *Secundo*: Men have always been fragile, but from now on it is admissible to say so, and we, Stan and Theo, recognize it. Women are equally fragile, except that they prefer not to think about it. Like Nivi, who is courageous but still has her 9,999 internal coups d'état. She lacks the Gascony wit, alas, and she doesn't know swordplay. *Tertio*: As fragile men, they are also full of cleverness. They cut seconds into sixtieths of seconds like Claude-Siméon, or even into a thousand billionths of billionths of nanoseconds, like Astro. They do really exist, but they don't let themselves get easily trapped, or even seen—not much, not often . . . Like God . . . And like Theo. They are in love with women—certain women—while still being happy bachelors . . . Their first names rotate between Athos, Porthos, Aramis, and d'Artagnan. Faithful to Louis XIII (for a change from Louis XV and his 9999), engaging in heavy combat with the cardinal's guards, they recuperate the queen's necklace while also unmasking milady, join the siege of La Rochelle (right near Ré again!), and end up reconciling with Richelieu before each returns to whatever life he likes . . . And the duo starts up: *We are the captains of Gascony*, to make Nivi laugh and pester her a bit.

"This time you swallowed the Big Bang, obstinate Athos! Long live eternal expansion!"

"You've about got it, d'Artagnan. New worlds are being born, and it's not over!"

"So there are no 'zero moments' left? Only sequences of beginnings? We relinquish *The Origin of the World* to Courbet, intrepid Aramis!"

"And one learns to tolerate contingencies! In the process, Porthos, we distance ourselves even more from theology. Because the laws of physics reside at the heart of the universe, not before, not afterward, we discover them as we go along, and we obtain their proof. That's all, that's huge."

"A little humility, d'Artagnan! There are still a lot of crazy dreamers in the cosmology tribe. You fabulate hypotheses; you take your math calculations for realities."

"Not untrue, captain, but this time your timing is bad, the very day when BICEP2 provides proofs, and what proofs!"

"We'll see, wait for the next scenario . . . Pardon me, the next 'scientific discovery,' with your permission . . . Not everybody can be a captain of Gascony . . . Shameless liars and fighters!"

And they start up again:

We are the Captains of Gascony,
Fighters and liars without shame,
From Carbon and from Castel-Jaloux,
We are the ones!

They've rehearsed their number; they like to play it for me from time to time; I pretend to disapprove, but I'm actually proud. Jealous, in fact! One jealous of the other, normal, and of Nivi, to be expected, Stan and Theo run their duel in the French manner, at a gallop, like a carnival, like a historical memory. It's their music.

She feels the happiness of being with them and also of not being, if it's only by intermittence. Nivi leans out the open window. A smile hovers over the park, but the houses around it stand as opaque, as stiff, almost as threatening as before. The light shimmers in the chestnut trees; the Lux looks like the décor for a solemn fairy theater. An airy radiance welcomes her; she seems to understand that a shadow has melted inside her, disappeared for good. The smile reigns upon the world, it is the world, and the Lux is its vivacious and colorful proof.

Nivi's sadness, always fleeting, lost, on the lookout, has molted into something luminous, unheard of, and fabulous. Not really a destiny but a unique reality, almost exalting, somewhat like morning, for which a single word comes to her lips: *serenity*.

That vision makes her possible.

In the sun-splattered street alongside the Lux, under her window, she sees a green hedge, the most delicate there is. Vibrating cords caressed by the breeze, foraged by clouds of bees. At the bottom of this cloth of transparent threads, scarcely higher than the height of a little girl of three, a rose laurel. Unique, slim, adorned with smooth dark green foliage, crowned by curly petals of cherry color. Which open to the pure light, the first light of the world.